A Covert War

Dedication

For my darling, patient wife Patricia.

A Covert War

Michael Parker

ROBERT HALE · LONDON

© Michael Parker 2010
First published in Great Britain 2010

ISBN 978-0-7090-9010-6

Robert Hale Limited
Clerkenwell House
Clerkenwell Green
London EC1R 0HT

www.halebooks.com

The right of Michael Parker to be identified as author
of this work has been asserted by him in accordance with the
Copyright, Designs and Patents Act 1988

2 4 6 8 10 9 7 5 3 1

A Covert War is a figment of my imagination. I've no knowledge of any illegal activity that goes on in Afghanistan apart from what I know is in the public domain. All the characters are imaginary but I hope they are lively enough to make them believable.

Michael Parker

Typeset in 10/13.5pt Sabon
Printed in Great Britain by the MPG Books Group, Bodmin and King's Lynn

PROLOGUE

I CAN REMEMBER when I realized that I was in love with Shakira. I had known her barely three weeks. It probably happened within days of our first meeting at the mission. Shakira was such a lively, extroverted character, so full of humour and yet with warm simplicity. I felt a connection with her that is difficult to describe, but one I believe was reciprocated. I knew without doubt that Shakira had warmed to me as soon as we met. There was something in her manner, the way she spoke and reacted to me. I can remember how her face would light up as soon as she saw me and how the atmosphere in a room seemed to change when she walked in; such was the effect she had. I felt the change in me and could see it in others. I loved the way she would throw her head back and laugh out loud at my terrible jokes, showing her beautiful, white teeth. And then she would stop laughing and look directly at me, her lovely eyes softening. And as her laughter died away, so her mouth would change into that wonderful, disarming smile of hers.

I had been working at the mission for a number of weeks, each day writing up my report for The Chapter on the work that the centre was undertaking. Shakira was the senior administrator there. Because of my project I often found myself in Shakira's company. In the evenings we would walk up to the high point above the mission and talk over the highs and lows of the day. We would sit on a fallen tree trunk that had been there for many years. It was divested now of its foliage. It had no branches; they had been lopped off so that it could be used to sit and look over the lovely countryside. The view from there down into the valley was charmingly beautiful, particularly as the sun was setting. As we sat together on that log, it was obvious to me that we were getting closer and I felt, instinctively that Shakira welcomed it.

And that was the moment I knew I was in love with her. I can see her now, tossing her head back, her mouth wide open in that delicious laugh. She had thrown her hands up in the air and slapped them down on the tops of her legs. Her red dress, patterned with large, white flowers seemed to dance like fire in front of me. I was mesmerized and happy that I knew I loved her and that she loved me.

And that was the moment the bullet slammed into me. The impact pitched me forward and sent me sprawling at Shakira's feet. The sound of the gun came seconds later. As I hit the ground I blacked out, but it could only have been momentarily because when I looked up I saw Shakira's lovely face turning into an image of shock and pain. The white flowers on her dress began to change colour as her blood seeped into the dress, and she rolled off the log, falling face down on to the hard, stony ground.

I opened my mouth to call out, but no sound came. I felt a terrible pain in my shoulder where the bullet had hit me, but the pain in my heart when I realized Shakira was almost certainly dead and I was probably about to die was unimaginable. It would be true to say that I wanted to die then; life without Shakira would be so empty.

I remember hearing a great deal of shouting and the sound of gunfire coming from below the slope, down at the mission. I could hear screaming and the sound of men's voices. Then the gunfire stopped and I heard the thud of footsteps as the attackers ran up the slope towards us. I lowered my head on to the ground and pretended I was dead. I prayed nothing else would happen.

But something else did happen; something even worse. I felt myself shrivel inside with an inordinate fear because I couldn't close my eyes; I had to keep them open. Several men appeared. They were all wearing camouflage uniforms and calf-length boots. Two of the men stopped beside Shakira and said something to each other in a language that I couldn't understand. One of the men put his boot on Shakira's body and pushed her. Then he leaned forward and pointed a gun at her head. He said something and shot her. I can see Shakira's body jumping now. I see it every night in my dreams; in my nightmares.

The killer walked over to me and pointed the gun at my head. I noticed the little finger of his left hand was missing. Why do we remember such trivial things in our darkest moments? Aren't we supposed to have no recall of events immediately preceding such trauma? Why wasn't I allowed to have no memory of what happened? I will never forget it. Never. He laughed and said something in English, and then he shot me.

ONE

SUSAN ELLIS SHUDDERED and closed the remnants of her brother's notebook very slowly and then lifted her hand and wiped away a tear from the corner of her eye with the tip of her finger. She thought David was dead. She had heard nothing for over a year, and now this; a few stained pages from where? She looked down at the grubby book and opened it again. Tears welled up and ran down her cheeks, dropping on to the pages where they mingled with the pencilled words of a brother she longed to see again, but never thought she would.

David Ellis was Susan's twin. He had worked as a freelance journalist and often found himself in some of the most dangerous hot spots in the world. His last assignment was with a group known as The Chapter of Mercy.

The Chapter was a mysterious organization which ran orphanages in and around Pakistan, India and Afghanistan. They rarely encouraged journalists or other media groups to highlight the work they did for deprived children, so David had found himself in something of a privileged position.

Her eyes misted over and she closed the book again. She looked across the table at the man sitting opposite. He had been watching her very intently, almost benevolently. Now he shifted and picked up his cup. He continued to watch her as he drank. His name was Cavendish – Sir Giles Cavendish. He had told Susan that he was something to do with the Foreign Office.

When he had called her that morning on the phone, he told her that he had something of her brother's. Susan's legs had weakened when he mentioned David. She had assumed her brother was dead. She couldn't speak for a while. He suggested they meet somewhere for a coffee. It was Saturday so Susan did not have to go into work at the bank. She tried to answer the voice on the phone, but all she could manage was a faltering, stumble of words.

'Look,' he said, 'there's a Starbucks in the Strand. Could you meet me there?' Susan said she could. 'Right, how about eleven o'clock?'

Susan nodded, 'All right,' she told him. 'I'll be there at eleven o'clock.'

She put the phone down and realized she hadn't asked him how she would know him. She immediately tried a call-back on her phone, but his number had been withheld. She shrugged and guessed it wouldn't be too difficult to identify her mysterious caller. Then she began wondering what it was he had of David's, and if this meant that her brother could still be alive.

When Susan arrived at Starbucks, Cavendish was waiting. She had no need to wonder how she might recognize him because he came straight over to her and introduced himself. He took Susan across to a table up against the far wall away from the windows. He then brought over the coffee that she had asked for and sat down at the table. That was when he pulled a small, tatty book from his jacket pocket and handed it to her. It only contained a few pages.

'This belonged to your brother,' was all he said.

Now Susan had read it and was looking at the man who sat opposite her.

'Where did you get this?' was her obvious question.

Cavendish put his cup down and leaned forward. He lowered his voice and spoke quite softly to her.

'It came to us in a diplomatic bag,' he told her, and leaned back in his chair.

'Where did the bag come from?' Susan asked.

He arched his eyebrows and gave an almost imperceptible shrug. 'Well, that's the devil of it; I don't know.' He could see words beginning to form on Susan's lips. He put up a manicured hand and splayed his fingers to stop her from asking the next question. 'Apparently,' he began, 'the bag was opened by a junior at the office a few days before it crossed my desk. I'm afraid he didn't attach much importance to it because it carried no official comment, no stamp and no signature.' He shrugged. 'Some of our new graduates can be like that; no brains, you see.'

Susan had taken a tissue from her handbag and was wiping her eyes carefully. She lowered the tissue. 'So why did it come to you?'

Cavendish pushed out his bottom lip as though he was giving it some considerable thought. 'I really don't know. It was probably being handed on from one desk to another until someone claimed it. But I remembered the story. It was about a year ago, wasn't it?' He didn't wait for an answer. 'There was a murderous attack at a mission in Afghanistan, close to the Pakistan border. Your brother was caught up in it. Most unfortunate,' he concurred, shaking his head. 'Most unfortunate.'

Susan wondered if Cavendish realized just how deeply distressing it was for her to be reminded of her brother's untimely death. But then she wondered if the civil servants who worked for the government perhaps encountered too many tragedies to be able to empathize with the victims. Perhaps Cavendish was no exception.

'But this means my brother must have survived the massacre,' she insisted, holding the book up. 'There's no way it could have been written after if he hadn't survived.'

'Obviously,' Cavendish agreed. 'And I have looked into it, I can promise you. There were survivors of course, and they were taken to a nearby hospital and treated for their wounds. But there was no record kept of who was taken to hospital.' He shrugged again and opened his hands out in an empty gesture. 'And that is all I know. I'm sorry.'

Susan picked up her cup, sipped at the coffee and then put it down. She then opened her handbag and put the book into it.

'If you find out anything else about my brother, would you let me know?' she asked.

Cavendish nodded. 'Of course.'

'How can I contact you?'

He smiled and pushed himself back into his chair. 'Just ask for me at the Foreign Office. The desk will patch you through.'

Susan stood up. Cavendish responded immediately and stood up as well. Susan reached over the table and shook his hand.

'Thank you, Sir Giles. You won't forget your promise, will you?'

He shook Susan's hand, taking care to do it gently. 'Of course not; as soon as I hear anything, I will let you know.'

Susan walked out of Starbucks into the Strand. It was a fine day so she decided to walk to Waterloo Station where she would catch a train to Clapham in south London where she lived.

Cavendish came out of Starbucks a few minutes after Susan. He hailed a cab and climbed in as he told the driver where he wanted to go.

'85 Embankment, please, driver.'

The driver pulled out into traffic. Another James Bond, he said to himself. Cavendish had just given him the address of the building that housed Britain's secret intelligence service, MI6.

Three days after her meeting with Cavendish, Susan stepped out of the underground at Old Street in the City of London. Since that meeting, she had trawled through the yellow pages and surfed the net looking for an agency that might be able to help find her brother. Susan had even tried persuading various editors of the national press that there might be a story to follow up, but in each case her quest was doomed to failure because of cost. There were agencies who were prepared to help her, but at a price that was well beyond Susan's limited means. As for the newspapers they wanted more than just a couple of pages from her dead brother's diary. And none of them were prepared to finance a quest that was almost certain to end in failure and would elicit little support from the newspaper barons. She tried the television companies, but there was no celebrity value in Susan and David Ellis. Not now.

And so it seemed that her search was doomed to fail. Until, that was, she came across a small advert in the classified section of the London *Evening Standard.*

Guard Right Security. Professional help at a price you can afford.

The advert gave a phone number and an address, but little more. Susan phoned and made an appointment. Guard Right Security was at an address in Oliver's Yard, just off the City Road, south of Old Street Underground Station, and it was in that direction Susan turned as she came up out of the underground.

There was no street number for her to look for, but an instruction that she would find a small doorway just a few yards inside Oliver's Yard with the small logo 'GRS' on the wall.

It took Susan a while to locate the logo, but she found it and then wondered if she had come to the right place. The doorway was set back into the large, old building that graced the main frontage along the City Road. The door looked a trifle shabby, but at least it yielded. It creaked noisily as she turned the handle and pushed.

The door opened on to a short passageway which was unlit, but

Susan could see a staircase leading up to a small landing. The floor was not carpeted. She walked in and closed the door behind her and very carefully climbed the stairs. If she had wanted to keep her presence quiet, she was out of luck; the bare steps creaked and groaned with each footfall.

Eventually she reached the landing and saw a door with an opaque window inset and the letters GRS etched on the glass. There was no doorbell to be seen anywhere. For some reason Susan found herself feeling quite nervous, and her hand shook as she rattled her knuckles on the glass.

She heard a sound coming from behind the door, rather like a chair falling over, followed by a shadowy silhouette of someone coming towards the door. Susan stepped back involuntarily as the door was thrown open. She put her hand to her mouth and made a sound as the young man smiled at her.

'Susan Ellis?' he said warmly. 'Please, do come in.' He made a sweeping gesture with his arm, inviting Susan to walk in.

She hesitated. 'Marcus Blake?'

He held the smile and brought his arm down. 'At your service, but please call me Marcus.'

Susan was immediately struck by his disarming manner, or at least what appeared to be a disarming manner. For all she knew it could have been affected. Nevertheless, she had made the appointment so she stepped willingly into his office.

Marcus closed the door and hurried over to a chair that was lying on its back. Obviously this was the chair that Susan had heard topple just after she had knocked. He straightened it and indicated that she should sit there.

Susan did as she was asked and began studying her surroundings. The office was quite plain, with little to indicate how busy Marcus Blake was. Behind his desk, hung crookedly on the wall, was what appeared to be a certificate. It was framed and probably related to some qualification Marcus Blake had achieved. There was nothing decorating the walls except for a poster depicting a musician by the name of Isao Tomita. Susan had never heard of him.

There was also a calendar with each day crossed off up to that day. In one corner of the office was a small sink. Next to this was a kettle, a carton of milk and a coffee jar. There was a small cabinet above. Susan had noticed as she walked into the office that there was a clothes peg screwed to the wall with what looked like a beanie hat hanging from it. A threadbare carpet covered part of the floor. There was precious little else in there to give Susan the feeling that she was in the realm of a true professional, and she was already thinking up her excuse to leave and put it all down to experience.

'Would you like a coffee?' Marcus asked her, before he settled himself in the chair behind his desk. Susan glanced at the sorry looking corner where the kettle resided and declined.

'Right,' he said, and rubbed his hands together as he sat down. He picked up a pen and held it poised above a notepad. 'So, what is it you would like to talk about?'

Before answering, Susan wondered if she shouldn't just make an apology for wasting his time and leave straight away. She had the feeling that this was developing into a farce and wished she had never seen the advert for Guard Right Security in the first place.

The only positive she could see so far was that Marcus Blake was quite handsome. He had blond hair that was parted in the middle, but not too severely. It fell loosely around his ears and had a natural curl to it; the kind of hair some women would die for, Susan thought to herself. His skin looked smooth and slightly tanned. He was broad and muscular without the look of someone who worked on his physique. He was a lot taller than her, and she judged his height to be about six feet. Altogether he looked the kind of man Susan would happily meet for a dinner date – once she had got to know him a little better.

'Well,' she began hesitantly, 'I'm not sure how to begin.'

'Why not try the beginning?' he joked, trying to put her at ease.

She took a deep breath, drawing the air in slowly through her nostrils in an effort to steady herself.

'I have a brother, a twin brother,' she told him, 'and I want to know if he's alive or not.'

Marcus tapped the notepad with his pen and began doodling. 'Go on,' he said.

'Well, David, that's my brother,' she added unnecessarily, 'worked for an organization known as The Chapter. He was a journalist.' She stopped. 'Sorry, he is a journalist by profession and was working on an assignment for them.' She hated herself for thinking of David in the past tense, but it was something she had slowly become resigned to. 'About a year ago David was working at an orphanage in Afghanistan, at Jalalabad. He was studying the work they do there. Orphan children,' she explained, then mentally kicked herself for fumbling her words. 'There was a massacre. Some insurgents attacked the staff and took the children. David was ...' She stopped and held back a sob. 'I'm sorry.' Marcus shook his head and made a slight, negative gesture with his hand. Susan continued, 'David was shot. I was told by The Chapter that the survivors had been taken to a hospital. Some of them weren't expected to live. I don't know what happened to David; he just, well, disappeared.'

Marcus stopped doodling. 'So what is it you want GRS to do?'

Susan, who had been looking down at her hands folded in her lap now looked up at him. 'GRS?'

'Guard Right Security,' he reminded her. 'What is it you want us to do?'

'Oh, yes, of course. Well, I want to know where David is. I want to find him.'

'In Jalalabad?'

Susan shrugged. 'I don't know. Wherever he is, I want to find him.'

'Are you sure your brother is still alive?' he asked.

Susan nodded vigorously. 'He must be, otherwise I wouldn't be here.'

Marcus leaned forward, his elbows on the desk. 'Miss Ellis, or is it Ms?'

'Susan, please.'

'OK, Susan. First of all you must understand that a lot of people who go "missing",' he emphasized the euphemism, 'do so because they wish to sever all contact with their current lives and have no wish to be found.'

'Not David,' she insisted.

'Of course not,' he rejoined, leaned back in his chair and carried on doodling. 'But how do you know, or why do you think your brother is alive?'

Susan opened her handbag and took out David's report of what happened at the mission. She passed it across the desk.

'This,' she said, and handed him the grubby notebook. 'It came into my possession three days ago.'

Marcus took it from her and frowned as he opened the dirty pages. There was only the one entry there and he read it carefully, his expression darkening as the report changed from a declaration of a man's love for a woman to an eye-witness account of a violent execution. He closed the book slowly and slid it across the desk towards her.

'Have you been to the authorities?' he asked.

Susan retrieved the book and put it back in her handbag. 'What authorities?' she muttered. 'It was a year ago.' She looked up. 'I don't want retribution: I just want to know where my brother is.'

Marcus looked up towards the ceiling and began swivelling in his chair. He had the aura of a man who had switched his thoughts to something entirely different from the moment in hand.

'You need a detective agency,' he said eventually, 'or the Missing Persons Bureau.' He lowered his gaze and looked directly at her. 'Why didn't you ask David's employers?'

'The Chapter? I assume they would have searched for him.'

'Don't you know?'

Susan shook her head. 'I didn't find out about this until a few days ago.'

This drew a guarded response from Marcus. 'How? What happened?'

Susan told him how Cavendish had phoned and arranged to meet her. She told him that Cavendish had been unable to offer any explanation as to how David's notes ended up in the diplomatic bag.

'So you see, I am left with a trail that is probably stone cold now.' She opened her bag and took out a tissue. She dabbed at her eyes. 'I'm sorry,' she said, 'but the more I think of how long it has been, the more I realize how little chance there is of finding my brother.' She put her hands in her lap. 'But I have to know.'

'Have you thought about contacting this chap Cavendish again and asking for his help? After all, he brought you the news of your brother.'

She shook her head. 'He made it quite clear that he knew nothing. What he was doing was simply a favour.'

'How did he know about you?' Marcus pointed towards Susan's handbag. 'There's no mention of you or David's connection to you in his notes.'

Susan shrugged. 'I don't know. To be honest I haven't given it any thought. He seemed to know me as soon as I walked into Starbucks. Why, is it important?'

Marcus didn't answer immediately. 'Perhaps he learned about you from The Chapter,' he said after a while. 'Would you have been registered as David's next of kin, do you think?'

She shook her head. 'I'm sorry, I keep saying no, or I don't know; but David was away so often on so many different assignments, I rarely saw him. I have no idea if he would ever have put me down as his next of kin. I suppose he must have done, though, wouldn't you?'

'I don't have any siblings, so I wouldn't know.'

After a few moments of thought and relative silence, Susan asked if they could move on to more pragmatic things. She found the discussion of her brother and whether he was alive or not distressing.

'Look,' she began, 'I have spoken to other agencies in the City but I'm afraid they are all far too expensive for me. What I want to know is what it would cost me for you to accompany me to Afghanistan while I look for the truth about my brother.'

'You want a bodyguard,' he said, 'a minder, is that it?'

'Yes, that's it exactly. I would feel vulnerable if I went on my own.'

Marcus was quiet for some time. It was fairly clear to him that the young woman sitting opposite was now down to the last noggins; the last scraping of the barrel. She had no money to speak of otherwise she would have taken on one of the bigger agencies. His own expertise extended little further than escorting celebrities, minor ones at that, and doing some courier work for other companies. What Susan Ellis was asking extended beyond his usual limits and would almost certainly end in tears, metaphorically speaking.

'My fees,' he said, suddenly, 'are two hundred and fifty pounds a day, plus expenses.'

Susan nodded her head slowly and sadly. 'I was afraid of that,' she told him, and stood up. 'I can't afford that kind of money, so I'm obviously wasting your time as well as my own.' She held out her hand. 'Thank you for listening, Mr Blake, but I can't do business with you.'

Marcus stood up. 'So what will you do?' he asked, as he shook her hand.

'Oh, I shall take a couple of weeks off work and fly out to Afghanistan. Try on my own for a while. I owe that to David,' she said.

'Why not give Cavendish a call?' he suggested. 'Perhaps he can come up with something.'

She shook her head. 'I don't have his number. I tried dialling him back, but the number had been withheld.'

Marcus gave that some thought, then came round the desk and opened the office door for her. 'I wish you luck,' he said, as she stepped out on to the landing. 'I wish there was something I could do.' He shrugged. He meant it too; she was too lovely a woman to have to relinquish so soon.

Susan gave him a brief smile. 'Thank you again,' she told him, and went down the stairs.

Marcus closed the door and went quickly to his desk. He tore off the top sheet of the pad on which he had been doodling and then he pulled a pair of sunglasses from his desk drawer and walked out of the office, lifting his beanie hat from its peg as he went out.

When he got down to street level, he checked to see which way Susan had gone, then turned round and locked his outer door. He slipped the hat over his blond hair and put on the sunglasses. Then he followed Susan up the City Road towards Old Street Tube Station.

TWO

TWO MONTHS EARLIER

ABDUL KHALIQ GLARED across the table at the American sitting opposite him. There was no love lost between the two men, particularly when it came to business, and the American was upsetting Abdul because he was demanding a little extra for his pains. The girl Abdul had offered him was little more than a passing bauble between men who had no scruples. The American wanted something with a bit of class; something a little more refined than one of Abdul's whores who would be passed off as rough trade.

Abdul Khaliq was a product of Afghanistan's turbulent history; very much like the warlords who held power with an iron grip. But his province extended beyond the vaguely drawn boundaries that defined the tribal fiefdoms of the country and reached into the very corridors of power in the Western World. Abdul bowed the knee to no man, but many bowed the knee to him.

Abdul's power lay not in fiefdoms, or the merchandise he traded with his Western counterparts, but in the more powerful element of knowledge; knowledge that could be useful as a bargaining chip, and deadly as a means of reprisal. His currency was fear, and men who traded with him were not to be found in the upper echelons of the Taliban or Al-Qaeda, but among those who hid behind some of the most powerful leaders in the West. It was these men who had most to lose, and from that spawned the fear that Abdul used as his ultimate weapon.

But Abdul was becoming unsettled by a subtle change in the way in which his British and American customers wanted to do business. It was almost like a collective change of philosophy; a change so fine it was almost undetectable. But pressure for results was being upped a little, and balancing the scales between his sources and his customers was causing extra friction.

In short, Abdul's almost inviolable powerbase seemed to be coming under threat; as though some others wanted to move in on his operation and effectively reduce his influence to that of a mere cog in a big wheel. His position as a warlord was becoming increasingly untenable.

Abdul's ability to sense danger was legendary; he had the awareness of a wild animal. He also understood that his position in the chain of operations between his powerbase and the big hitters in the West could only be undeniable so long as he held the upper hand. And he knew there was a sense of impatience in the demands being made on him, and powerful men were becoming restless.

But the American guy sitting across the table from him was not in that league, and he would often try to extract more from Abdul whenever he negotiated the deals on behalf of his paymasters. Despite his power, Abdul was no mug; he needed to keep the Americans and the British happy. But keeping the big guns happy didn't mean he had to listen to the inflated ego of a minion. The man was becoming a nuisance and Abdul was losing his patience fast.

'The girl has been spoken for,' Abdul told the American. 'She is part of my next shipment.' He waved a dismissive hand. 'It was a mistake that you saw her. Believe me, she is not for you.'

The American persisted. 'Abdul, my friend, who is to know if the girl has been used?' He shrugged. 'And we have been doing business for some time. I think you owe me.'

Abdul put out a restraining hand and stood up. 'I owe nothing to anybody but to keep my word. And my word is that this girl will be delivered clean and untouched.' He went to move away from the table when the American reached forward and grabbed his arm. Abdul looked down at the man in surprise. Then that emotion turned to disbelief that the American should have the temerity to lay hands on him.

He pulled his arm away and stepped out from the table. 'You will not do that again,' he said quietly, but venomously. Then he walked over to the door of the room and pulled it open.

The American stood up and was about to say something when the two men who had been in the room with them stepped forward and blocked his path. Abdul nodded his head sharply and left the room. If the American was wondering what was happening, he was about to find out. The moment Abdul closed the door a crashing fist sent the American into oblivion.

Fifteen minutes later the two men carried the American's body out of the farmhouse and tossed it into the back of a Toyota pick-up truck. There was no sign of Abdul, just the faint trail of dust from his Landcruiser that signalled his departure.

The two heavies climbed into the pick-up. Beyond them was an enormous expanse of wasteland; an enormous expanse in which to dump the dead American.

THREE

MARCUS FOLLOWED SUSAN into Old Street Underground Station. He had put on the sunglasses and zipped his leather jacket, relying on an amateur like Susan to have no idea she was being followed by a professional. Marcus liked that word; it made him feel good. Susan was easy to keep in sight, probably because she had her mind on other things. Marcus was intrigued as well, but not by what she had said; more by what she had unwittingly revealed to him.

He used his Oyster Card to walk through the turnstiles at the station and followed Susan down to the Northern Line platform. She was heading south. He stood about twenty feet away from her, losing himself among the other travellers and listened out for the rush of air that would signal the presence of an oncoming train.

From time to time he would glance at Susan and have little fantasies about her. He wondered what she would be like on a date, and how far he could get with her. Would dinner be sufficient, he wondered? Would he have to impress her with conversation, with his dress sense, or with his worldly knowledge? She was certainly an attractive woman, and she hadn't said anything about having a husband, or a boyfriend, or a partner even.

He spun round quickly as Susan turned and looked in his direction, then he turned back after a suitable pause and saw that she was no longer facing him, but was staring directly ahead towards the huge adverts on the far side of the track. He began to fidget with an imaginary object in his pocket, and then cursed himself for being so unprofessional. He had to act normal, cool he told himself. If he was to persuade Susan that he was worth employing, he had to convince himself that it was worth a gamble; after all, it could end terribly for them both.

The train rumbled in and eased to a halt. The doors slid open and the people on the platform crowded on to the train. Marcus sat half a carriage length away from Susan and kept an eye on her as covertly as he could. He tried to remember what he had read in the police training manuals about surveillance techniques. Not that he had been in the police force, but there was an enormous amount of information on the internet and in the public libraries.

During the time he was on the train, he kept amusing himself by imagining all kinds of scenarios that could fit the picture as far as Susan's brother David was concerned. He came to the conclusion there was no chance of ever finding out, but he conjured up vivid pictures of himself performing a heroic rescue straight out of the pages of a Special Forces novel. And at the end of the epic adventure, Susan would fall into his arms and pledge undying love and devotion for rescuing her brother.

The train jolted a little as it stopped at Clapham Common and woke Marcus just in time to see Susan stepping off the train. He leapt up and made it through the sliding doors as they were about to close. He was the only other passenger to alight at that station, but Susan did not notice because she had disappeared down the exit tunnel before Marcus could compose himself.

He ran to the exit and saw her walking out on to the street, turning right out of the station. He followed and kept a safe and reasonable distance from her until she turned into a road of semi-detached, Victorian houses.

Marcus was about fifty yards behind Susan when he saw her turn into a gateway. He kept his eye on the opening where she had disappeared and walked past it, glancing at the bay windows and patterned glass door beneath a small arch. He saw the number and continued on until he was well past the house.

The next stage of Marcus's master plan was to find an internet café and pay for a booth. He found one in the High Street populated by a mixture of gangsta rap aficionados covered in bling. The owner of the café looked like he could have easily gone the distance with the world heavyweight boxing champion, and won.

Once he had logged on, Marcus went on to British Telecom and entered Susan Ellis into the search box for residential numbers. He added Clapham and came up with fifteen people named Ellis. Nine of them had the initial 'S'.

Using the back of the sheet of paper he had been doodling on in his office, he wrote all the numbers down and then logged off. He paid for his time and then went in search of a public phone box.

Some of the numbers rang and eventually left him with an answering service to talk to. When he did get through to a person on the other end of the line, he pretended he was an Eco representative who could insulate the house and reduce its carbon footprint. He got short shrift for that and Susan Ellis was no different; she certainly wasn't interested because she lived in a flat. Sorry and all that.

Marcus smiled as he put the phone down and underlined Susan's number on his scrap of paper. All he had to do now was move on to stage two of his plan and find out more about the mysterious Mr Cavendish.

Chief Master Sergeant Danny Grebo drove out of the gates at Royal Air Force Lakenheath in Suffolk and motored the four miles to the town of Brandon with a lot on his mind. The information he had received was not good; it looked like the far end of the operation was experiencing some unexpected difficulty, but it hadn't come to his attention soon enough. That was part of the reason for having a great deal to think of; the lack of a strong link between his end of the operation and the source. When information came in at such a slow rate, it was difficult to act upon it with any degree of confidence. Everything had to be locked down tight, no gaps. But now a single crack was beginning to show and the organization was having to act on it.

He pulled into the car-park of The Flintknappers in the Market Hill and pulled the Buick over to the far side, away from the main road. He knew he was expected and hoped that he wouldn't be kept waiting.

Danny Grebo was a naturalized American. His parents were Bosnian immigrants who had moved to America before the civil war broke out in Yugoslavia. Danny's real name was Danvor, but the kids in his neighbourhood always called him Danny. The name had stuck, even though Danvor was the name he used when he joined the United States Air Force.

Grebo was in logistics. It was not his choice of employment when he enlisted, but service in some of the hotspots of the world had taught him an invaluable lesson: good logistics was the key to a successful campaign. Whatever the guys up front wanted or needed, the people in logistics had to come up with it. And Grebo was good; so good he had made a substantial living out of supplying what was needed at the right time, legit or not.

He was a wealthy man, but most of his wealth was secreted in offshore banks in the Caribbean. It wouldn't do for a non-com to show considerable wealth on a chief's pay packet. He was due for release within six months and he intended moving up the ladder of the organization and taking a more proactive role in it. For now he was a small but important cog in a big chain, and part of his role meant acting as a messenger from time to time. And that was his role for the present; to pass on a message to another important cog in the wheel.

The man waiting for Danny Grebo was propping up the bar, his big fist wrapped round a bottle of Budweiser. He turned as Grebo walked in and straightened up.

'Hey, Danny!'

Grebo winked at him. 'Hey, Chuck.'

They shook hands. Grebo asked the bartender for a Budweiser.

When the bottle had been opened, but not poured – the Yanks couldn't get used to the quaint idea of having their beer poured into a glass – Grebo and his companion adjourned to a table beside a window. There was a loudspeaker above them with soft music burbling from it, mingling with the occasional roar of traffic from outside. His friend took a swig of beer and banged the bottle down on the table.

'What's the panic, Danny?' he asked.

His name was Dale Berry, and he and Grebo went back a long way. He was called Chuck after the sixties pop singer, Chuck Berry. He was in transport, but not motor vehicles. Chuck Berry flew; he was a Hercules pilot. He had been an F15 combat pilot, but an accident in the Iraq conflict had meant an enforced change for him and he had converted from single engines to the multi-engined Hercules.

'We lost a guy,' Grebo answered, and took a mouthful of beer. He belched and studied the label on the bottle for a moment. 'I didn't find out until yesterday.'

'What happened?'

Grebo glanced around the bar and then at Berry. 'He disappeared, never came back.'

'Did he do a runner?'

Grebo shook his head and curled his lips. 'Not this guy, he was making too good a living out of it.' He shrugged. 'I got word that the fucking ragheads have topped him.'

Berry studied Grebo's expression for a few seconds. His own was stern and thoughtful. 'When did this happen?' he asked.

Grebo leaned forward and whispered through clenched teeth, 'Two fucking months ago.'

Berry knew better than to press Grebo on the details, but it was important to him, for his own sake that he knew why it had taken so long for the news to filter through.

'Why did it take so long?'

Grebo relaxed. 'Diplomatic sources,' he told Berry. It was a euphemism that Berry understood. He didn't know who Grebo worked for directly, but he did know that Grebo was a small link in a very big chain, and it was these very senior people that Grebo was referring to as the diplomatic sources.

'So what happens now?'

Grebo took another pull at his beer. 'They're gonna try and smoke the raghead out. They're gonna put a team in and they want you to do the drop.'

Berry nodded thoughtfully, rolling the Budweiser in his hand, and settled back in his chair. 'What will be my cut?'

Grebo shrugged. 'The usual, but there'll be no pick-up this time. That's all I can tell you. But listen up; none of the team that goes in knows of the connection between the raghead and the diplomats. By using you, we are keeping this in-house. The drop has got to be right.'

'What about getting them out?' Berry asked, knowing that once the team had been parachuted in from the Hercules, they were no longer his responsibility.

'Once the job is done, the team will be brought out by helicopter.'

Berry understood the reasoning behind the decision to get him to fly the Hercules transport. He was due to begin another tour of duty in Afghanistan the following week at the American military base at Khost, and he was one of the very few men who were part of a highly secret cartel who owed little allegiance to their flag. There had been times before when he had flown a covert mission to extract a live cargo, but the live cargo had always been women and children and he had never flown them to any allied air force base, but always to a remote strip somewhere near the Turkmenistan border, in the north-west of Afghanistan. For that he had been paid a handsome sum. And he had never questioned the morals or ethics of what he was doing.

Marcus picked up the phone and dialled the Foreign and Commonwealth Office. There was very little delay and a charming female voice told him that he had reached the Foreign and Commonwealth Office and how could she help him?

'Could you put me through to Mr Cavendish, please?'

'One moment, sir. Who may I say is calling?'

'Marcus Blake.'

'Thank you Mr Blake.'

Marcus relaxed and gazed around the impoverished walls of his office, rattling the tips of his fingers on the desk top while the music played softly in his earpiece.

The music stopped and the operator came back on the line.

'Mr Blake, I'm sorry, but there is no one of that name here at the Foreign Office.'

Marcus sat upright. 'Are you sure?' he asked without thinking.

'Yes, sir; I have just checked the computer directory of employees here and there is no one listed under the name of Cavendish.'

'Oh.' It was all he could think of saying at that moment. Then, 'Oh well, thank you anyway.'

'Thank you, sir.' The phone went dead.

Marcus put it back in its cradle. He sat like that for a while, his hand still lying on the phone and began to think of those points he had written while doodling and listening to Susan Ellis.

Cavendish. There had been something puzzling him about the man. When Susan Ellis told Marcus about her brief encounter with him, she had told him that she didn't have Cavendish's phone number and that she couldn't call him back because his number had been withheld.

It was also odd that he seemed to know her the moment she walked into Starbucks, although that in itself was not significant. But the nonsense about the diplomatic bag was stretching things a bit, Marcus thought. His father had worked for the diplomatic corps all his life and

Marcus wondered how much credence he would put in a story like that. He picked up the phone, hit the speed dial and waited. A minute later his father came on the line.

'Sir Henry Blake.'

Marcus chuckled. His father always answered the phone sounding as though he was looking down his nose at the caller.

'Hallo, Dad, it's Marcus.'

He sensed, rather than heard his father pull away from the phone.

'Emily, do we know anybody called Marcus?'

Marcus rolled his eyes and waited. Then he heard his mother's shout of joy in the background and the click of the phone extension as she picked it up.

'Marcus, how lovely to hear from you. It's been ages since you last called.'

'A month, Mother.'

'Four months, Marcus.'

Marcus contested that. 'Well, maybe three.'

'How are you, Marcus? Are you keeping well? When are you going to visit us? Your father and I would love to see you.' Marcus just kept nodding. 'And are you still working?'

'Yes to all that, Mother,' Marcus butted in. He loved his mother dearly, but she wouldn't stop if he didn't say anything. 'Now, can I speak to Dad, please?'

'I'm still here Marcus, as always.'

'I know, Dad. Now look, I need a favour.'

His father made some kind of grunting sound down the phone. 'Trouble with that escort agency of yours, is that it? Not enough Z-list clients?'

Marcus rolled his eyes again. 'Dad, I do not run an escort agency. I provide minders for important people.'

'And how many minders do you have on your books?' his father asked.

'Well, it's mainly me,' he admitted. 'But I do have men I can call on.'

'As I thought; you're sitting on your backside all day pretending you're a big operator in the City. Why don't you come home and get a proper job?'

'I don't need one, Dad; I'm happy and have enough money to keep my head above water.'

'Your grandmother's inheritance? Thought you would have blown that by now.'

Marcus had been left a generous annuity by his grandmother, part of which he had carefully reinvested and was now more than just comfortable.

'So what do you need me for?' his father asked.

'Do you know anybody by the name of Cavendish?' Marcus asked him. 'A guy probably your age, might have gone to public school, university. Might have been in the military. Member of one of your clubs, perhaps?'

'Hmm.' The sound rolled down the phone line. 'I knew a Cavendish at Westminster. Went into the City, I think.'

There was silence for a while and Marcus knew his father was thinking. It was a positive sign because his father would never dwell on something that he knew he couldn't possibly recall, so this was promising.

'Of course,' his father said suddenly. 'I met a Cavendish a few years ago in Hong Kong, Something to do with military intelligence. It wasn't the Cavendish I knew at school, but I do remember when I met this chap I asked him if we were at school together. He must have thought I'd lost my marbles.'

Marcus clenched a fist and gently punched the air.

His father went on, 'So yes, I do know a Cavendish, but if he's your man, he doesn't know me. Well, maybe he does. If he's in Intelligence he'll know every bloody diplomat going. Does that answer your question, dear boy?'

Marcus nodded. 'You're a diamond, Dad, thanks a million.'

'Wait, wait!' his father called down the phone. 'Don't think I'm letting you off the hook that easy. Now, your mother and I want you to come up for a day or two. Can you pull yourself away from your not so busy schedule to see us?'

'Tell you what, Dad,' Marcus began, trying to come up with all kinds of imaginative reasons for delaying the inevitable. 'Let me run this Cavendish bloke down and I'll get back to you.'

'Marcus.' This was his mother. 'Your father is talking about Sir Giles Cavendish. We met him at the handing-over ceremony in Hong Kong. I think he was rather taken with me, but your father saw him off. Spoil sport,' she added, with a chuckle.

'Take no notice, Marcus,' his father urged him. 'And be sure to come up here and see us.'

'I will, Dad. Promise. Love you both!' He put the phone down and leapt out of the chair. 'Yes!' he shouted. 'A result.'

FOUR

THE MERCEDES ROLLED smoothly to a stop outside one of the large residences in a leafy avenue in St John's Wood in London. It was almost midnight and the occupants of the car could not be seen through the blackened windows. There were a few lights showing from the windows of other houses in the road, but not enough to deter the man who stepped from the car.

He was wearing a long black overcoat with the collar turned up. He had sunglasses on, despite the darkness, and was also wearing a fedora hat, pulled down low to avoid recognition. The driver of the car had opened the door for the passenger and, now that the man had gone through the gate and was striding up the path towards the house, he closed the car door and slipped his bulk effortlessly into the driver's seat and moved the car away from the kerb.

The passenger reached the door of the house which was opened for him without the need for him to announce his presence, and he stepped inside where he stood quite still while another man patted him down, searching him for weapons.

Once the procedure was completed, he was shown through a door into a large drawing room where two other men were seated. The lighting in the room was subdued, but this was used to create shadows in which the two men were sitting and where the third man now joined them.

Once the trio had nodded their introductions, none of which was verbally necessary or even allowed, another door opened and three young girls were brought in through the open doorway. They were all dressed in very little clothing, and what they were wearing was carefully arranged to leave very little to the imagination.

A brutish-looking man followed the girls into the room and closed the door behind him. He was dressed completely in black and wore no jewellery. He wore his hair close cropped, rather like the style favoured by American servicemen, but he wasn't anything of the kind; his name was Milan Janov, cousin of Danny Grebo.

Janov was carrying three folders and he handed one to each of the men sitting in the room. He gave them time to browse through the folders until he was satisfied that they were aware of what they contained. Despite the shadows, the men had no difficulty in picking out the inventory of weapons that was printed therein.

'Do you have any observations?' he asked the men once they had finished looking through the folders.

It was the man who had been a passenger in the Mercedes who answered first.

'Do they speak English?' he asked, nodding towards the girls.

'Simple words,' he said, shaking his head, 'but not enough to understand a conversation.' He looked at the girls who were standing forlornly in the line, and smiled knowingly. 'But they will soon understand the words you will need to encourage them.'

'Are they virgins?' the man asked.

Janov nodded emphatically. 'Yes. I would not offer you anything less. Once you have finished with them, they can go into the system.'

'If there is anything left of them worth keeping,' one of the men said. They all laughed; the man who had made the remark was well known for his sadism.

'The list,' the passenger said, raising the folder, 'it is comprehensive, but fairly simple. When would you expect delivery?'

Janov stepped forward so that his face came into the shadows. 'As always you will be given ample time to get the weapons together. I expect you to deliver within two weeks. They must be in the warehouse by then.'

'What about the other merchandise?' one of the men asked.

Janov turned his head away in a quick movement. 'It is waiting for you and will be handed over once you have confirmed you have the weapons. Agreed?'

They all nodded their acceptance of what was a very simple contract made by men of honour; if that was the right word to describe men who held positions of immense power in their respective fields.

'Good,' Janov said, with satisfaction. 'Now, you can take the girls upstairs. There are drinks in the room and the usual equipment. I will give you two hours. The room is well soundproofed, so go upstairs and enjoy yourselves.'

The three men stood up with smiles beginning to gather on their faces and followed Janov who was leading the three girls from the room. At that point, the three young teenagers had no idea exactly what was waiting for them in that room upstairs.

Marcus saw the punch coming and turned inside his opponent's swinging arm, bringing his elbow snapping into the man's rib cage. But the jab did not affect his opponent because he brought his knee up and drove it into Marcus's thigh. Marcus yelled and jumped back, then spun and lifted his leg to kick out at the man's face. All this succeeded in doing was to unbalance him slightly. This gave his opponent an opportunity to drive forward as Marcus struggled to regain any momentum. The blow to Marcus's face was not unexpected, but he was able to deflect most of the effect by lifting his forearm and grabbing the man's wrist. He pushed it away and dived underneath the upraised arm, spun and kicked the man sharply in the rib cage. The man winced and Marcus seized the moment and drove his fist into the man's side. The man collapsed on to the floor, then spun like a street dancer. His rotating legs caught Marcus across the ankle and whipped his legs from beneath him. Marcus went down, flat on his back. His opponent leapt up and pounced, driving his knee into Marcus's chest and pushing a hand down hard on to his throat.

'You lose, Marcus,' he declared triumphantly. 'Now you've got to buy me lunch.'

'Sod you, Maggot,' Marcus cried, and tried to wriggle free as his opponent eased the pressure on his throat. 'You always seem to get the better of me.'

Maggot laughed and stood up, hauling Marcus with him. 'That's because you don't try,' he told him, as he slipped off his protective headgear. 'You know, Marcus, you would be so much better if you bloody concentrated.'

Marcus got to his feet. 'I let you win, anyway,' he joked. 'It's the only way to stop you moaning all week.' He pulled off his headgear and followed Maggot across the gymnasium floor to where their towels were hanging from coat hooks.

'So, where do you want to go for lunch?' Marcus asked his friend. 'McDonald's?'

'Now, now,' Maggot complained. 'You know I'm a vegetarian. I don't eat meat.'

'That settles it then,' Marcus answered, 'we'll go to Dimitri's Burger Bar.'

Maggot flicked him with his towel. 'Bloody cheek,' he said. 'Next time I beat you up, I'll do it for real.'

Marcus had known Maggot for years. Nobody knew how he came by the name because his real name was Rafiq Shah. His mother and father were from the remote region of northern Pakistan. They came from the small town of Beraul Bandal, about ten miles from the Afghanistan border and had arrived in England as working doctors when Maggot was an infant. Marcus had met Maggot at university. They struck up an instant friendship and took up martial arts together. Maggot said it was because he wanted to compensate for his naturally slight frame, while Marcus took up the sport because Maggot had persuaded him to.

Maggot went into teaching once he had left university, but he found it difficult because of the struggle he had at the boys' school where he taught. He told Marcus that young boys needed an alpha male role model to look up to and respect, and that he felt he was failing to supply that need. Marcus told him that it was because he was a bloody lousy teacher and they laughed about it. But in the end, Maggot gave up teaching and opened a small gymnasium south of the River Thames, and it was there that he and Marcus spent many a happy hour beating the living daylights out of each other.

'Why don't you get a proper job?' Maggot asked.

'That's what my dad says,' Marcus answered.

They had finished the lunch that Marcus had willingly paid for and were now having a drink. Marcus had a beer while Maggot had a Coke. Beside them the Thames flowed past effortlessly and the sun tried desperately to come out from behind the clouds. The weather was being kind and allowed them to sit in the garden of the pub without getting too cold.

'How about next week, Maggot, can you make it?'

Maggot shook his head. 'Sorry, Marcus, but I'll be in Pakistan.'

'Visiting family?'

Maggot nodded. 'Something like that. And what about you, what's your latest project?' he asked.

Marcus explained briefly about Susan Ellis and Cavendish. 'So I want to know who this Cavendish bloke is,' he finished.

'Do you think he has a connection with the girl's brother then?' Maggot asked him.

'Got to,' Marcus said sternly. 'Otherwise it doesn't make bloody sense. He's not a do-gooder, is he? I mean, how come he brings her a piddling bit of information about her brother yet lies about who he really is?'

'You say he's Secret Service,' Maggot reminded him. 'Could be a bit dodgy poking your nose in there, you know.'

Marcus shot him a sideways glance and lifted the glass to his mouth. 'I haven't done anything yet,' he said.

Maggot shifted on his chair. 'No, but you will, won't you?'

Marcus took a mouthful of beer before answering. He put his glass down. 'The way I see it,' he began, 'is that I could find out who this Cavendish bloke is and pass that on to Susan Ellis. Then she could go to the Press and maybe stir up a little mischief; find out about her brother that way.'

Maggot leaned forward, his expression taking a more serious tone. 'You know, Marcus, my mother and father have always loved it here in this country. Always believed it was truly the land of the free and the fair, but now they admit their adopted nation is no longer free and fair; it's no longer safe. Since we climbed into bed with the Americans after 9/11 we have been forced to submit ourselves to the security forces. We've given them *carte blanche* to decide what the meaning of freedom is for the British people. They blame terrorism, the Muslims, other people, other countries. But they use those reasons as a stick with which to beat us and subdue us.' He pointed a finger at Marcus. 'Just be very careful who you get tangled up with, Marcus. Let Susan Ellis find her own way in this. Her brother is probably dead anyway. Don't add to the body count.'

Marcus tipped his head over to one side and regarded Maggot with a curious expression.

'You know, Maggot if we all gave in like that, we'd have been under the jackboot years ago. That Cavendish bloke has dumped on Susan Ellis and simply added to her grief and worry. She has no way of ever learning the truth, and if I don't help her, no other bugger will.'

Maggot smiled at him. 'You always were a softy, Marcus. That's why I keep beating you.'

Marcus leaned across the table and lightly punched his friend in the arm. 'As long as there is breath in my body ...'

Maggot leaned back and started laughing. 'Oh come on, Marcus, don't give me that bullshit; you just fancy the girl, don't you?'

'Well,' Marcus admitted, 'she is a bit tasty. Got to get in with her some way, haven't I?'

Maggot pulled a face. 'It's up to you, Galahad, but, like I said, don't add to the body count.'

Marcus laughed. 'As if I would,' he said. 'As if I would.'

David Ellis stared at the far wall and thought about a story his father had once told him. During the days of National Service in Britain his father knew a married soldier who spent time lying on his bed staring at the ceiling because he had no money and didn't want to sponge off his mates. He couldn't afford to anyway. He said the soldier was able to find all manner of interesting things on the ceiling, providing he let his imagination run away with him.

So David was staring at the far wall and trying desperately to let his imagination run away with him. But all he could think of was why there was no paint on the wall and what he would do if he had to redecorate. Which was silly, anyway because he was imprisoned in a bloody cave and the walls would probably look worse if he tried painting them.

This was where they brought him during the day. He didn't know why, but it was what they did, and when evening came and the sun had set, he was taken back to a place which was little more than an old farmhouse inside a compound.

He had no recollection of time; it simply passed by and had no impact on him. The days merged, one into the other, and his only joy, if it could be called that, was the walk from the house to the cave in the morning, and the return journey in the evening.

He tried applying the soldier's mind games to that journey and imagining he was going on a trip. But the trouble was the trip only lasted about two minutes and there was precious little time to get his mind into gear and let his imagination run away with him.

Each morning, before leaving the house, David was allowed to have a good breakfast. He was also allowed to wash and have clean underwear. The cave was little more than a deep hole in the rock. It had a slight curve so that he couldn't see outside while he was in there, but at least he had sufficient light by which to see. He wasn't allowed to read anything, so his own attempt at playing that soldier's games was the only distraction he could employ. He was always shackled to an iron ring set into the wall of the cave.

David had overcome his appalling injuries and was now nursing little more than an arthritic shoulder, a deep furrow along the side of his skull and a broken heart because of the loss of Shakira. He had no idea why he had been taken from the hospital, and guessed it might have had something to do with being a hostage and being useful as a negotiating tool. But he had been in the kidnappers' hands for almost a year now, a time he could only really judge by the seasons, and he was no closer to being released than he was when they first brought him there.

He was still contemplating the wall when he heard the sound of footsteps and realized the light had almost faded away to nothing. He had learned long ago that the sun didn't set in the Middle East; it simply fell out of the sky and disappeared within a minute of touching the horizon.

He began struggling to his feet when the Arab appeared brandishing some keys. David had a set of handcuffs hooked on to his belt. The Arab put a gag round David's mouth and then unlocked the cuffs and put them on David's wrists, ensuring that his hands were behind his back. Then he unlocked the chain which was attached to the iron ring set in the wall and nodded to David; the unspoken permission for David to leave the cave.

The two of them were halfway to the cave entrance when the sound of gunfire came crashing through the evening air. The Arab immediately pulled David back into the cave and held him there for a while. He then peered cautiously from where he was standing and suddenly darted forward, running from the cave leaving David behind. He was pulling the machine-gun from his shoulder as he ran.

David hurried forward and stopped by the cave entrance. He saw men running towards the compound firing their weapons as they went. Return fire started coming from beyond the wall, but suddenly a rocket propelled grenade hurtled into it and blew open a large section. Immediately the attackers ran towards the gaping hole, running through the smoke and dust that had billowed up.

As the sun disappeared completely, so the light dropped to a yellowing gloom. Explosions began coming from the compound as grenades were being lobbed in by the attackers. David could pick out the sounds of rifle fire as the defenders in the house returned volley after volley. Suddenly, one side of the house fell away as another grenade launched at it found a weak spot, and the ancient, crumbling walls collapsed into a smoking, dusty heap.

David could see men pouring out of the house and being picked off by the attackers. Then he saw flames blossoming up from the old place and could see there was little more the defenders could do; whoever was attacking them was a well-drilled team.

David had never witnessed a fire fight, but had heard many reports of the bedlam, the fury and the fear that is felt and experienced by all who are involved. The fear gives an adrenalin rush to many of the combatants, and those who are left behind are usually dead. There are certainly no prisoners taken, and those who lie on the ground wounded will probably die of their wounds anyway.

It was over in minutes. The attackers had come swiftly and taken the men in the house completely by surprise. David watched as the attackers moved around the compound, rolling bodies over and dispatching those who had not been killed. He wondered what he should do, whether to run out of the cave and let himself be seen by the men or not. He couldn't shout at them because he was still gagged. If they had been sent to rescue him, they would not have destroyed the house as they would have secured it and left it reasonably intact so they could search for him.

He began to think that possibly these men were not there to rescue him. So what were they up to? And would he be of any use to them? Would they kill him as they had those who had survived the fire fight, or would they ignore him? Did they even know he was there, he wondered?

As if to answer his question, David heard the sound of a helicopter thundering its way towards the scene of the battle. And as the last rays of the sun disappeared completely, the silhouette of the chopper came into view and landed on the hard ground, throwing up clouds of dust. Very quickly the attackers ran towards the chopper and merged with the billowing sandstorm until their figures could be seen no more. Then the helicopter lifted and thundered up and away, the chopping sound of its blades reverberating through the evening air until the sight and sound of it was no more.

It was over. Only David was left. And he was still gagged and hand-cuffed.

FIVE

MARCUS KNEW THAT unless he had a good reason, he would get short shrift if he went to the headquarters of MI6 at Vauxhall Cross and asked to see Sir Giles Cavendish. He thought he might try using his father as a reason for asking, perhaps by intimating that his father and Cavendish were old schoolfriends, which of course they were not; he might be able to use that as an angle. If he played the idiot, it might work. He also knew that if he walked into MI6 headquarters and asked somebody to point out Cavendish to him, or show him a photograph, he would be arrested and thrown in jail for a couple of days until he had been checked out by the police. So that was not an option. So he found another way, and that was why he was sitting on a bench on the Embankment with his father on a very cold day.

What Marcus had done was to agree to spend a weekend with his parents if his father would agree in return to help him identify Cavendish. So, on the Monday morning after Marcus's weekend visit, he travelled down to London on the train with his father and went immediately to his father's club, Whites in St James's Street. There was no way Marcus was going to suggest to his father that they went to his office in Oliver's Yard.

At about midday, Henry Blake phoned MI6 headquarters and asked to speak to Sir Giles Cavendish. He was put through by the operator and reached Cavendish's secretary. He was asked his business.

'I'm an old school chum of Sir Giles. Thought I'd look him up while I'm in London. Surprise him.'

'Who shall I say is calling?'

'Sir Henry Blake.'

'One moment, sir.'

The silence that followed was interrupted by music. Then, a minute or so later, the secretary came back on the line. 'I'm sorry, sir, but Sir Giles has no recollection of anyone by that name from his school years. He does apologize and hopes this hasn't inconvenienced you. Good day.'

The phone went dead. Blake looked at his son. 'Well, Marcus, I said they would be a suspicious lot. At least we know he's there, don't we?'

Marcus nodded his approval. 'OK Dad, now we go and wait until he goes to lunch.'

And that was why they were sitting on the bench, and had been for an hour or so when Cavendish came out of the building and hailed a cab. Blake stiffened and nodded in the man's direction.

'That's him, Marcus. I remember the randy old goat as if it were yesterday.'

'Did he really chase after Mum?' Marcus asked.

'He wasn't the only one,' Blake muttered. 'They were like flies round the jam pot sometimes.'

Marcus smiled at the thought. 'Never make a pretty woman your wife, so the song goes,' he said to his father, and put his arm up to a passing taxi.

'I'll remind you when it's your turn to get married,' his father said, and stood up. 'OK my boy, time I caught the train back home and let you get back to this mysterious job you've got.'

'I haven't got it yet,' he lamented. 'But I may be able to provoke a reaction and get into someone's good books,' he said, as he climbed into the cab.

'Pretty, is she?'

Marcus looked up at his father's smiling face. He held out his hand. His father took it and then leaned forward and gave him a hug. He felt Marcus's body stiffen slightly.

'Be careful, Marcus. No heroics. And don't let your mother know what we've been up to; she'd have a fit.'

Marcus winked at him. 'Thanks, Dad. I'll see you around.'

He turned to the taxi driver and pointed up the Embankment to where Cavendish was getting in his taxi. 'Follow that cab.'

Sir Giles Cavendish paid off the taxi outside Covent Garden and wandered down the stairs through the throng of tourists watching the classical musicians busking in the small area allocated for the acts that performed there. Not far behind, Marcus followed using his camera like any tourist, and making sure Cavendish was in every shot.

Cavendish had not bothered to wear a coat and was now beginning to wish he had. But his business in Covent Garden wasn't going to take up too much of his time, and he knew the man he was meeting would probably not want to linger either.

He saw him sitting at an outside table, still with his black overcoat buttoned up. It was one of the little foibles of The Right Honourable James Purdy, Secretary of State for International Development, that he was never without the coat. He stood up as Cavendish pulled out a chair and sat down. Purdy glanced over at the inconspicuous watcher in black whom he knew would be carrying a gun, and nodded that his visitor was bona fide.

Cavendish sat down and ordered a cup of English tea with milk. He looked across the table at the minister and noticed a bruise on the side of his face. Cavendish touched the side of his own cheek.

'Fall over?' he asked.

The minister chuckled. 'Didn't take enough water with it, old boy.'

Cavendish noticed he had three scratch marks beneath his ear. 'My, my, you certainly have been in the wars.'

'Nothing a good nurse can't handle.'

Cavendish mumbled something and then spotted the waitress walking towards him with his tea. He waited until it was served and the waitress had left before opening up his conversation again.

'Thank you for agreeing to meet me here, Minister. I find it useful to have the public around with all the noise and what have you. And I'm sure we can keep this in-house as it were.'

The minister smiled. 'So long as what you wish to talk about does not fall within the parameters of my role within the Cabinet,' he replied.

Cavendish shifted slightly, moving his body in such a way that it opened up into a friendly gesture. 'It has nothing to do with your job, Minister, more to do with you.'

The minister's eyes widened. 'Oh, in what way?'

Cavendish looked across at the minder and held his hands open above the table for a brief moment. Then he reached into his jacket and pulled out a small envelope.

'I would like you to look at these photographs and say nothing or do anything.'

He slid the envelope across the table. The minister reached forward, a curious expression beginning to scramble his features. He opened the envelope and pulled out the photographs. Immediately the colour drained from his face and he looked across at Cavendish.

'What the blazes...?'

Cavendish held up his hand. 'I know how you got the bruises and the scratches on your face, Minister. Now, would you like to arrange to speak to me privately, with or without your lawyer?'

Cavendish's expression was as hard and cold as iron. It also looked regal; rather like an eagle on its eyrie, its prey struggling beneath the vicious talons that were sunk deep into its victim's flesh.

And standing above them, leaning against the railings, Marcus was busy photographing the whole thing.

David Ellis heard the sound of a vehicle grinding its way across the rocky ground towards the compound. He sat up and struggled to his feet, then edged his way carefully to the cave opening.

David had hobbled out of the cave once the attack was over and struggled down to the compound. In all he counted about twenty bodies as he searched among the ruins and the devastation. There was nobody left alive.

He made it into what was left of the house and began searching around for something to help him get off his gag. He came across an old wooden coat hook and managed to remove his gag by slipping the edge of the hook between his cheek and the gag and pulling down sharply.

Once the gag was off, David was able to find a container of water. Although it was lying flat on its side and most of the water had dribbled out, he was at least able to get down to it like a dog and fidget with it until he had drunk enough to quench his thirst.

He knew he would find some food because the men would have been preparing supper when the attack came. He came across a cupboard, its door shattered and hanging from its hinges. He found fruit, bread and some meat. But before he attempted to eat anything, he went in search of the man who had been his gaoler. If he could find that man's body, he was sure he would find the keys to his handcuffs.

It took David about twenty minutes to find the man and another twenty minutes of sheer frustration before he could bring his hands round to the front of his body and get the key to his handcuffs. Once he had removed them he had to rub his wrists gently to restore some life into them. He picked up the dead man's Kalashnikov machine-gun, took a bandoleer from the man's shoulders and went back into the house to eat.

David woke suddenly as the noise of a diesel engine invaded his sleep. He realized that he must have slept through the night because there was daylight penetrating the cave. He had chosen to stay there because he was afraid of being alone in the shattered house.

He looked down towards the compound as a Toyota pick-up truck bumped its way across the terrain. He tightened his grip on the Kalashnikov and waited, not really knowing what he would do. He wasn't sure if the men in the pick-up were hostile or not. It was an irony that didn't escape him because his kidnappers were hostile by definition, and the previous night's attackers were not concerned about searching for him, so they obviously had no interest in his predicament – if they even knew he existed.

So he watched and waited, and what he saw began to convince him that the men who had turned up were friends of those who had died fighting. He could see by their body language the despair that would have been seen on their faces. And that put him on the horns of a dilemma; should he go out to them, or remain hidden?

Suddenly one of the men barked out some instructions and began sweeping his arm round in a gesture that looked like he was urging them to search for something, or somebody; survivors, perhaps?

It took no more than five minutes before they were back together in a small group. There was a huddled conversation and the one who appeared to be the leader began looking around again. Then he suddenly pointed towards the cave where David was watching, and David realized then that it was over; there was no way he could offer up any resistance to these men because he was outnumbered and, in a sense, defenceless. So he dropped the Kalashnikov to the ground and the bandoleer and walked out of the cave with his hands in the air.

There were five men in the group and, as soon as they spotted David they broke into a run and came rushing across the rocks towards him. David stopped and let them come to him.

They were all wearing caftans, a traditional, hooded garment, but no headgear. Each one had a large leather belt around his waist with a fear-some-looking knife and sheath hanging from it. One of them spoke to David in English.

'Ellis, what happened here?'

David remembered him although he had only seen him once since he was taken from the hospital: it was Abdul Khaliq.

David simply gestured towards the compound and the house and explained what happened. His explanation was succinct and left Abdul in no doubt that the attackers were intent on one thing: murder.

'They didn't find you?'

David shook his head. 'They didn't look. Unfortunately it wasn't a rescue mission.'

Khaliq considered this for a moment, not taking his eyes off David. Then he said, 'You will help my men bury these people. We must cover them so the wolves and jackals cannot finish what they started during the night.' He turned away and began walking off towards the grim scene that lay before him. Then he stopped and turned towards David.

'They may not have come for you, my friend, but this may be the beginning of your freedom.'

And with that curious statement, he wheeled away and hurried towards the morbid task that awaited them.

Susan Ellis had been home from work little more than an hour when the phone rang. She lived on the ground floor of a Victorian house that had been converted into flats, and was in the kitchen at the rear of the house preparing her evening meal. She had no idea who could be calling her. She put the knife down that she had been using and wiped her hands on a paper towel, pulled off her apron and went through to her front room to answer the phone.

'Susan Ellis.'

'Good evening, Susan, this is Marcus Blake.'

She frowned and did not recognize the name for a moment. Then she realized who it was. 'Marcus Blake? How did you get my number?'

'With high skill, extreme perseverance and a modicum of luck. Can we talk?'

'What about?'

'Well, I would prefer to speak to you face to face.'

Susan wasn't keen on inviting a comparative stranger round to her home. 'Can't you tell me what it is you want to say over the phone?'

'I could,' he replied honestly, 'but I have something I want you to see and I can't exactly show you that over the phone.'

'Oh, well, why not try to explain what it is that you want to show me?'

Marcus sensed her extreme reluctance, but he was determined to push her until she relented.

'I cannot do that, but what I can do is invite you out to dinner and we can talk. It will be in public and you can leave whenever you wish. How does that suit you?'

She found herself nodding. 'Well, that's reasonable, but I was already preparing a meal for myself.'

'It's no fun dining alone, Susan. I know, because I do it so often.'

'Is this about my brother?' she asked him. Susan felt a little lift in her spirit and her skin tingled in anticipation. It was a momentary thing and passed quite quickly.

'Have dinner with me, Susan; there's something you need to know.'

'Bad news?'

'No, no,' he said quickly. 'Sorry, Susan, I didn't mean that kind of news. Look,' he urged her, 'meet me at the Regent Restaurant. It's at the bottom of your road. Eight o'clock. I'll see you there.'

Marcus put the phone down and looked at his watch. One hour; plenty of time to get across to Clapham Common and wait for Susan to turn up, as he was sure she would.

James Purdy sat opposite Cavendish in an office in the House of Commons. He looked mortified as the security man spelled out the consequences of his predilection for young girls, particularly those who were brought into the country illegally.

'You want me to resign, is that it?' Purdy asked.

Cavendish shook his head. 'That isn't for me to say, Minister. But I'm sure you can see the problem; we have here a Minister of State knowingly consorting with illegal immigrants for reasons of sexual perversion. It's clear that you are laying yourself open to blackmail, and that would, or could, jeopardize the security of our nation.'

'How did you get the bloody photographs?' the minister demanded to know.

Cavendish shrugged. 'Well, unless you want a detailed account of why we have been suspicious of you and what you've been up to for ages, I'm sure it doesn't take brains to realize that we do have our ways and means. We usually succeed in the end.'

Purdy stood up, quite angry and obviously worried. 'I could deny it all,' he ranted. 'Say I've been set up, the photos have been doctored. I'm a Minister of the Crown, for God's sake. And why on earth are MI6 involved in this? Aren't you supposed to be looking after our overseas interests?'

'Charity isn't the only thing that begins at home, Minister,' Cavendish reminded him. 'Our overseas responsibilities begin here as well. Something as Secretary of State for International Development you seem to take very lightly.'

'Damn it, Cavendish!' he shouted, slamming his hand down on the desk top. 'What are you trying to do? A little harmless, private fun and you poke your bloody noses in.' He stopped. Cavendish was holding up his hand.

'Your harmless, private fun resulted in the death of one of those girls. She was found in a rubbish skip not fifty yards away from where you sodomized and raped her; you and your companions. So don't talk to me about private, harmless fun, Minister. You are in deep, deep trouble and will go to prison for a very long time.'

Cavendish was getting angry and it was the last thing he wanted to do. He also wanted the minister to have a clear head and be given an opportunity to redeem himself by co-operating and agreeing to what it was Cavendish had in mind. He wished he'd been lying about the girl being found dead in a rubbish skip; for all the good that men like the cabinet minister do for those poor girls, and the life they put them into, they might just as well be dead before they were used and abused.

'But there is a way out for you,' he told him, 'for your own peace of mind and for the security of our country.'

The minister looked up expectantly, his brow furrowing into deep creases. 'What are you talking about?' He snapped out the question, his demeanour now very much like the cornered animal he was; no longer the urbane, cabinet minister who was seen so often in the debating chamber of the House.

Cavendish had no pity for him or his ilk. All he wished to do was get the truth out of the man and then rid the country of the vermin that he was. It galled him to offer him a way out.

'First of all, Minister, I want the names of the two men who were with you during your little bit of "fun", as you so describe it.'

The minister shook his head vigorously. 'Out of the question; I don't even know them.'

Cavendish looked at his watch. 'You can begin by telling lies if you wish,' he said, looking up, 'but eventually you will tell me what it is I want to know.'

The minister stretched his hands out across the table; his manner more compliant. 'Look, it's the truth; I do not know those men. We have to arrive incognito and remain so, for obvious reasons.' He dropped his voice a little. 'But I can get their names for you. Would that be enough?'

'That would depend how long it would take you.'

The minister drew his hands back and relaxed a little. He thought he recognized the beginning of the bargaining; the dealing that would be done in order to minimize the risk of exposure and subsequent scandal, to say nothing of a stretch in prison. He also thought he could see a way out of the danger he would undoubtedly face once others higher up the chain learned of his own misjudgement.

'I could have the names by midnight,' he told Cavendish.

The security man didn't trust him, but ironically the cards were in the minister's hands. If Cavendish had him arrested by Special Branch, the news would break immediately and be splashed all over the front pages. The prime minister would have no need to sack his Cabinet colleague because the minister would have resigned immediately, and the faceless ones, those whom Cavendish was really after, would fade away into the background and put their operation on hold. No, arresting the minister would serve no useful purpose at the moment.

He looked at his watch again. 'I will give you until this time tomorrow,' he told him. 'If you come up with those names and anything else you can tell me about them, I will withhold any action against you.' He stood up. 'I'll be here tomorrow. Oh, and please understand that you will now be under surveillance until then – just in case you decide to skip the country.'

The minister didn't bother to stand. 'I won't,' he said. 'You have my word on that.' He watched as Cavendish left the office and immediately began considering the quickest and most effective way of silencing him.

SIX

MARCUS WAS SEATED inside the Regent Restaurant when Susan walked in. He stood up immediately and waved at her from across the room. She half smiled when she saw him and came over to the table. Marcus thought she looked lovely. She had put on a coat to ward off the evening chill, but it was fitted and accentuated her figure. She had on a white beanie hat, but unlike a lot of people Marcus had seen wearing them, it looked lovely on her and emphasized the brunette shade of her hair that curled from beneath it.

Susan unbuttoned her coat and pulled off the hat, tossing her head a couple of times to get her hair to fall naturally into place. She was wearing a black turtle-neck sweater which made it all the more difficult for Marcus to take his eyes off her. He took her coat and hung it on a coat stand that was close by.

Susan was just settling into her chair when Marcus came back. She looked up at him and smiled.

'Thank you.'

Marcus sat down and asked her what she would like to drink. Susan said she would only have water, which was already on the table. He poured a glass for her and handed her a menu. Five minutes later the waiter had taken their order and they toasted each other's good health – Susan with her water and Marcus with his small beer.

'So, how did you get my phone number?' Susan asked him.

He smiled at her disarmingly. 'Dead easy; I followed you.'

Susan looked a little startled. 'You what?'

'When you left my office, I followed you. Once you reached your house, I went into an internet café and logged on to British Telecom.

Simple.' He couldn't help looking a little triumphant when he had finished.

'OK, so you got my phone number, but you wouldn't be the first to have it.' She sounded a little sharp with him. 'And what is it you have to show me? The reason you made me come here?'

Marcus put his hand in his jacket pocket and pulled out a couple of photographs. He passed them over to Susan.

'Recognize this man?' he asked, pointing at the picture.

Susan looked through the photographs, then back up at Marcus. 'This is Cavendish.' There was surprise in her voice. 'How did you—?' She stopped in mid-sentence, then her shoulders drooped a little. 'Of course, you went to the Foreign Office, right?'

Marcus shook his head and had a tight little smile on his face. 'He doesn't work at the Foreign Office. They've never heard of him.'

This brought Susan up straight. 'Then how did you?' She waved the photos at him. 'How did you find him? Why did you find him?'

Marcus reached across the table and took the photographs from her.

'Cavendish works in Intelligence. He is highly placed in MI6 and his name is Sir Giles Cavendish.'

Susan frowned. 'I don't understand.'

Just then the waiter appeared with the first course of their order. Susan had chosen pâté. Marcus had plumped for soup.

'When you told me how Cavendish had contacted you, how he had met you and all that,' Marcus said between mouthfuls, 'it struck me as most odd. You couldn't call him back because his number was withheld; he knew you as soon as you went into Starbucks, didn't give you his phone number, but gave you a long story about the diplomatic bag.'

Susan took a bite of toast. 'You thought of all this while I was talking to you?'

'I wrote it down.'

'You were doodling.'

'Sez you!'

'Well,' she said, through a mouthful of crumbs, 'you're crafty.'

He finished his soup, pushed his plate away and dabbed his mouth with his napkin.

'The question is, Susan; why did he do it?'

Susan just looked absently across the table and shook her head gently. 'I don't know,' she said softly. 'I really don't know.'

'He gave you nothing but a little hope, and then disappeared.' He leaned into the table. 'Susan, men like that do not do this kind of thing unless it's for a reason.'

Susan shook her head. 'Perhaps he wanted me to stir up something. Go to the Press or the television people.'

'And did you?' he asked.

She nodded. 'Didn't do any good, though; I don't think me and my brother are newsworthy enough. And I certainly couldn't afford the agencies, not even you,' she said pointedly. Marcus ignored the remark.

He watched her finish her pâté and toast. 'What are we going to do about it?' he asked.

'We?' She nearly choked on a piece of toast and had to take a drink of water to clear it. 'What do you mean, *we*? You know I can't afford to hire you.'

Marcus could see she was getting a little upset. He reached across the table and put his hand over hers.

'Let's see how far we can go with this, Susan,' he suggested. 'And don't worry about the fee; I'll cover it.'

An expression of disbelief came over Susan's face. 'Really?' she said softly.

He squeezed her hand. 'It's no big deal at the moment. Like I said, let's see how far we can go with this. Perhaps we can ginger up the newspapers; get them interested.'

'Do you think we can?' she asked him hopefully.

Marcus shrugged. 'I don't know, but we can try. First things first though; let's eat, get to know each other and tomorrow we'll confront Cavendish. How does that sound?'

Susan's eyes began to fill with tears. Marcus lifted her napkin off the table and handed it to her.

'Don't cry, Susan. Somehow, some way we will learn the truth about your brother, and something tells me that Cavendish will have the answers.'

It was shortly after eight o'clock in the evening when Marcus and Susan sat down to dine, and it was at precisely the same time that a signal arrived at the American Embassy in Grosvenor Square. It was for the Military Attaché, Commodore John Deveraux. The signal was encrypted, which prompted a phone call to the commodore's residence should he wish to come to the embassy and pick it up. This he chose to do and at nine o'clock that evening, Deveraux was sitting in his office with the signal in front of him on his desk. He had decoded it and was now shaking his head in frustration.

He picked it up and took a cigar lighter from his desk drawer. The flame blossomed, which he touched to the paper. As the charred remains dropped into his empty, metal wastebin, he picked up the decoded signal and torched that as well. He then picked up the wastebin and took it through to the small washroom that was attached to his office. He emptied the contents of the bin into the lavatory and flushed them away.

The next thing Deveraux did was to go to his wall safe and open it, taking out a cell phone. The phone was not one that he used for anything other than a very, very private conversation with some extremely unsavoury people.

He dialled a number and waited for a reply. He heard the connection being changed to another exchange until he was eventually connected to a voice that answered without a name. Deveraux spoke briefly, his last words delivered with a slight tremor.

'He's compromised. I want you to deal with it.'

He cancelled the call and put the phone back in his safe.

Marcus and Susan were now in a relaxed mood. Neither of them had drunk too much – a bottle of wine between them. They had let the evening roll by, enjoying each other's company, being silly, being serious. Marcus enjoyed every minute of it and hoped that Susan felt the same.

He was in such a good mood when the bill came, that Marcus gave the waiter a generous tip. Then he helped Susan on with her coat and took her arm as they walked out of the door.

It was fairly late and there was a chill in the night air. Because there was no wind about, they decided to walk a while before going back to Susan's flat. Marcus had no knowledge of the area and Susan, being a local girl, had very little reason to show caution at that time of night.

They strolled, arm in arm, talking of very little until they found themselves in a road where the streetlamps were not working. Suddenly Marcus felt Susan stiffen. He turned towards her and saw that she was looking directly ahead of them where two men had just walked from a doorway and were now standing motionless on the pavement just a few yards from them.

Marcus hadn't noticed them, but he did now, and could see that they were not standing there for fun. The men took a couple of steps forward. Then one of them stepped into the road and came up beside Marcus, standing about six feet from him. He was holding a knife.

Susan instinctively put her hand up to her mouth to scream, but nothing came out of her throat. Marcus felt her go absolutely rigid. As the man on the pavement advanced towards them, Marcus shoved Susan away and turned, bringing his leg up at the same time and lashed out at the attacker, catching him on the arm.

The force of Marcus's heel catching the man on the tip of his elbow made the man shout and curse loudly, and he dropped the knife. Before the man could react, Marcus dropped to the ground and supported his body on the heel of his hand, spun and brought both legs slashing across the mugger's knee caps. It dropped the man instantly.

Pushing the element of surprise and not giving either of the two men time to think, Marcus turned to face the second man who was advancing towards him. The attacker suddenly made a stabbing feint in Marcus's direction but then moved towards Susan. Marcus leapt forward, fending off the slashing knife thrust and jammed the heel of his hand into the man's face pushing his nose back up into his forehead.

The sound of the cracking bone and gristle made Susan scream out loudly. The man cried out in pain and immediately clutched his face. Marcus didn't pause and clenched his fist and swung it sideways, chopping him across the windpipe. This made the man gag and he fell forward on to his knees, putting his hands out to stop himself from falling. Marcus then drove his shoe into the man's face, knocking him back and then kicked him fiercely in the head.

As the man straightened up by the force of the kick, Marcus swung his arm downwards in a chopping motion and brought the heel of his hand down on to the busted nose. Blood erupted from the wound as the man screamed again and fell. As the man's hands touched the pavement, Marcus slammed the heel of his boot on to the man's fingers and broke those too.

He spun round and looked at the man whose kneecaps had been shifted severely and whacked him with another devastating blow, using his foot across the man's forehead. The man groaned and passed out.

Susan was still screaming and crying when Marcus had finished. He looked at her with the venom of his attack still burning fiercely in his eyes, and in the poor light, Susan knew she was looking at someone she didn't know. She pulled her hands away from her face and they were trembling violently.

Marcus grabbed her and dragged her away, shouting at her, 'Run! Run!'

Susan felt herself being propelled away from the hideous scene where the two men lay badly beaten and ran as fast as her legs would go. Marcus kept close behind her, keeping hold of her elbow as they fled.

Eventually they ran into a road where there were a number of shops, all closed, but there were a couple of public houses and an all night taxi rank. They ran up to the first of two taxis in the queue, yanked open the rear doors and dived in.

'Where to?' the driver asked.

'Just drive, we'll tell you when to stop.'

The taxi pulled away and Marcus flopped back into the soft seat. He looked at Susan and smiled. Susan continued to stare at him, still stunned.

'Marcus,' she managed to say eventually, 'who are you?'

He turned his head away, not in anger or anything like that. Then he laughed and glanced back at her.

'Maggot would have been proud of me tonight,' he answered, and just kept on laughing.

SEVEN

J AMES PURDY FINISHED reading *The Times* newspaper and turned his attention to the *Guardian*. There were various sections of both papers that had been marked as relevant for the minister, and it was simply a case of scanning the pages until he came across a section that merited some interest. After that he would turn his attention to the tabloids.

But, try as he might, Purdy was unable to absorb much of the written word; his mind was still on the meeting with Cavendish the previous afternoon and the unquestionable consequences once the news was out in the public domain.

Immediately after his meeting with Cavendish, Purdy had made a short, but discreet phone call. He vented his anger on the person he had called and remarked that the reason for falling into the trap set by the security service, was simply down to incompetence of the organization. He said he believed Cavendish would be operating on his own, for now, and to avoid any problems for the organization Cavendish should be eliminated.

Purdy had promised to deliver the names to Cavendish of those who had taken part in the orgy and subsequent murder of one of the girls, but now he expected that to be unnecessary; Cavendish would not be a problem.

Despite his own conviction that the organization would deal with the problem swiftly, Purdy still carried a sense of doom and foreboding in his heart. He tried desperately to ignore the constant, nagging doubts that assailed his mind and concentrate on his work, but it was useless, no matter how he tried. So, one hour after arriving at his office in the House of Commons, he informed his secretary that he felt unwell and would be returning home.

Purdy took the lift down into the underground car-park of the House of Commons and walked across to his designated parking space. The garage was well lit and it wasn't unusual to bump into a colleague there and take time out for a chat. He saw someone climb into a car and pull out of a parking bay. Although he barely knew the woman driving the car, he acknowledged her as she drove by.

His own car's flashers flickered into life as he triggered the security locks. He opened the car door and tossed his briefcase on to the passenger seat. He climbed in, sat for a moment letting the silence seep into his thoughts, then pushed a button on the dashboard.

A light came on informing him the engine was running. He slipped the gear lever into drive and released the handbrake. The car moved away smoothly and he could barely hear the sound of the tyres on the resin floor of the garage.

He turned towards the ramp out of the garage, lifting a hand in acknowledgement to the security guard and accelerated up the ramp. Beneath the front wing of the Lexus, a mercury tilt trigger switch responded to the action as the car's front end lifted on the ramp and completed a circuit to a compact bomb. The detonator fired causing the bomb to explode.

The car ballooned outwards as the explosion was confined within the walls of the ramp and burst into flames. Immediately, the security guard ran to a panic button, one of many fitted around the garage and struck it hard with his hand.

And all hell was let loose.

Marcus was just leaving Vauxhall Bridge Tube Station when he heard the wail of police sirens screaming through the streets somewhere. He took no notice of it because it was such a familiar sound in central London. He even dismissed the thought again as two fire engines clamoured past. But when the ambulances appeared, he began to think that there might have been another terrorist attack on the city.

He knew that when these atrocities happened, the security forces literally tied London down and closed the entire area around where the attack had occurred. He hoped he wouldn't be inconvenienced because he had decided that morning to secure an interview with the mysterious Sir Giles Cavendish.

It wasn't long before Marcus realized that his efforts to get to the headquarters of MI6 were going to be severely hampered. The police had closed off several of the road bridges across the river and brought the centre of London to a grinding halt, although being on the south side of the river he couldn't foresee a problem. He pulled his mobile phone from his pocket and dialled Maggot's number for no other reason than he wanted to check if there was any chaos further up the river where his friend had the gymnasium. His phone was dead, so he figured the security people must have put a block on the networks.

He put his phone in his pocket and began walking along the Albert Embankment towards the headquarters of MI6, but when he was within about 200 yards of it, he knew he would not get in; there were armed police everywhere.

He picked a side street leading away from the river looking for a bar where he would find a television and learn what had happened. He came across a small public house, walked in and asked for a beer. The television was switched to Sky News and already they were reporting from Parliament Square; the closest the cameras were allowed to get. It soon became clear that a cabinet minister had been assassinated, and the attack was already being attributed to Al-Qaeda terrorists or Muslim sympathizers. There was also a rumour that it was the Secretary of State for International Development, but details were not being released until the family of whoever it was had been informed.

True to the sensationalist character of the media, a picture of the minister was flashed up on the screen. Marcus sat bolt upright. He was looking at the man whose photograph he had taken in Covent Garden; the man he had seen talking to Cavendish.

Marcus felt numb. It was a weird sensation and only lasted a few seconds, but it was if his entire body had lost all feeling. He shuddered and took a mouthful of beer. Little prickles of fear seemed to run up and down his spine. His mind began to consider the implications of what he knew and what had happened. Cavendish had involved Susan Ellis in something that appeared to be generated by a spirit of kindness and generosity. But it was also open ended; there was no answer to the question he had put into Susan's mind, not at home anyway. No, the answer to her brother's situation lay abroad somewhere.

Yesterday he had seen Cavendish talking to James Purdy. Could there be a connection, he wondered between the grubby booklet Cavendish had handed to Susan and the member of government whom Marcus had seen him with?

He looked around the bar. There were several people in there, all watching the television screen as the reporter did his best to keep up the momentum of the sensational event that had taken place at the heart of government. He thought about the best way to handle what could be a potentially dangerous problem. Should he go to the police with a copy of the photograph? Probably not. He decided there was no way the police would consider anything sinister about the photograph of two men taking tea together. At least, they wouldn't admit it. And they would probably suspect that Marcus had taken the photos for sinister motives. He knew then that if the police saw those pictures, he would be thrown in jail and left to rot.

He pulled his mobile out of his pocket and tried it again, but the network was still down. He looked around for a public phone and saw one in the corner. It was reasonably quiet over there, so he picked up his beer and went across to the phone. He lifted the receiver off the rest and put it to his ear. He could hear a buzz. He dialled the number of MI6 after putting a one pound coin in the slot. It rang briefly.

'Good morning, Intelligence Service. How can I help you?'

'Could you put me through to Sir Giles Cavendish, please?'

'I'm sorry, sir, but Sir Giles will not be taking any calls today.'

Marcus could understand why. 'It's rather important I speak to him,' he told the receptionist. 'I have something he should see.'

'You could make an appointment if you like, but it wouldn't be until next week at the earliest. Sir Giles is a very busy man.'

'I'm sure he is,' Marcus told her, 'but it is imperative that he sees what I have to show him.'

'Perhaps you could post it to Sir Giles, recorded delivery. Or fax it if that's possible. Would you like to leave your name, sir?'

Marcus shook his head. 'No, I wouldn't. Goodbye.' He put the phone down. He was annoyed because he had to find a way to rattle Sir Giles Cavendish's cage, and maybe find some answers for Susan.

David Ellis was under no illusions; he was still a prisoner despite the fact that he was no longer in chains, or confined to a darkened room. He had been bundled into the back of the pick-up truck by the men who had turned up at the compound, but not until he had helped bury their fallen comrades. Their leader, Abdul Khaliq, had not taken part in the arduous and grisly task, but had spent a great deal of time in the ruined house and generally wandering about encouraging his men as they worked.

David wondered if he would be taken somewhere else later on, but for the time being he was sitting at a table with a stew of lamb in front of him, a bowl of rice and fruit on the table. The others, who were ignoring him, ate heartily, and he was surprised to see that they were all in good spirits; there seemed to be no remorse or tears over their fallen comrades in arms.

David understood the hearts and minds of these men, and knew that in their self-proclaimed fight against the infidel, they lacked nothing in courage and had an amazing self belief, not only in themselves but in the rights of their cause and what they believed was the defence of their faith.

David had seen Abdul briefly before the meal had been served, but the man had said nothing to him, especially about the strange remark regarding David's freedom. Once the men had finished and women appeared to clear the table, the room began to empty until there was only Abdul and David remaining.

Abdul Khaliq cut an imposing and dominating figure. He was an intimidating man and had an aura about him that demanded allegiance from his men. His reputation went before him, and to be in his presence was almost to be subdued.

He carried himself well, having a fine physique, although it was difficult to detect beneath the traditional Arab clothes he was wearing. There was no sign of any weapon on him, not even the pantomime belt and scimitar. And in front of David, who did not have an imposing presence at all, Abdul had no need for a display of weaponry of any sort.

Abdul moved along to the end of the table where David was sitting and took a seat. David waited patiently, having no other option, until Abdul spoke.

'Your freedom,' Abdul began, 'can now be exchanged for something.'

David felt a surge of relief, but he said nothing because he knew that men like Abdul and his kind were always very patient, and their words and arguments could be stretched almost indefinitely.

'We have kept you with us for a long time because it is always good to have somebody who may be of use to us in our war against the infidel.' He stopped there and regarded David with a look that seemed to search deep into his soul. 'I know you were working for British Intelligence at the mission.'

David opened his mouth in surprise, but Abdul held up his hand.

'Please, do not try to deny it. Your work for The Chapter was simply a cover, but now that is no longer important. What is important now is how I can use you, and how we can secure your release.'

David waited until he believed he could say something. 'You mean a hostage exchange, or something like that?' he asked.

Abdul didn't answer the question; he simply ignored it.

'The men who attacked the compound were not soldiers.' David frowned at that assertion. 'They were mercenaries employed by the same group who attacked the mission.'

'What group?' David asked immediately.

Abdul shook his head. 'At the moment, that is not important. But I believe those men were being used by someone within British and American Intelligence to bring discredit on the Taliban.'

'But you are not Taliban,' David pointed out.

Abdul put up his hand. 'That is not important; it was done for other reasons. Your people in the West will believe anything. But there was another reason behind the attack on our compound.'

David waited for an explanation but nothing came for a while. 'What was the reason then?' he asked eventually.

'At the moment it isn't necessary for you to know or even to understand the reasons why,' Abdul told him. 'But what you must understand is that I want you to do something for me that could bring you your freedom.'

David could think of nothing he could do, given the circumstances of his confinement, that could help Abdul in any way. But he asked, naturally.

'What can I do?' He shrugged his shoulders.

'You wrote something, a long time ago. Remember?'

David thought back to when he had been taken from the hospital. One of Abdul's men had given him a notebook and asked him to write down what had happened at the mission. David needed time to bring himself to recall on paper exactly what he had seen and what had transpired. And when he had written just a couple of pages, the book had been taken away from him. He decided then it was the beginning of their mind games; deprivation: giving something and then taking it away.

While David was thinking, Abdul watched him carefully.

'We took the book and removed a lot of the empty pages. Then we soiled it, made it looked as though you had written it while desperately ill.'

'Why did you do that?' David asked, frowning.

Abdul smiled. 'Pretence,' he said, then he took an apple from the bowl of fruit that was on the table and bit into it. He carried on talking as he was chewing the apple.

'I want you to write a letter to the man you served in British Intelligence. I will tell you what to write. But first I want to know how much you trusted him, and if you still trust him.'

David lifted his hand and ran his fingers through his hair. He felt some comfort in being able to do that in front of the man who could order his death as easily as ordering a hookah pipe. It was an absurd notion, but it implied a degree of relative ease within himself.

'How can I answer that honestly?' he queried. 'I was working for a man who held many secrets; someone who has worked in powerful positions in the military. He was my boss and I was his employee. Do your men trust you?'

'We trust Allah, who knows everything.'

'That doesn't answer my question, Abdul. How can I say to you that I trust my boss when I have been your prisoner for …' He stopped; it occurred to David that he wasn't really sure just how long he had been in captivity. 'How long have I been here?'

Abdul shrugged. 'No matter, you will write the letter and then, one day, you might be a free man.' He stood up. '*Inshalla!*'

And with that he walked out of the room leaving David to wonder if this was to be another mind game.

Marcus found a newspaper shop and bought a packet of envelopes. Then he went looking for a photocopier, finding one in an internet café. He took the photograph of Cavendish from his wallet and copied it a few times. Then he disfigured the face of the Minister and wrote the words 'Covent Garden' on the top of the picture. Beneath this he wrote the words: *I will call midday for three days*. Then he slipped the copy into an envelope and wrote: *For the attention of Sir Giles Cavendish only.*

Satisfied with what he had done, he retraced his footsteps to the Embankment and MI6 headquarters.

EIGHT

THREE DAYS AFTER Marcus had delivered his envelope by hand; there was a reception at the American Embassy in Grosvenor Square. John Deveraux, the Military Attaché caught up with Chief Master Sergeant Danny Grebo and parted him from an attractive female journalist representing CNN. He led Grebo away to a reasonably quiet area in the large reception room.

'I think it looks less obvious if we talk here rather than in my office, Chief,' Deveraux told him. 'But we do need to talk.'

Grebo smiled and tried to look as though he was simply indulging in pleasantries. 'Yes, I know, sir, but it depends what you want to talk about.'

'Cavendish is getting too close,' Deveraux admitted. 'He freaked the English minister out.'

Grebo thought he detected a sense of strain in the attaché's voice. He hadn't been involved in the assassination of the British minister, but was fairly confident that Deveraux had called the shots; it had been his decision.

'I thought it was too public, whatever the reasons,' Grebo told him. 'The crap has really hit the fan now.'

Deveraux took a drink from a passing waiter, leaving his empty glass on a sideboard nearby. 'The British are blaming Muslim terrorists.'

'Very convenient,' Grebo offered. 'But why so sudden?'

'We have a shipment due in. Cavendish wanted names; he had the minister over a barrel.'

Grebo frowned. 'How come?'

So Deveraux told him. Grebo whistled softly through his teeth. 'I thought the girls were makeweights; something to sweeten the pill for these perverts.' He paused and sipped consciously at his champagne. 'They lost one?' he asked eventually, disbelief all over his face.

'That's not important; the girls mean nothing.' He put on a smile for the benefit of whoever might be looking in their direction. 'We're sitting on a billion-dollar operation here and those idiots can't keep their disgusting habits out of it. They could pull a couple of frigging whores out of the city and do it without dragging The Chapter into it.'

It was unusual for The Chapter to be named in any conversation between those men who headed up the organization, unless there was a specific need for it. For that reason, Grebo realized that Deveraux's action in ordering the assassination of the government minister smacked of a keenly felt worry about the organization's security.

'How many were involved?' Grebo asked him.

'Three,' Deveraux replied. 'Fortunately, Cavendish was only interested in the Cabinet minister.'

'As far as you know,' Grebo put in.

'As far as I know,' Deveraux admitted, and looked around the room, smiling at whoever was looking directly at him. He caught the ambassador's eye and regretted it immediately. He turned to Grebo.

'Looks like we'll be splitting up. Ring me later.' He checked his watch. 'About five this evening? Remember, we have to stop Cavendish.' He raised his voice a little as the ambassador came up beside them. 'So, when is it you leave the service, Chief?' he was saying. Grebo looked at the ambassador, Deveraux turned. 'Ah, Ambassador, allow me to introduce Chief Master Sergeant Danny Grebo.'

The two men shook hands and began a desultory conversation as Deveraux made his excuses and left them talking.

The phone rang and Cavendish picked it up. 'Sir Giles Cavendish.'

'Thought you'd been avoiding me,' Marcus said to him. Twice he had rung and twice he had been fobbed off with somebody purporting to be from Sir Giles Cavendish's office saying he was sorry that Sir Giles was away on important business.

'I presume you've seen the photograph?' Marcus asked him.

Cavendish sighed deeply. 'I hope this isn't a very feeble attempt at blackmail, whoever you are.'

'No blackmail, I promise. Well,' Marcus said hurriedly, 'perhaps a little persuasion.'

Cavendish listened for some background noise. He could hear the muffled sound of traffic, so assumed the caller was in a public call box somewhere. It didn't sound as intense as London traffic might.

'Isn't that the same thing?' Cavendish asked. 'Unless I do as you ask, you will take a copy of the photograph to the newspapers and try to implicate me in something that could seriously jeopardize my livelihood. Or something like that.'

'Not quite, Sir Giles,' Marcus told him, 'but I do need your co-operation.'

'Co-operation about what, may I ask; co-operation for what you want?'

Marcus grinned on the other end of the phone and looked at his watch. Another minute and he would have to hang up. 'Co-operation on behalf of a client of mine,' he told the security chief.

'A client? So you are a professional, are you?' Cavendish asked a little mockingly. 'And exactly what profession is it you practise?'

'I'll ring you again tomorrow while you think about it today,' Marcus answered and put the phone down.

Cavendish looked at the phone and put it down gently on its cradle. Whoever it was, he thought to himself, was playing a dangerous game. It would be interesting to track him down and learn the real reason for his phone call.

There was a knock at his office door.

'Come in,' he called.

A young man came in clutching a notepad. He closed the door behind him.

'We traced the call to a phone box in Clapham, sir. That means he has phoned twice from the same box in the City and once from a box in Clapham.'

He waited for Cavendish to make some comment, but it was obvious that his boss was mulling something over. He wouldn't go until he was dismissed. Eventually Cavendish moved and opened a drawer in his desk. He took a pad from it and began leafing through it. Then his face brightened triumphantly.

'Susan Ellis,' he said to the young man. 'Susan Ellis lives at Clapham. I want you to check her phone records and find out if she has been in touch with any professional organizations within the last week. Let me have the list as soon as you can.'

The young man dipped his head in acknowledgment and left the office. Cavendish looked at his watch, feeling pretty good. Time, he thought, to have lunch.

Deveraux made the call that would see the end to Cavendish's pursuit of those connected with The Chapter. It was short and to the point. He advised extreme caution because of Cavendish's position within British Intelligence. And there was little point in trying to make it look like an accident, he warned the person on the other end of the phone; scientific analysis of a crime scene was so sophisticated now it was almost impossible to fool the crime scene investigators.

'Just make sure,' he insisted, 'that the target is dead.'

Cavendish finished his lunch at The Crown, a Victorian pub on the Embankment opposite the Tate Gallery. He would often use the pub and then spend an hour or so wandering among the paintings hanging in the Tate, enjoying the ambience and the quiet. Cavendish found that the peaceful atmosphere often helped him to unlock difficult cases or come to terms with operations that had gone badly wrong.

His mobile phone vibrated in his pocket, dragging his mind back to reality and he walked out of the Tate and dialled his office.

'We've got a couple of names, sir. Best you look yourself, but I think we have the man you're looking for.'

Cavendish smiled and put the phone back in his pocket and caught a taxi back to the MI6 headquarters a short distance away.

The information in front of him on his desk showed the phone calls that Susan Ellis had made over the course of a week. There were several professional organizations that Cavendish recognized and dismissed immediately, but one organization which stood out was that of Guard Right Security. And the address placed it within yards of the public call box that had been used by the mysterious caller when he made the calls from a City of London call box. It had been highlighted as the 'most likely' among all the others. And alongside the name of the company was that of Marcus.

Cavendish looked across the desk at the young intelligence agent who had supplied the information.

'I want you to find out as much as you can about this Marcus Blake.' He paused because the name seemed to ring a bell but he couldn't place it. He shook his head; it wasn't important. 'Then I want you to make an appointment to see him tomorrow morning, if possible. Use any name, but I will be going along myself. Oh yes, and I want you to put someone on Susan Ellis; she may be entirely innocent in all this, but I think it might be pertinent to keep an eye on her and any callers she has.'

Abdul drove the minibus with all the skill and assurance of a man who had been doing it for years. It was a kind of disguise for him; because his presence outside his own fiefdom would mean grave danger if he was recognized. He had discarded the *shalwar kadiz* dress of long shirt and baggy pants or pantaloons, that were *de rigueur* for all Taliban converts, even though he wasn't one. Now he was wearing a traditional Afghani *pakol* hat, a *chapan* jacket and loose fitting pantaloons.

Beside Abdul in the front seat was his right-hand man, Habib, and behind him, sitting next to David, was his third-in-command, Kareem. Abdul went nowhere without these two men, and it was a testament to them that he was prepared to trust them with his life this far away from the relative safety of his own people.

The three men had travelled with Abdul from the northern province of Zabor beyond Kandahar. They were now driving through the hills approaching Jalalabad, about a hundred miles or so east of the capital, Kabul.

David understood that this strange new treatment of him by Abdul did not mean he was now considered a 'trusty', or whatever the equivalent was in this troubled country. No, David was still bound, although discreetly, and there was no way in which he could flee from his captors.

Abdul had made it clear to David that he was something of an investment now, but it had not been made too clear exactly what he had meant by that. Shortly after being told that he wanted him to write a letter, Abdul had appeared with pen and paper and instructed David to write to his sister, Susan.

David was staggered at the request; he thought the letter he was going to write was to have been to his old boss, Sir Giles Cavendish. He was also surprised when Abdul mentioned Susan, and when David asked what he should write, Abdul simply shrugged and told him to write the kind of things he would normally write to a member of his family. Once the letter had been written, and David had put as much in as he felt would be allowed, one of Abdul's men took it away.

The minibus pulled off the main highway leading away from Jalalabad and turned on to a dirt road that wound its way towards the foothills and eventually the mission orphanage.

David recognized much of the countryside and immediately began to feel a hurt deep inside. He recalled fond memories; memories he no longer wanted to have, but the lush green vegetation, the old road and the backdrop of the mountains were dragging him back to that moment when his heart had died with Shakira.

The minibus bumped and groaned its way up the dirt road until the mission came into view. It was a single-storey building with other, smaller outbuildings scattered around it. There was a fenced compound and a set of gates that were now closed. David remembered they had always been open.

He glanced up towards that place in the hill above the mission where Shakira had died and, metaphorically speaking, so had he. He turned away and looked at the back of Abdul's head and wondered what part he had played in the massacre.

Abdul pulled up at the gates and a turbaned Afghani walked over to the minibus. He was carrying a machine-gun over his shoulder. Abdul put the window down and jabbered away at the man. David understood much of what was said. Eventually the man sauntered over to the gates and pulled them open. Abdul shoved the minibus into gear and accelerated through the opening, throwing up clouds of dust.

It was all very bewildering and not making a lot of sense to David. He couldn't for the life of him think why Abdul had taken all this trouble to drive some distance from his own province down to Jalalabad. Whatever it was, it must be important and probably worth a lot of money to the warlord.

They pulled up outside the front doors of the mission. Above the doors was the legend; The First Chapter. David glanced at it and remembered Shakira telling him that it meant the first chapter of a journey that deprived and orphaned children would embark upon to a new life in the West. He could see the bullet holes, unrepaired, still in the woodwork.

David was ordered out and scrambled down from the minibus, helped by the two minders. The four men walked into the mission, but once inside, Abdul gestured to his men to take David along the passageway to another room. He then made his way to the office.

It crossed David's mind that he might be recognized by one of the staff there, but considering it was a year ago that the attack happened, plus the fact that David was now wearing a full beard and was also dressed like Abdul and his men, it meant that he was literally unrecognizable.

After about ten minutes, and also having been escorted to the lavatory, David was pleased to see some food and drink brought in. The man who brought it in said nothing. He even avoided eye contact, which didn't surprise David either. He ate a good meal, which also included English tea much to his delight and surprise.

It was about an hour later when Abdul appeared and signalled that they were leaving. Once again David was herded like the prisoner he was by the two minders to the minibus. Still not sure why all this was happening, David began to adopt a kind of philosophical attitude, and had been ruminating on all kinds of theories when Abdul suddenly appeared with three young children. A woman, dressed in the Catholic style nun's outfit, accompanied them. She spoke warmly to Abdul and then bobbed courteously before turning and going back into the mission.

The children had a very small bag each. Abdul took the bags from them and shepherded them into the minibus. Without any words spoken between them, the three children were settled into the empty seats. Abdul gunned the motor into life and roared out of the mission gates. And, just as he cleared the gates, he turned and said to David, 'Your letter is on its way.' Then he looked back at the road ahead and up at a darkening sky. 'We stay in a safe house tonight and tomorrow we return home.'

Marcus checked his watch for the about the tenth time that morning. He had only looked at it a few minutes earlier. He was getting fidgety, waiting for a client who had been very close mouthed about what it was he wanted Guard Right Security to do for him. But Marcus had little or no option when asked for an appointment; after all, he was supposed to be in the security business.

It was past midday and the appointment had been made for twelve o'clock. Marcus wasn't the best timekeeper in the world, but he did expect others to be; one of his failings probably.

It was 12.30 when Marcus heard the door at the bottom of the stairs creak open. He then heard the familiar tread of someone on the stairs as the steps creaked and groaned beneath the person's weight. His mind went back to a few days earlier when it had been Susan Ellis who had trodden that path to his office, and found himself wishing he had a good reason to call her and offer to take her out to dinner again. But after the incident with the two muggers, Susan seemed quite reluctant to want to see him. He decided to phone Cavendish as soon as he had finished dealing with the next appointee and then maybe he would have a good reason to call Susan.

A figure appeared behind the opaque glass and Marcus got to his feet as the sound of a knock came at the door. He walked across to the door and pulled it open. The man standing there was a lot older than Marcus had expected, recalling the sound of the person's voice who had made the appointment. He did a swift mental appraisal of the man and put his age at about sixty. He was about the same height as Marcus and looked in reasonably good condition for his age. All that took Marcus about two seconds as recognition clicked in.

'Sir Giles Cavendish,' Marcus said, with marked surprise. 'How did you...?'

'I'm in the intelligence business,' Cavendish answered abruptly, and stepped into the office. 'How else could I have tracked you down?'

Marcus closed the door behind him and continued to stare at Cavendish, his mouth slightly open while wondering just how he could have tracked him here?

Cavendish sat down on the chair facing the desk. Marcus walked round the desk and put his finger on a desk diary, open at that day's date.

'I presume it wasn't you who made the appointment?'

Cavendish gave a winsome smile. 'My office,' he told Marcus.

Marcus looked at the name. 'Trotter?' He thought of the TV character in the series 'Only Fools and Horses'. 'A sense of humour, then,' he said.

'We do have our moments,' Cavendish admitted lightly.

Marcus grunted and sat down. 'Can I offer you tea or coffee?'

Cavendish shook his head. 'Thank you, no, but what you can offer me is the memory card from your camera and any pictures you have printed out.'

Marcus reached into a drawer and pulled out an envelope. He dropped it on the desk. 'I had this ready for when I was supposed to meet you, but you've pre-empted me.'

Cavendish leaned forward and reached across the desk to take the envelope, but Marcus kept his hand on it and shook his head. 'Not until you've done me the courtesy of answering some questions.'

Cavendish leaned back and waited, saying nothing.

'Why did you lie to Susan Ellis?' Marcus asked.

Cavendish frowned. 'So that's who you're working for,' he said without answering the question.

Marcus stood up and turned his back on Cavendish. He stood by the window, looking down on to the street. 'I'm not working for anybody,' he told Cavendish, watching two men get out of a black Mercedes. 'Susan came to me because of you, but she couldn't afford me.' The men were dressed in black. They were fairly well built and looked as though they had a purpose in whatever it was they were about to do. 'I decided to do a little investigating and discovered that you did not work for the Foreign Office as you claimed.' The two men crossed the road as the Mercedes pulled away from the kerb. It moved off quickly and Marcus watched as it reached the top end of the City Road. He glanced back at the two men who had crossed the road and were walking towards the street door leading to his office. When he glanced back towards the top end of the City Road, the Mercedes had completed an illegal turn and was now slowly driving back towards the point where it had dropped the two men, but now on Marcus's side of the road.

Marcus swung round and looked at Cavendish. 'Did you bring two thugs with you, just in case I put up a struggle?'

Cavendish looked askance. 'Of course not; I have nothing to fear from you.'

The door creaked at the foot of the stairs and he heard the first groan of the step. Marcus knew they were not coming up the stairs to ask for an appointment. Suddenly he leapt round the desk and hauled Cavendish to his feet, throwing him up against the far wall.

'Stay there!' he hissed. 'Whatever you do, don't bloody move!'

He then positioned himself against the wall beyond the door, flattening his back up against it. Cavendish now looked bewildered, but had the sense to see that Marcus was not threatening him with any kind of violence. He could also see something in the expression on Marcus's face; something he would describe later as frightening.

The door swung open and a gloved hand holding a Glock handgun appeared. Marcus swung his left arm up and grabbed the wrist of the man holding the gun and pushed it upwards, turning the hand at the same time. Then he rotated inwards towards the man and brought his right arm up beneath his armpit, locking his right hand on to his left wrist and pushed down with a tremendous force.

The gunman cursed as his hand opened dropping the gun and Marcus brought his knee up swiftly, driving it into the man's crotch. As the gun fell from the gunman's hand, Marcus let the man drop and swooped down, picking up the gun.

Only about two seconds had elapsed between the gunman opening the door and Marcus disarming him. But it was enough time for the second gunman to fire a shot at Marcus. The bullet zipped through Marcus's clothing, scorching a deep line across the top of his shoulder.

Without thinking about it, Marcus turned and fired the Glock he was now holding straight into the second gunman. There was a terrible cry of agony and pain as the gunman toppled down the stairs, falling into a heap at the bottom: he was dead.

The speed with which Marcus was thinking didn't slow because he knew there was still a risk from the first gunman. The man was on one knee and struggling to get up. Marcus brought the gun crashing down on the man's skull, which flattened him. He dropped on to the man, driving his knee in between his shoulder blades and jammed the barrel of the Glock into the soft flesh behind his ear.

'Don't move!'

Cavendish had hardly had time to breathe and, by the time he realized what was happening, it was all over. He looked at Marcus who was now bent over the gunman, his knee pressed into the man's back and the gun jammed hard behind the man's ear.

'Don't kill him,' Cavendish snapped at Marcus.

Marcus turned and looked at Cavendish, his face a mask of fury. 'Why, is he one of your fucking hitmen?'

Cavendish put both his arms forward and shook his hands desperately. 'No, no; he's not one of my men. I don't know who he is.'

Marcus nodded his head in the direction of the small sink across the room. 'See that tea towel? Bring it over here so I can tie him up.'

Cavendish hurried across to the sink and lifted the grubby towel from the draining board. He brought it across to Marcus and helped tie the man's hands behind his back. Marcus handed the Glock to Cavendish.

'I presume you know how to handle this,' he said firmly. 'Keep him covered while I look for something else.'

Cavendish took the gun and waited until Marcus had finished rummaging around his office and finally came back with a length of cord. He lashed the man's arms to his ankles, and pulled the cord tight. He then took the gun from Cavendish and flopped down in his chair.

Cavendish pointed at the phone. 'I'd better make a phone call.'

Marcus needed no telling; he knew what Cavendish was about to do. What had happened was something that needed to be kept out of the Press and police notebooks. Suddenly Marcus remembered the Mercedes and went to the window. The car was immediately below him, which made it impossible to read the number plate. He heard Cavendish asking for a team, on the double, and knew some people would arrive who would remove the dead guy, clean the place up and leave no trace of anything that could connect him and Cavendish to what had happened.

The Mercedes pulled away from the kerb which meant Marcus was able to read the number plate. He went back to his desk and wrote the number down on his doodling pad.

Cavendish put the phone down and looked at Marcus. Marcus turned his head and glanced down at the man. Then he put his fingers to his lips and pointed towards the man trussed up on the floor. There was no reason for either of them to say anything until the team arrived. Now all they could do was wait.

The children were taken from the safe house and driven away in a black car with darkened windows. Abdul had not tried to keep David from seeing the children leave, and David wondered what the significance of the warlord's change of attitude meant. He asked Abdul what was going to happen to the children.

'There are many people in this world who are desperate to have children, but through no fault of their own, it cannot be.'

'So you provide the children for these desperate people?' David's remark was acerbic; making no attempt to hide his true feelings about what he believed was child trafficking.

Abdul smiled, showing his white teeth beneath his beard. 'The First Chapter is in a good position to take advantage of the war in Afghanistan and find homes for orphaned children. What can be so bad about that?'

'At a price, no doubt,' said David.

Abdul closed his mouth and changed his expression to one of a more philosophical stance, arching his bushy eyebrows in response to David's cutting rejoinder.

'There are people willing to pay and I am willing to help.' He got up from the table. 'Enough now; time to leave.'

The brief discussion was over and it left David wondering if there was really a benevolent heart beating beneath Abdul's powerful exterior. He doubted it; after all, Abdul was known for his ruthlessness in dealing with his enemies. And it left David wondering once again why he was being dragged round with the man like a token of some kind. And why on earth was he asked to write a letter to his sister?

His thoughts were cut short as the men took David out of the house and bundled him into a Toyota Landcruiser. David wondered if Abdul had decided to change vehicles because of the pilotless drones flying high overhead, watching the movements of known insurgents and warlords. He hoped and prayed that Abdul had not been picked up by the remotely controlled aircraft. If that was the case, he was sure their journey would end in death by a missile fired from the drone.

Perhaps, he thought, that was why Abdul was hauling him round the country – as protection from a missile attack. He slunk into his seat and began to feel an uncomfortable frisson of fear trickling down his back.

The team arrived and ushered Marcus and Cavendish from the building. Marcus wanted to protest but knew he was involved in something too big for him to deal with. He clambered into a white van that was waiting outside and, as soon as he and Cavendish were settled into their seats, the van pulled out into traffic and sped away.

They motored out of the city and travelled for several miles into the countryside, travelling at normal speeds and obeying all the road signs and taking care with the varying traffic conditions. Marcus was impressed with the unspoken professionalism of Cavendish's men.

Eventually the van pulled into the driveway of a house shaded by a combination of oak and elm trees. It stopped outside the front door and Cavendish immediately climbed out, beckoning Marcus to follow him.

Once the two men had got out of the van, it sped off, leaving them standing by the front entrance. As the door was opened for them, Cavendish looked at Marcus.

'After you,' he said, indicating that Marcus should go on ahead of him.

Marcus stepped into a large hallway. There was an umbrella and hat stand: very old-fashioned, thought Marcus. On one wall was a mirror with a gilt frame. The carpet on the floor looked as though it had seen the passage of many feet over many years. It had a dull, military colour and lacked any kind of style. There was little else in the hallway to suggest a family might live there. And considering the game that Cavendish was in, Marcus doubted if anybody did; it was probably a safe house.

Cavendish led Marcus into a lounge which was sparsely furnished. It added to Marcus's opinion that the house did indeed belong to the intelligence department. They were followed into the room by the man who had opened the door for them. He waited until both Marcus and Cavendish were seated.

'Care for a drink?' he asked.

Cavendish glanced at Marcus, giving him the opportunity to order something first.

'Tea, please; bog standard English.'

Cavendish grinned. 'I think I'll have a whisky and soda, thank you, Eric. Oh, and would you bring in the first-aid box? Our man needs a plaster.'

Marcus's wound was superficial and he had almost forgotten about it, but he thought that it was probably the right thing to do; get it looked at.

Eric disappeared to get the drinks. Cavendish turned to Marcus.

'Now,' he said, 'we can talk.'

Marcus thought Cavendish looked more comfortable now; he had been trembling earlier, which Marcus put down to adrenalin after the shock of the attack. The man was too old for excitement really, he decided. He thought about what had happened knowing that only Cavendish could come up with the answers.

'Who were those men?' Marcus asked.

Cavendish shook his head. 'I have no idea, but I'm sure I will find out.'

'Who were they after, me or you?'

Cavendish arched his eyebrows. 'My, you do value yourself highly,' he said mockingly. 'They were professionals: it had to be me they were after.'

Marcus thought that would be the case. 'Not very good at their job then, were they?'

Cavendish frowned. 'Where did you learn to do that?' he asked.
'Do what?'

'I've seen a lot of very skilful men in my career; hardened professionals who would walk through hell to defend their country and their colleagues. But they have all been trained professionals; taught how to react instinctively to any threat, and to deal with it without thinking of the consequences. You reacted like one of those men,' Cavendish acknowledged. 'You saved my life and your own simply by reacting and not thinking of the consequences. I must say you were exceptionally quick. So I say again: where did you learn to do that?'

Marcus shrugged. 'I'm a quiet sort of guy. I like to be easy come, easy go. Enjoy life. You know the sort of thing. I just get very pissed off when people try to spoil my day, that's all.'

Cavendish allowed himself a rueful smile; seeing Marcus 'pissed off' was indeed a sight to behold. One he decided he might be able to make use of.

'As you say, Blake, they were not very good at their job. If they had been, neither of us would be here now.'

'So who were they?' Marcus asked again. 'If they weren't after me they must have been after you. That makes them Russian then, right?'

Cavendish laughed out loud. 'You've been reading too many spy books. If the Russians had wanted to dispose of me they would have been far more discreet and far more successful, I can assure you.' He let the laughter subside and shook his head. Marcus waited for him to continue. 'I don't know who they were,' he went on, 'but I will find out.'

'How?' Marcus asked.

Cavendish looked at Marcus in surprise. 'You only killed one of them; the other one is still alive. He might have a few bruises, Blake, but he is well enough to tell us what we want to know.'

There was a knock at the door and Eric walked in. He placed a tray on the table, nodded at Cavendish and left the room. Cavendish got up and poured out a cup of tea for Marcus. He brought it over to him and then retrieved his whisky and soda. He then went back to the tray and lifted a first-aid box from it.

'Take off your shirt, Blake; let's see what's needed.'

Very little was needed, in fact. Cavendish cleaned the wound and rubbed some salve on to it.'

'You'll live,' he said, and returned the first-aid box to the table while

Marcus put his shirt back on. Marcus then lifted his cup and sipped his tea, which was surprisingly good.

'Suppose he doesn't want to tell you anything?' Marcus asked, referring to the comment Cavendish had made about getting information from the man who had survived Marcus's show of anger.

Cavendish tilted his head a little. 'Oh, he will; I've no doubt about that.'

'What will you do, barter with him? You know, freedom for some information?'

Cavendish said nothing.

'Or will you torture him?' Marcus said, and lifted his cup to his mouth.

'How we get the information has nothing to do with you; just be assured that we will.' Cavendish sounded quite abrupt.

Marcus decided to push him a little. 'Rendition,' he said.

Cavendish screwed his face up. 'What?'

Marcus put his cup down. 'Rendition. It's what the Yanks have been doing; sending their prisoners to other countries who don't give a toss about extracting information under torture.' He studied Cavendish for a while. 'But you don't do that kind of thing in MI6, do you?'

'What we do and what we don't do is not your concern,' Cavendish told him levelly. 'But what should concern you now is your own safety, and what we must do about that.'

Marcus shrugged. 'I don't think I have anything to worry about,' he told Cavendish. 'They weren't after me, so I'll just get back to my business and leave you to get on with yours.'

Cavendish shook his head. 'Don't be so naïve; they will be back, and this time they will be more careful. So, for your own safety, you need to remain under my protection until we can nail the bastards who tried to kill us.'

'I don't think I fancy your kind of protection,' Marcus told him. 'It nearly got you killed.'

Cavendish laughed. '*Touché.*' He drained his whisky and got up, walked over to the table and put his empty glass on the tray. 'It is probably connected with the assassination of the secretary of state, and until I can learn more, I suggest you trust me and my department to keep you out of their clutches.'

Marcus stood up. He put his empty cup and saucer next to the empty whisky glass. 'No, thank you. Just get me a taxi and I'll be out of here. If you want to speak to me about any of this, you know where to find me.'

Cavendish accepted the rebuttal and offer of protection gracefully. 'Very well, but I cannot be held responsible for your safety. There is one thing though,' he added.

'What's that?'

'I wouldn't go back to your office if I were you.'

Marcus agreed. 'I know; it wouldn't make sense.' He put out his hand and held it there for a moment. 'Now, can you order a taxi for me?'

Cavendish sighed. 'Very well, if you insist; I'll ask Eric to call one.' He shook Marcus's outstretched hand. 'Where can I reach you if I need to ask you anything?'

Marcus rummaged through his pockets and pulled out his wallet. He took a business card from it and handed it to Cavendish.

'My mobile number's there if you need it.'

Cavendish thanked him and left the room. Ten minutes later Marcus was in a taxi heading back to London, and happy to be away from the dark world of the secret service. But there was one thing Marcus had promised himself: he would do his level best to trace the number plate he had seen on the Mercedes and try and spoil someone else's day.

Five minutes after Marcus had left, Eric walked into the room where Cavendish was waiting.

'Are we in touch with the taxi?' Cavendish asked.

'Yes, sir, same firm as usual.'

Cavendish seemed satisfied. 'Good. Whatever else happens, I don't think we want to lose that young man.'

NINE

SUSAN ELLIS WAS beginning to regret not keeping in touch with Marcus. Although he had frightened the life out of her the night he fought with the two knife-wielding thugs, she wondered if she had over-reacted to his show of inherent violence. She had made the decision that night, and told Marcus so, that she did not want to see him again. Marcus had been visibly disappointed, and she thought it was rather sweet of him to show that disappointment. But her mind was made up and she had been determined to display her own feminine character and individuality by refusing to see him again. She had been kind to Marcus and had let him down gently, but he had left her at her front door looking rather disconsolate.

The doubts had set in within twenty-four hours. Marcus was such a warm and generous person; a fun guy to be with. And she had been drawn to him the moment she saw him in his office. She had tried to put him out of her mind, trying to add determination to the effort. And then something happened that blew her plans out of the water: she had received a letter from her brother.

She found the letter on the mat as she opened the front door of the house. Normally all mail was sorted by the tenants – there were only four of them – into neat little personal piles that lay on a convenient table in the hallway. But this letter had no stamp, which meant it had been delivered by hand, probably while none of the tenants was in, which was why Susan found it there when she arrived home.

Now Susan was standing at the entrance to Guard Right Security at Oliver's Yard, the letter from her brother in her handbag, wondering if she should resurrect her brief encounter with Marcus.

She pushed open the door and stepped into the hallway. Immediately she sensed that there was something different about the place. There was no longer the musty smell she had noticed on her first visit to Marcus's office. Now it was as though a cleaner had been in to clean up and had used a lot of disinfectant because there was a hint of it in the air.

She let the door swing closed behind her, its hinges groaning noisily. She stepped on to the first step, which creaked as her weight came to bear on it. Something teased at her senses and she felt a little uncomfortable as she climbed the stairs, one at a time.

She kept looking up towards the opaque window on the door at the top of the stairs. It still bore the legend 'Guard Right Security' and naturally, Susan expected no less.

But there was still a sense of something being wrong. Susan told herself to stop being silly and shook herself. Then she breathed in deeply and held herself upright as she reached the top step.

She gripped the handle of the door and pushed it down gently. The door gave to the pressure and swung open. Susan stepped into Marcus's office and stopped abruptly. There was nothing there.

She felt herself going weak at the knees and thought she was going to faint. But what she could see, or couldn't see for that matter, was the fact that Marcus's office had been completely stripped. There was no furniture, nothing on the floor, nothing on the walls, no grubby tea towel tossed on to a dirty draining board. There were no cups, no kettle, no coffee and no milk; just the slight odour of disinfectant.

Susan stood perfectly still for several seconds, feeling a little scared. It wasn't for herself, but for Marcus.

And then a voice said, 'Who are you?'

Marcus had concealed himself on the edge of a small copse of silver birch trees that overlooked the house. He had been there for three hours now, since dawn, and had kept as still as he could while he peered down at the property through the binoculars he had borrowed from his father, his bird watching binoculars.

Marcus had plagued the life out of his father to come up with another favour, much to his disquiet. What Marcus had asked his father to do was to help him trace the Mercedes that had been used by the men who had tried to kill Cavendish. His father had ruled it out of the question when Marcus had first asked, but eventually he was able to persuade him that he would not ask for any more favours. He had said nothing of what had happened.

Henry Blake still had contacts within the Diplomatic Corps and the Foreign Office, and it wasn't unusual for people within that clique to ask for favours in return for favours previously rendered. Blake asked one of his ex-colleagues in the Foreign Office to run a check on a licence plate. The description of the car matched that which Marcus had seen, and the address at which it was registered was in Suffolk.

Marcus had travelled up to his father's home by train and found himself in need of a car, so he had borrowed one of his father's collection of 'runabouts' as his dad liked to call them. But rather than use one of the more upmarket models, Marcus had taken a Ford Focus. He did this deliberately because he wanted to preserve a sense of anonymity.

He located the house on Google search and drove to the village of Elveden, close to Thetford Forest. The house was about a mile or so from the village on the Thetford Road. Marcus drove past it a few times before deciding to drive into Thetford and find a pub where he could have a meal and a room for the night.

The following morning, Marcus drove to a small, supermarket car-park and left his car there. Then he used the cover of Elveden forest and walked to the area where he was concealed now, in the copse of silver birch trees.

Marcus couldn't see the Mercedes there, but that didn't mean it wasn't; it could have been inside one of the two garages Marcus could see in the grounds of the house. But what intrigued him was the fact that there was a Dodge pick-up truck in USAF colours parked out front. Shortly after making himself comfortable, Marcus had seen an American airman come out of the house and climb into the truck. The airman had driven away from the house and taken the road to Barton Mills, in the direction of the American base at Lakenheath.

Marcus turned his attention back to the front door of the house. It was set deep into a portico type entrance with columns either side. It meant that the main door was set back from the lip of the porch by about five feet. It also meant that anybody who called at the front door would be virtually unseen from the road. He gave it some considerable thought and filed it away in his memory bank.

About an hour after the airman had left the house, one of the garage doors swung open. Marcus focused his binoculars on to the door as a

Volvo Estate was driven out of the garage by a woman. The garage door closed behind her as she swept out of the drive and on to the road to Thetford.

Marcus spent the next three hours monitoring the house, but all that happened was the woman returned, the garage door swung up and over and the Volvo disappeared into the garage. The door closed again and this gave Marcus the beginning of an idea. All he needed was the balls to carry it out, but it meant waiting until he was confident he would be undisturbed, and that his estimation of what he had seen meant he had a good chance of carrying it off.

Susan almost leapt out of her skin when Maggot spoke to her. Because her mind had been drawn to the unexpected emptiness of Marcus's office, she hadn't seen him. He was standing by the door that led into a small toilet. He had been on the point of opening it when he heard Susan open the main door. And when he spoke to her she jumped visibly.

'Oh my goodness,' Susan cried putting her hand to her mouth. 'You frightened the life out of me.'

Maggot apologized. 'I'm sorry, but if I had said nothing, you would still have jumped when you turned round.'

Susan looked at the stranger. She guessed he was from India or Pakistan although he spoke excellent English.

'What are you doing here?' she asked him.

Maggot shrugged. 'I could ask you the same thing,' he pointed out.

'I'm a client of Mr Blake,' she told him.

Maggot tipped his head back as something dawned on him. 'I see; you must be Susan Ellis then.'

Susan was surprised that the stranger knew her name. 'How did you know that?' she stabbed at him. 'Doesn't Marcus understand client confidentiality?'

He smiled at her. 'Marcus mentioned that you are no longer a client; that is why I know who you are.'

'Well client or not, I am here to see Marcus.'

He made a sweeping gesture with his hand. 'But, as you can see, Marcus is no longer here.'

Susan looked round the empty room as though it might make some difference and Marcus would suddenly appear.

'Are you his business partner or something?' she asked.

Maggot shook his head. 'No, I am just a friend. The only one in the whole of London, I think.'

'Well, where is he? Has he moved or something?' she demanded to know.

He pursed his lips and gave a little shake of his head. 'I've no idea. But why don't you and I go and find a coffee shop and we can talk about what we know and what we may be able to find out?'

Susan agreed because it seemed so silly the two of them standing there face to face in an empty room. He was still holding his hands out, palms uppermost and, as he relaxed and dropped his hands to his sides, Susan noticed they were heavily calloused, and the little finger on one hand was missing.

That evening Marcus went back to Thetford; different pub, different meal. Before choosing the pub, Marcus bought a Maglite torch in the supermarket where he had parked his car. Once he had fed and watered himself, Marcus drove back to the house and parked his car in a lay-by a short distance away, locked it and made his way through the edge of the forest to continue his watch.

As darkness closed in and the temperature fell, Marcus decided to get closer to the house. He knew he would have to be alert for any kind of alarm system there might be, or even dogs.

There was very little in the way of security around the perimeter; simply a stout wall made from Norfolk stone. It was a little higher than six feet, but it proved no obstacle for Marcus, and as he landed on his feet inside the rear garden, he dropped flat and lay still.

He heard no alarms ringing and no dogs barking, so, after five minutes, he ventured closer until he was up against the outside wall of the double garage. He was about to edge round the front of the garage when he heard the sound of a car pulling into the drive. Its wheels crunched across the gravel and it stopped outside the front door.

Immediately, the front door opened and the man whom Marcus had seen earlier that day in uniform came out of the house. He greeted the man who was climbing out of the driver's side of the car and they both turned and went inside.

As soon as they had disappeared, Marcus ran across to the car and peered through the windows to make sure the car was empty. He had noticed that the driver hadn't bothered to lock the car, probably comfortable with the idea that while it was on the premises, it was safe, or he had simply forgotten.

He eased the car door open and, using the small Maglite torch, began checking through the glove box and under the seats to locate the car's documents. He pulled out a plastic folder from beneath the passenger seat. Flipping it open he saw the certificate of insurance and other sundry paperwork. He slipped the certificate into his pocket, put the wallet back beneath the passenger seat and went back to the far wall of the garage.

Marcus began to consider his next move. He had no way of knowing if the visitor to the house was simply a family friend or someone who was in league with the American who lived there. At the same time, he still didn't know if the Mercedes used in the attempted hit on Cavendish was actually in the garage or not, and he had to find out. He did think about following the visitor once he had left the house, but with the man's car insurance certificate in his pocket, there was no need for that. So he decided to wait until the visitor left and then he would go back to Thetford, stay the night and come back to the little copse of trees in the morning.

Just then Marcus heard the sound of a door closing somewhere. He realized it was coming from inside the garage, so was almost certainly the internal door. He heard the muffled sound of a car starting and then a slight squeal as one of the garage doors began to open.

Marcus hoped it might be the Mercedes, but instead it was the Volvo, and it was the same woman he had seen that morning who was driving. She roared out of the garage and disappeared down the drive. Marcus seized his chance and ran into the garage as the automatic door began its slow drop until it was closed.

He pulled the Maglite out of his pocket and switched it on. The Mercedes was there. He checked the licence plate; it was the same one. He then tried the passenger door and found it was open. He began searching for the car documents and eventually learned that the car was registered to one Danvor Grebo. His occupation was given as 'Airman, USAF'.

He put the paperwork back and began a cursory check around the garage. His torch beam fell on the internal door, and immediately Marcus thought it might be a good opportunity to get into the house unseen and undetected.

He tried the door, turning the handle very slowly and felt it give until the catch was free of the striker plate. He eased the door open and found he was looking into a utility room. He could see a washing machine, tumble drier and a central-heating boiler. There were a lot of boots and shoes lying about around the edges of the floor, golf clubs, a golf trolley and a great deal of impedimenta one would expect to find in a utility room. Hanging up with the other outdoor clothes was also an American Air Force uniform jacket and top coat.

Marcus crossed the room and gently opened the far door which led into a kitchen. He could now hear voices that sounded like the two men. He walked across the kitchen floor and stopped beside the work surface by a serving hatch. He could hear them quite plainly. The visitor was American.

He stood by the hatch for about ten minutes, listening to what could only be described as desultory conversation. Then he heard the sound of someone getting out of a chair and Marcus immediately went back to the internal door to the garage and pulled it closed behind him. As he did so, the kitchen light came on and he heard someone moving around there, probably getting a drink or something.

He then heard the sound of the kitchen hatch being opened and a voice said, 'When is the shipment due in?'

A voice from the lounge came back. 'Couple of days, Kings Lynn Docks. It's quiet there; not a lot of traffic and we have the right Customs man on that night.'

'What's the return?'

'Couple of crateloads; semi automatics, RPGs. Fairly low-grade stuff. Shouldn't give you too much trouble, Danny, shipping that lot out.'

'Where is it?'

'In the warehouse at Feltwell.'

Marcus heard the man in the kitchen, who he presumed was Danny Grebo, make some kind of comment as he went back to his companion in the lounge.

Marcus crept back into the kitchen. Grebo had left the hatch open.

'Who's handling the exchange?' Marcus heard Grebo ask.

'Station chief.'

Marcus peered carefully through the hatch, taking care not to let himself be seen. He kept himself to one side and was able to see the back of Grebo's visitor.

The two men started laughing at a remark one of the men had made that Marcus had not heard. Grebo stopped suddenly as though he had seen or heard something. Then he shook his head and carried on talking to his visitor.

Marcus decided it was time to get out, but how? The garage was now a cul-de-sac. He looked through the open kitchen door along the passageway that led to the front door of the house. He could see from his vantage point that the door into the lounge was closed. That meant that Marcus could get to the front door without being seen and, with luck, could get out of the house with the two men being none the wiser.

He made his way down to the door that opened on to the entrance lobby. He opened it quietly and stepped into the small area. He then took hold of the front door handle and began to turn it.

Then a man's voice said, 'Where the fuck do you think you're going?'

Marcus swung round and found himself looking down the twin ends of a double-barrelled shotgun.

Maggot put a cup of coffee in front of Susan and sat down at the table facing her. He had a Coke and took a sip before taking up the subject of Marcus.

'Let me get this straight,' he began. 'You went to Marcus because you thought he could help you find your brother; is that it?'

Susan shook her head. 'It wasn't quite like that. I wanted someone who was experienced in security to advise me and keep an eye on me while I went out to Afghanistan. I wanted to find out if David was still alive. I didn't know if Marcus had the necessary experience; all I knew was that he sounded quite confident on the phone.'

Maggot arched his eyebrows. 'Hardly a reason for trusting someone,' he remarked. 'All Marcus was doing was running a glorified escort agency. He had no one on his books; did most of the escorting himself.'

Susan's mouth fell open. 'He wasn't a gigolo, was he?'

Maggot laughed out loud. 'No way; Marcus just needed something to do to relieve his boredom. He's financially independent, you know.'

'It's just a hobby for him then?' she asked.

He watched her as she stirred the coffee and lifted the cup to her lips. 'You could say that. He kept threatening to find something "in the City" as he would say, but Marcus is a very impromptu man; very instinctive. He's had his so-called security firm for about a year. Chances are he will give it up before another twelve months has passed. It doesn't make him any money; just gives him a tag he can hang on himself.'

'You sound disparaging.'

Maggot shook his head. 'No, I love the guy. He's good company and good to have around when there's an argument going on.'

Susan made a dismissive noise. 'I can vouch for that,' she told him.

'Why, what happened?'

So Susan told him about the muggers and how Marcus changed from a calm, likeable sort of guy into a person she didn't recognize. 'He said you would be proud of him.'

Maggot laughed. 'He said that? Good old Marcus.' He stopped laughing and became quite solemn. 'But I wonder where he is now. He's not answering his mobile, and that's worrying.'

'Why would his office have been stripped bare?' Susan asked him.

Maggot shook his head. He picked up his drink and sat there for a while just looking at the glass.

'I don't know,' he admitted. 'But Marcus would not have done that without letting me know.'

Susan frowned. 'Why should he let you know?'

Maggot shrugged. 'I'm his mate; probably his only mate.'

'So somebody else did it for him?' she suggested.

Maggot became very serious. 'Something has happened to Marcus, and I don't like what I'm thinking.'

Nor did Susan; as much as she had liked Marcus, she had promised herself that she would not become involved with him. And now she found herself worrying about Marcus's fate with a complete stranger.

'Do you think it's connected with my brother David?' she put to him. Susan hadn't told Maggot about the letter she had just received, thinking it might be wise to err on the side of caution.

Maggot considered the suggestion carefully. 'If your brother is still alive,' he said eventually, 'it's entirely possible that Marcus has become involved in something that's way over his head. And if he's involved in big boys' games, he's in serious trouble.'

Marcus knew a lot about shotguns. He had often used them on his father's estate during pheasant shoots while following the beaters, and had proved himself to be a remarkably good shot. He knew what choke size was best for whichever bird or clay you were shooting, and the range and spread of the buckshot when it came rocketing out of the end of the barrel. A full choke would give a ten-inch spread over ten yards. Ten inches was about big enough to cover most of his stomach. And if Grebo pulled the trigger now, he wouldn't have to worry about peppering the doorframe because all of the buckshot would go straight through Marcus and probably through the glass door pane in front of which Marcus was standing.

Grebo stood in the passageway pointing the gun at Marcus. He was wearing jeans and a sweatshirt regaling the Dallas Cowboys. His hair was cut very close to his head and he stood about the same height as Marcus. He was overweight, but probably carried a lot of power in his frame. Not that it mattered because he carried the ultimate power in his hands.

Marcus didn't move, but looked steadily at Grebo. He knew he would not survive if he allowed the American to take him prisoner. There were deep woods behind the house and plenty of places to hide a body.

Marcus was thinking furiously. He knew he was in desperate trouble and couldn't see a way out of his dilemma. Grebo wasn't going to shoot him there, but with another man in the house, it wouldn't take long to gag him and tie him up. The gun would be sufficient to keep Marcus compliant while they tied him.

Grebo's visitor suddenly appeared in the passageway. 'What's up, Danny?' He stopped when he saw Grebo and Marcus.

At that moment, Grebo turned his head a little to say something over his shoulder. Marcus knew that there would not be another chance. Grebo was standing too far away from him to be brought down with a high kick, but Marcus still had his hand on the door handle of the front door, and in that fraction of a second he knew it was time to either die or fly.

As Grebo turned his head a little, so the twin barrels of the shotgun wavered and pointed away from Marcus. It was only by a small margin, but it was all Marcus needed. He whipped the door open, pulling it wide, dived forward and down and rolled to his right as a blast of buckshot roared out of the open door and flew over his tumbling body.

Marcus leapt to his feet and sprinted away towards the forest behind the house, zigzagging as he ran. Another roar of buckshot followed him and he felt some of the small pellets peppering his shoulder. He veered away, hearing Grebo in pursuit.

When Marcus got to the wall he didn't bother to consider how badly damaged his shoulder was, but took the leap without thinking. He grabbed the top of the wall and hauled himself over. A second gun opened fire and thudded into the wall as Marcus dropped to the other side.

Because it was pitch black behind the wall, Marcus fell awkwardly and turned his ankle. He straightened up and limped away from the wall into the bracken and ferns that edged the dark forest.

A few minutes after limping into the woods he saw a torch beam flicker, its light catching the foliage of the trees. He heard Grebo call out to his visitor, telling him to head the 'bastard' off. Another shot echoed into the night air and Marcus guessed Grebo had fired a chance shot, hoping to bring him down.

He could now feel the pain in his ankle worsening and also his left shoulder was beginning to throb and feel sticky. But worse still was the fact that he could feel himself getting a little weaker and nauseous.

He crashed through the undergrowth, not knowing which way to run, and knowing that as he blundered through the forest he was sending out loud signals to Grebo and his visitor.

He heard a voice shout out; 'He's over there!' A torch beam flickered across the trees about six feet above Marcus's head.

He dropped lower and turned right, crashing into tree trunks and falling over logs that had been cut and were lying there ready for shifting by the Forestry Commission during the working day. Eventually Marcus came out on to a forest track. It was wide enough for articulated lorries to drive along, and it gave Marcus a chance to move further away from his pursuers. But it also gave the two men a chance to get a shot off without the trees getting in the way.

Marcus could feel his strength draining away and he was beginning to stumble now. Each time he fell he knew this gave Grebo an edge. He also knew it wouldn't be too long before Grebo caught up with him, and it would be there that the American would shoot him.

And, as he fell again for probably the tenth time, he almost blacked out. He waited until he could think clearly, but now he could hear footsteps. He scrambled to his feet and collapsed again. This was it, he thought; the end.

He heard the footsteps again. They were hurried and came thudding up beside him. He felt an arm go round his waist and a voice say, 'Come on, son; get your arse in 'ere.'

He felt the softness of a car seat and heard the door closing behind him. Then the surge of acceleration as the car picked up speed and motored away from the forest.

TEN

MARCUS WOKE UP. He lay still for a moment enjoying the relaxed comfort of a warm bed and a soft pillow beneath his head, his last dream still lingering in the outer reaches of his consciousness. He opened his eyes and moved his head a little. He could see a saline drip hanging from its steel hook, the clear tube snaking down towards his arm. He lifted his head off the pillow and saw Cavendish sitting in a small armchair a few feet away from him.

'At last, Blake, you are awake.'

Marcus groaned and dropped his head back on the pillow. 'Where am I?' he asked, his voice cracking a little because of the dryness in his throat. 'And why are you here?'

Cavendish looked a trifle smug. 'Well, dear boy, first of all you are in a private clinic. But don't worry, Her Majesty's Government is picking up the bill. And the reason I'm here is because I saved your life.'

Marcus lifted his head sharply. 'You? There's no way you lifted me off the ground, Cavendish.'

'A mere detail, Blake. But you blundered into something well out of your league and we had to drag you out.'

Marcus regarded him quite severely. 'What do you mean?'

Cavendish shifted in his chair and leaned forward. 'We have had Grebo's house under surveillance for some considerable time. And because we followed you from the moment you walked out of the safe house, we knew there would be trouble once you showed up.'

Marcus struggled into a sitting position. 'You weren't there, were you?'

Cavendish shook his head. 'No; I'm too old for that kind of thing. I let the younger ones do that. And fortunately the man I had on duty recognized the possibility of a disaster in the making and called up the local police. It was one of the local coppers who saved you.'

Marcus leaned back against his pillow which he had pulled up behind him. 'So it's all blown; Grebo knows you've been watching him.'

Cavendish allowed himself a little triumphant smile. 'No, we were able to explain that there had been a report of a suspicious character in the neighbourhood and we were doing close checks on all the houses in the area.'

'And Grebo fell for that?'

Cavendish shrugged. 'Who knows? That was the explanation we gave; it was all we could come up with. What it means now, of course, is that we will have to pull our detail back for a while, just in case Mr Grebo has any suspicions.'

The door opened and a nurse came in. She walked over to the bed and removed the drip from Marcus's arm. Then she hung the tube up over the empty bottle and pushed the stand to the rear of the bed.

'Can I go home, Nurse?' Marcus asked.

The nurse smiled at Marcus and walked out of the room, closing the door behind her.

'What I want to know, Blake, is how on earth you learned of Danvor Grebo and the house?'

Marcus looked away from the closed door, giving up all thoughts of the nurse and turned his attention back to Cavendish. 'First of all, please call me Marcus; I got used to not being called Blake once I left school. And Grebo's house? I traced it through the number plate of the Mercedes I saw in the City Road: the one used in the attack on my office.'

Cavendish looked mortified. 'How on earth did you catch on to that?'

So Marcus told him. 'I saw the whole thing beginning to unfold through my office window. I didn't realize then what was happening, and by the time it clicked I didn't have time to say anything to you because I was busy, as I'm sure you will recall.'

'I'll give you that,' Cavendish admitted drily. 'Who do you know who can trace vehicle plates?'

Marcus shook his head. 'Can't tell you that; client confidentiality.'

Cavendish laughed. 'It isn't important, but it very nearly got you killed. And I'm sure your father would have had apoplexy if that had happened.'

'You know my father?' Marcus asked.

Cavendish nodded. 'Your name rang a bell. Then I remembered: Sir Henry Blake. He rang my office a few days ago. I didn't speak to him but later I remembered that he was on my radar for a while some years back during a "catch-all" enquiry we were doing.'

It was Marcus's turn to laugh. 'Seems to me it was my mother who was on your radar, Cavendish,' he told him.

Cavendish frowned. 'I'm not sure I know what you mean.'

'Hong Kong; the handover.'

It suddenly dawned on Cavendish. 'Ah, yes; the lovely Emily. Your father is a lucky man, Marcus; your mother is quite a beauty.'

Marcus gave an emphatic nod. 'Good; now you know where I get my good looks and intelligence from.'

Cavendish held up his hand. 'You leave the intelligence bit to the professionals. You'll learn nothing by getting yourself killed.'

'I did learn something though,' Marcus told him.

Cavendish immediately adopted a cautionary look. 'Oh, what was that?'

'I heard Grebo's visitor tell him that there's a shipment due in at Kings Lynn docks in a couple of days and a return load is now in a warehouse at Feltwell. I also heard someone say that the station chief is responsible for organizing the shipment going out.'

Cavendish looked as though he had been run through with a sword. His expression turned to stone and he sat in complete silence for a minute.

'Say that again please.'

Marcus knew he had said something of extreme importance. More so than that, he realized there was now far more to this man Grebo than he had first assumed. So he repeated it again, but slowly this time.

Cavendish muttered something and left the room. Marcus was now beginning to feel as though he had walked into a nest if vipers when he broke into Grebo's house. He could see how lucky he was to have escaped from the man's clutches because it wouldn't have been a quick shot to the head, but more than likely a severe beating before being shot. And he was basing that premise simply on the way Cavendish had reacted to his news.

When Cavendish came back he had Susan Ellis with him. Marcus was stunned at seeing her there with him. She looked quite helpless somehow; as though it wasn't her fault for being there. She gave Marcus a sorry look with a weak shrug of her shoulders.

'What are you doing here?' he demanded to know.

Cavendish offered Susan the chair he had been sitting in earlier. Then he spoke to Marcus.

'Let me explain something,' Cavendish began. 'I have been investigating a case that spans many borders and involves citizens of many countries. I have had to be extremely careful and sensitive about whom I approach and on whose toes I tread. Miss Ellis received another letter from her brother two days ago.' Marcus looked quickly at Susan who nodded. 'She went to see you, although goodness knows why, and found an empty office.' At that moment, Marcus did not know his office had been cleaned out by Cavendish's men. 'So she contacted me, which, of course, was the sensible thing to do. I brought Miss Ellis here so she could talk to me on the way. When Miss Ellis mentioned her brother, some pieces of my increasingly complex jigsaw began to fall into place. You, Marcus, have just added another piece.'

'Are you going to tell me what piece of the jigsaw I'm supposed to have supplied?' Marcus asked.

Cavendish shook his head briskly. 'Not yet, Marcus: all in good time.' He turned to Susan. 'Now, my dear, if you don't mind, I need to talk to Marcus alone. I'll see you out.'

Susan stood up and came over to the side of the bed. 'I hope you'll soon be up and about, Marcus. And I do hope one day we can both see David.'

'What are you going to do now?' he asked her. Susan glanced over at Cavendish before looking back at him. 'Well, if Mr Cavendish will arrange a taxi for me, I'll go home and get on with my life. I intend going to the newspapers about David again; they're the only ones who might be able to help.'

'I wish you luck.' It was a poor but well-meant offering from Marcus; he couldn't see any way Susan was going to make progress with her self-imposed task.

'Thank you, Marcus,' she said quickly, and leaned forward, planting a kiss on his cheek. 'Goodbye.'

She left the room with Cavendish behind her. Five minutes later the

MI6 chief came back. He shut the door and walked over to the bed and sat on the edge.

'I believe,' he began without preamble, 'that Danny Grebo is smuggling drugs into the country and shipping arms out. That is why your information has been so vital.'

Marcus frowned heavily. 'Where the bloody hell would Grebo get arms from?' he asked disbelievingly.

'That's my problem,' Cavendish replied. 'I believe I know, but I cannot prove it. It isn't actually Grebo who is shipping the arms out: it's the CIA. Danny Grebo is part of a chain. His cousin, Milan Janov is another link, but he's based in Turkmenistan. There are a lot of top, top people caught up in this, Marcus. There are billions of dollars involved too. That's why you nearly got yourself killed; you blundered into something that is way beyond you. But you opened a door for me and it has given us the opportunity to step through.'

'Us?' queried Marcus.

Cavendish nodded. 'Yes, us; from now on, Marcus, I want you to work with me.'

John Deveraux, the American Military Attaché at the American Embassy knew that Randy Hudson, the CIA chief was worried about something by the way in which he had asked for some of Deveraux's time. They often spoke about common links within their remit in the United Kingdom, but there was one area in which they were both involved that was rarely discussed, and that was the covert organization within The Chapter. And it was because of the CIA chief's look of concern that Deveraux knew their meeting would not bring good news.

He waited for Hudson to make himself comfortable before asking him why he wanted a meeting. Randy Hudson was in his fifties and beginning to show the ravages of time versus exercise. With fewer and fewer field operations and more desk work, Hudson looked his age.

'There was an incident at Grebo's house the other night,' he told Deveraux. 'Grebo was in the middle of discussing the weekend shipment with one of his men. He'd gone into the kitchen to get some drinks; noticed this guy's reflection in a mirror. He went back to his visitor and kept him talking while he got hold of a shotgun, then went out and faced the guy. Unfortunately the guy got away. Grebo chased him out into the woods at the back of the house, but the local cops were on the scene mighty quick; Grebo had to back off.'

'Has the operation been compromised?' Deveraux asked him.

Hudson shook his head. 'I don't think so, but I think we should call a halt to the operation for a while.'

'Why is that?'

'There was something that didn't ring quite true with what happened. Grebo couldn't figure out how the local boys got to the scene so quick. He said there was no phone call made, no alarms ringing off. The house is fairly secluded, too. Grebo had chased the guy into the forest. Said he would have despatched him there if he had caught him. But the guy stumbled into the main road and into a policeman's arms.'

Deveraux considered the implications of what he had been told. It certainly sounded like some kind of connivance with the local force.

'There's a shipment due in this weekend, right?' Hudson nodded. Deveraux went on. 'And one due out in a couple of days?'

'We'll hold that,' Hudson told him. 'It's in a bonded warehouse. It should be OK.'

'How long do you want to hold off for?' Deveraux asked him.

'Couple of weeks. No activity until then.'

'Will you tell Grebo?'

The CIA chief nodded. 'I'll tell him to close everything down.'

Deveraux whistled through his teeth. 'That's a long time; our client will think we're reneging on the deal.'

'Our client will do as he's told,' Hudson remarked angrily. 'He's getting a good deal out of us, and we're an easy market for his goods.'

Deveraux put his hand out. 'Be that as it may, Randy, it's always a tricky operation shipping those arms out; we don't always have a smooth run.'

'I know, John, but Cavendish is getting too close for comfort, and I can't afford to throw caution to the wind just because some fucking raghead in Afghanistan is getting impatient.'

'So why is Cavendish still around to worry the life out of you?' Deveraux put to him. 'What happened to the hit?'

Hudson shook his head. 'They fucked up. I don't know why. All I know is that Grebo's man waited for the full two minutes in the road, but the guys didn't come out. He left.' Hudson lifted his hands in a gesture of helplessness. 'That was the agreed plan. I know Cavendish put a team in and cleaned the building totally. We lost one guy and the other is probably on his way to the Intelligence Bureau in Pakistan.' It was there that the alleged questioning of MI6 suspects was carried out in order to bypass the interrogation laws in Great Britain. 'No doubt they'll get the truth from him.'

'How will that affect us?' Deveraux showed a little concern.

Hudson shook his head. 'It won't; the guys were hit-men. They only know their own names. The Brits will get nothing out of the one who survived.'

He sounded supremely confident, which made Deveraux feel a little more comfortable.

'So what are we going to do about Cavendish?' he asked the CIA man.

'We're going to leave it. It might be a good idea to let him have his head for a while. We'll just have to be extra vigilant and extremely careful.' He stood up, ready to leave. 'We've got a good operation here, John, and we've got to keep the lid screwed down tight. We have to be patient. The Chapter has to keep running for the sake of all those poor kids out there,' he said, cynically.

Deveraux chuckled and stood up. 'And for the sake of the twenty million bucks you put in your offshore account last year.' He reached across the desk and shook Hudson's hand. 'Keep me informed, Randy.'

Hudson nodded. 'You bet.'

He walked out of the office and left Deveraux wondering if the operation was becoming too unwieldy, too big and with too many fingers in the pie. But he had also put $20million into an offshore account and decided you don't earn that kind of money without taking a few risks.

The MV *Odessa* inched its way towards the quayside as two dockers stood waiting for the heaving lines to be tossed over to them. Once this was done, they pulled out the large ropes that would tether the ship and dropped the loops over their respective bollards. Their job now done they waited while two crewmen on the deck of the ship, one fore and one aft, waited for the captain's signals from the bridge before taking up the slack on the capstan winches.

The ship stopped and the capstan winches groaned beneath the deck lights as the slack in the hawsers was taken up. When all was secure, the ship's captain moved the bridge telegraph to 'stop engines' and handed over control of the bridge to the duty officer. He then went down to his cabin and waited the arrival of the local Customs Officer who would inspect the ship's manifest and then do a physical check of the ship's cargo holds.

Marcus watched the arrival of the MV *Odessa* with a growing feeling of excitement, tinged with anticipation. He was concealed in the dark recesses of some timber stacks that were waiting to be loaded on to lorries during daylight hours. He didn't know what cargo the *Odessa* was carrying beneath her decks, but he suspected that she was carrying something else that was worth a great deal more than the cargo that would be declared on her manifest.

Marcus had been sent up to Kings Lynn by Cavendish. He had even been furnished with a British Ports Authority Pass and a reason for visiting the docks. But all Marcus had been asked to do was observe and nothing else. He had been given the name of three ships; two of which had already docked and unloaded an enormous quantity of timber on to the quayside and departed. The third ship on Marcus's list, the *Odessa* was not due to dock until midnight because of the tide. And it was the unearthly hour of its expected arrival that intrigued Marcus.

He glanced at his watch and saw that it was almost midnight. He had no idea how long it would be until the crew bedded down for the night, but he had decided to chance his luck and get on board for a look in the cargo holds.

Marcus had got over his wounds from his previous escapade. His ankle hadn't given him any trouble and his shoulder had suffered only a minor peppering; nothing much at all. He was quite confident he no longer had to worry about them.

He saw a single gangway hauled up to the ship and a man in uniform immediately hurried up on to the deck. Someone was waiting for him and the two of them disappeared into the accommodation block at the stern end of the *Odessa*.

Marcus walked out from the timber pile, crossed the quayside and clambered up the gangway on the ship's deck. Without stopping to think of what he should do next, he opened one of the doors set into the bulkhead and stepped inside.

Marcus had chosen that moment to go on board because it was time least likely that anyone would have any suspicion of strangers going on to the ship, so long as it was done with a sense of purpose. All Marcus had to do now was to learn as much as he could about the cargo and get himself off the ship while most of the crew were sleeping.

He made his way down to the lower decks by following a common sense approach and using stairs, or ladders as they were known on ships, which went down until he came to a long passageway that ran forward.

Although it was the middle of the night, the bulkhead lights were on and he could see a closed, watertight door at the far end of the passageway. He made his way to this and swung the handles down, pulled the door open and stepped inside. He swung the handles up to secure the door and took his Maglite torch out of his pocket.

Marcus knew he wouldn't be able to break open any crates inside the holds without attracting attention and letting the crew know there was someone in the cargo hold causing damage. And Cavendish had been quite specific as to what he expected Marcus to do, and that was to learn as much as possible and then get out.

After about thirty minutes, Marcus had seen as much as he was likely to. All of the crates that he could actually examine closely were identified by labels and serial numbers, which were painted on the sides of the crates. It meant nothing to Marcus, but he dutifully made a note of what information there was in a small notebook.

Marcus was getting to the end of the hold when suddenly the door at the far end opened and all the lights came on. He spun round and immediately dropped into a crouch, keeping well behind the stack of crates.

He heard two men talking to each other and risked taking a look, but such was the way that the crates were stacked that he was unable to see who they were. As the two men walked along the stacks, their voices dropped to a murmur, but, as they came closer to where Marcus was hiding, their voices grew louder.

Marcus inched his way along the crate wall and peered carefully round the edge. He could now see the Customs Officer who had gone on deck the moment the gangway had been put in place. He assumed the seaman with him was the ship's captain, although he had no way of knowing. He was wearing a seaman's cap with gold braid round the peak, and on his shoulder epaulettes were four gold stripes.

The Customs Officer tapped a crate with his knuckle.

'This one,' he asked, 'with the X in the serial number?'

The captain nodded and said something which Marcus presumed meant 'yes'.

'How many?'

'Four.'

The Customs Officer seemed satisfied. 'Tomorrow afternoon, on the quayside, I'll sign them off.' He tapped a clipboard he was carrying with the tip of his pen. 'It all seems in order.' He then tucked the clipboard under his arm and turned on his heel. It seemed to catch the captain unawares and he was left standing there for a second. A minute later and the hold was in darkness once again.

Marcus knew he had just seen a crooked Customs Officer verify the crates containing the drugs were on board and had identified those he would attend to the following day. He had a vague notion that ships' cargoes had to be cleared officially by the Customs and Excise people before they were allowed to be offloaded on to the quayside. And he had no doubt that they did a thorough and excellent job in the main. But here was a classic case of smuggling with the collusion of the authorities; in this case the bent officer. All Marcus had to do now was to get off the ship, notify Cavendish and get himself back to the Duke's Head Hotel for a good night's sleep.

He made his way carefully along the crate wall to the door at the far end. He turned off his Maglite and put it in his pocket, then opened the door handles one by one until the door swung freely on its hinges.

He stepped out and turned to close the door when a crewman came through an open door a few feet away. He saw Marcus and stopped. Then he called out something in a language Marcus didn't understand. The crewman had shouted back through the door from which he had appeared, obviously calling for some help.

Marcus didn't wait to think of any consequences; he simply ran at the man and drove his fist into his face. It sent the crewman crashing to the deck and Marcus leapt over him. There was a shout from behind as two men came through the doorway. They saw their friend lying on the floor and immediately went after Marcus.

Marcus ran as fast as he could until he came to a closed door. In the few seconds he took to open it, one of the two men chasing him threw something at him. It caught Marcus on his injured shoulder. Although Marcus hadn't suffered any real ill effects from his wounds, when the heavy weight that had been thrown struck him, it seemed like a thousand fragments of steel had cut into him. He gasped out loud and fell up against the edge of the open door.

This gave the two men an advantage and within seconds they were on him. Marcus felt their hands pulling him away from the bulkhead, cursing at him. The look on their faces left him in no doubt what they were about to do.

But, as hurt as Marcus was, he felt the anger rising up in his chest and he swung his elbow out, catching one of the men full in the face. The man yelled out and fell away clutching his jaw. Then Marcus lifted the heel of his shoe and dragged it down the shin of the second man. It was enough and Marcus was free.

He ran as fast as he could until he reached a ladder and sprinted up two steps at a time, pulling himself clear on the upper deck. Another crewman happened to be at the top and wasn't aware of the fracas going on below. Marcus drove his fist into the man's face without stopping and kept up his dash for the gangway.

Suddenly a shot rang out and he felt the bullet zip past his head and clang into the bulkhead. It almost stopped him in his tracks, but he turned away from the shooter and ran to the far side of the ship.

Without giving thought to what the consequences might be, Marcus hurled himself over the side and plummeted into the water below.

ELEVEN

SUSAN HADN'T BEEN home from work more than a couple of minutes when the doorbell rang. She put the milk back in the fridge and went through to the front door. When she opened it she saw a uniformed policeman standing there holding out his warrant card. He looked impossibly young to be a policeman.

'Susan Ellis?' he asked brightly.

'Yes,' Susan answered, with the long drawn-out reply that suggests caution.

'Constable Evans,' he told her. 'I wonder if you would be good enough to call in at the local nick.' He corrected himself. 'I'm sorry; the local police station. Just routine,' he assured her. 'Whenever is convenient. Well,' he added, 'if you could make it this evening, that would be really helpful.'

'What's it about?' she asked the young copper.

'I'm sorry, ma'am, I can't say. You're not under arrest; nothing like that.' He looked quite concerned as he said it.

Susan smiled. 'I'm sure I'm not. Very well; give me five minutes and I'll walk down to the station with you. Is it far?'

He pointed over his shoulder. 'I've got the car here. I'll bring you back as well.'

'Five minutes, then,' she said and closed the door.

About fifteen minutes later, Susan walked into the police station with the young constable. He took her up to the station desk. The young female police officer looked up at them.

'Susan Ellis,' the constable told her, pointing over his shoulder at Susan. 'Chief wants a word with her.'

The young woman reached across to a box with an array of buttons and held one down. 'Chief, desk here. Susan Ellis to see you.'

She looked up. 'Take Miss Ellis through, John,' she told him, and looked back down at whatever she had been doing when they walked in.

Evans took Susan through a small maze of people working at their desks, on the phones, checking data on computer screens and busy chatting away as though they were anywhere but in a working police station.

Evans knocked on a closed door marked 'Detective Chief Inspector Rendell.' He didn't wait for a response but opened the door and stepped inside.

'Evening, Chief. Got Miss Ellis for you.'

Rendell looked across the top of his half-moon glasses and signalled with a crooked forefinger to bring her in.

Susan followed Evans into the office as Rendell stood up. 'Thank you, Evans. I'll call you when we're finished.'

Evans left the office as Rendell shook Susan's hand and asked her to take a seat.

'Can I get you a coffee, glass of water?' he asked Susan. 'Anything?'

Susan shook her head. 'No, thank you, Chief Inspector. So long as you don't intend keeping me here too long, I think I'll manage.'

Rendell was in his fifties and looked fit for his age. He reminded Susan of her father a bit. He had a warm, inviting face and seemed to exude friendliness, although she doubted he would show that countenance to offenders.

'I'll try not to keep you.' He hadn't taken his seat yet and immediately went across to a filing cabinet set against the far wall. On top of the cabinet was a folder which he brought across to the desk. He sat down and spun the folder round so that it was facing Susan.

'Now, do I call you Miss, Ms, or what?'

'Susan will do fine,' she told him.

He smiled and seemed to relax. 'Good. Now, I have it on highest authority that you are a little bit special. I haven't been told why, not yet anyway, so I'll assume you're related to the prime minister, or something like that, eh?' He allowed himself a little chuckle at the joke.

'Now, there are some photographs in there,' he told Susan, pointing to the folder. 'If you wouldn't mind, would you look through them and tell me if you recognize anybody.' He passed the folder across the desk and sat back and watched as Susan opened the folder.

She began turning over the pages and saw a photograph of one of her neighbours coming out of the front door. 'My neighbour,' she muttered, and kept on turning the pages.

It was obvious to Susan that someone, no doubt a police officer, had been stationed outside her flat with the instruction to photograph everybody who came in or went out, and even those people like delivery men or salesmen who simply called at the front door or posted mail through the letter box.

Then she stopped at a photograph of a man putting something through the letter box. In the next photograph he had turned round and was now walking away from the door. The photograph was very good; she recognized him immediately.

'That's Maggot,' she said, looking up. 'What the hell is he doing there?'

Marcus sat in his hotel room thinking about his next move. He had thrown himself off the MV *Odessa* deliberately because he knew there was not much of a drop from the main deck down to the water, and the option of remaining on board and trying to make a fight of it hadn't come into it; especially as someone was firing a gun at him.

As soon as he had surfaced, he had swum away from the ship as fast as he could. He could hear the sound of shouting, but mercifully no more shooting. The darkness helped to cover his escape and he hoped that the captain of the *Odessa* would assume he was an illegal immigrant making a run for freedom.

Eventually, more by luck than judgement, he ended up someway along the river, and, by the time he had dragged himself up on to a small, wooden landing stage, he was breathless as well as soaked through to the skin.

He had put about a hundred yards between him and the *Odessa*. There was no obvious sign of pursuit, so Marcus had walked away from the river and out on to a road. He took his bearings and made his way back to the hotel. Fortunately for Marcus his clothes were not in too bad a state when he walked to reception and asked for his room key. The night porter barely glanced up at him.

He had taken a hot bath, then a shower before slipping into bed. His shoulder was beginning to hurt a little but he ignored it. The flesh wound that Cavendish had dressed at the safe house hurt as well, but he ignored that too. He felt a little troubled by them but soon fell asleep.

When he woke that morning he showered again, put on a pair of jeans and a check shirt, called Cavendish and then went into the town to buy another change of clothes.

He had watched an early morning television broadcast on the local news channel carrying reports of an illegal immigrant shooting his way out of a trap on board the MV *Odessa* in the docks. It suited Marcus to see the incident reported that way, and it probably suited the captain of the *Odessa* too.

Now he was sitting in his room contemplating his next move. He had been reticent about explaining to Cavendish exactly what had occurred the night before, so kept much of the detail to himself. He was surprised when Cavendish suggested he went back to the docks and tried to identify the illegal cargo once it was on the quayside, and find out where it was heading.

He wondered if the security chief was really concerned about what happened to him; whether he really cared that Marcus was not exactly a trained agent. After all, he had literally been given free rein to follow his own instincts and to come up with some answers. Perhaps Cavendish trusted those instincts to the point where he believed Marcus was more than capable of achieving a satisfactory conclusion to whatever objective he set him.

Or maybe not; maybe Marcus was a pain in the arse and Cavendish wanted shot of him. The drugs coming into the country through Kings Lynn Docks couldn't have represented more than a fraction of what was flooding into the country anyway, and there was a National Drugs Squad, or something, to take care of that. So why him, why Marcus?

Susan Ellis sat staring at Chief Inspector Rendell. She found it difficult to believe what he had told her; that Maggot was known to them and was listed as having links with Al-Qaeda, the Muslim terrorist organization.

'Don't misunderstand me, Susan,' Rendell was saying. 'Just because a person is listed as suspect, doesn't mean he or she is guilty of terrorism. A lot of people come up on our radar and we have to investigate them as thoroughly and discreetly as possible.'

'But I was only talking to him a couple of days ago,' she told Rendell. 'I didn't know who he was when I met him. He said he was a friend of Marcus Blake.'

Rendell looked down at a file in front of him. 'Who is Marcus Blake?' he asked, looking up.

Susan explained who Marcus was, more or less repeating what Maggot had told her without going into detail about her own reason for contacting him in the first place. She thought her description of Marcus as a private detective would be sufficient and left the description at that.

'Marcus and Maggot are good friends. His name is Rafiq Shah, by the way,' she added.

Rendell leaned forward and put his elbows on the desk. He rested his chin on the knuckles of his hand.

'Yes, we know him as Rafiq Shah, not Maggot.'

'Is this serious?' Susan sounded concerned. 'I don't want to get involved in any trouble.'

Rendell shrugged. 'The devil of it is, you are involved simply by association. It's a bugger, I know, but that's the way it is.' He was being gentle with her because he recognized innocence when he saw it. 'It might help,' he continued, 'if you could let us see what it was Rafiq, or Maggot as you know him, put through your door.'

Susan blanched and Rendell sensed he had touched a nerve.

'I can tell you what it was,' she admitted, 'but you will have to take my word for it; I cannot show it to you.' Susan did not want David's letter taken from her because she wanted to go to the national press with it.

Rendell tipped his head slightly. 'Why not let me make up my own mind about that?'

'Very well,' she began reluctantly. 'Have you ever heard of David Ellis?'

Milan Janov would have looked completely out of place had he not adopted the standard Afghani *pakol* hat and *chapan* jacket, such was his size and east European appearance. But he wanted to appear as inconspicuous as possible in the northern region of Faryab in Afghanistan for his meeting with Abdul Khaliq.

The two men had met in this way before, but there had never been any obvious tension between them apart from a natural proclivity for sharpened senses and awareness that comes from clandestine meetings. Abdul felt it more than most because he suspected that Janov was trying to muscle in on his operation.

The two men were seated in the house of a hill farmer at Maymaneh, a small town nestling in the foothills twenty miles from the border with Turkmenistan. With Janov were two very powerful and ugly-looking minders. Abdul knew he would have more men stationed outside up on the high ground overlooking the meeting place.

With Abdul were his own trusted men, and David Ellis. David was under instruction to say nothing and not respond to any questions. Abdul knew that Janov could speak fluent English and wanted to avoid David falling into any traps. David was now easily passed off as an Afghani, providing nobody spoke to him. Abdul had still not explained satisfactorily to David why he was being dragged around like a trophy prisoner. All he would say was that David's freedom depended on him remaining with him at all times and at all costs.

The two men sat facing each other with barely disguised hostility.

'I spoke to my cousin in England this morning,' Janov began. 'He told me there was a problem in the port when the ship docked.'

Abdul opened his hands in surprise. 'So why are you telling me?'

Janov explained. His voice was steady but full of implication. 'The authorities in England must have known about the shipment. We need to find who is supplying them with the information. I have no reason to suspect any of my men. So you must make sure you are confident with yours.'

Abdul would have laughed had he not felt insulted by the suggestion that there was a leak in his organization. His side of the operation meant that he dealt with the Afghanistan farmers when it came to buying up their opium yield, the men who converted the milky sap from the poppy into heroin, and the Taliban warlords who allowed the poppies to be grown on their territory. None of those men had any reason to jeopardize their own part of the operation; they were all well paid and had a virtually guaranteed market.

Each year the farmers produced about 4000 tons of opium; roughly eighty per cent of the world's supply. The market in Great Britain alone was worth about £6 billion, to say nothing of the markets *en route* from Afghanistan to the points of entry into the United Kingdom.

Abdul's part in the drug route covered most of the northern provinces of Afghanistan; Janov's covered the entire European route once the drugs had entered Turkmenistan. But Janov had another finger in the pie – weapons.

The Taliban needed weapons and money to support and maintain their so-called *intifada* against the infidel and the great Satan, America. The beauty of it for the Taliban was that they were allowing farmers to grow opium for which the Taliban took a share of the profits, and the money earned from the drugs was used to purchase arms from the British and the Americans to prolong the war in Afghanistan. It was a continuous loop and Janov sat in the middle of it, sending misery into the world and filling his pockets with money and feeding his power-hungry aims and ambitions.

Janov was convinced that Abdul was causing him a problem and wanted shot of him.

And Abdul knew it.

But Janov could not declare open war on him without alerting their paymasters to a split in the 'ranks'. As far as Janov was concerned, Abdul's demise had to be made to look like a dispute that had gone tragically wrong, and Janov needed more time to set something up.

The reason they had met was routine; money was to exchange hands and deals to be concluded. But because of the problem at the docks in England that Janov had referred to, and the fact that the operation had been closed down for the sake of security, there was to be no money and no deal.

It made for a very tense meeting between the two men, but they had no reason to blame each other, although that was exactly what Janov was trying to do: lay the blame at Abdul's feet.

The meeting ended with a lot of angry words on both sides, and left Abdul hoping that the letter David had sent to England would elicit some kind of response. If not, then he and David were dead men.

TWELVE

MARCUS SAT BESIDE an enormous policeman in the back of a nondescript but very powerful Vauxhall Vectra. He had met him when the lorry that he had been following had pulled into a truck stop just outside Brandon in Suffolk. Marcus had contacted Cavendish and asked for instructions. Cavendish told him to wait at the truck stop until he was contacted. Half an hour later the Vectra turned up and pulled into a parking space a few yards from Marcus.

The two men who climbed out of the car were defying the laws of ergonomics because there was no way the two of them should have been able to get into the car. They were dressed in plain clothes and for a moment Marcus thought the villains had caught up with him. One of them put his hand on the roof of his Mondeo and tapped on the window. Marcus opened it.

'Marcus Blake?' He pulled a warrant card out of his pocket. 'Detective Sergeant Whelan,' he told Marcus, in a heavy Irish brogue. He looked across to the passenger door. 'And that's Detective Constable Iverson; "Yorkie" to his mates. If you want to speak to me, call me Paddy.' Whelan straightened up and beckoned Marcus. 'Now, sir, if you'd like to follow me?'

Marcus got out of the Mondeo and went over to the Vectra with the two policemen. Yorkie Iverson got into the driver's seat while Whelan and Marcus climbed into the back.

'Is that the truck?' Whelan asked him.

Parked among the lorries in the lorry-park was a flat-bed articulated lorry stacked with large crates.

Marcus nodded. 'That's the one.'

'Right,' Whelan began after a short pause. 'It's like this: we follow the truck as far as it goes. It will probably be Feltwell according to our sources.' Marcus didn't have the heart to tell him exactly who those 'sources' were. 'We'll make a decision when we get there.'

'Make a decision about what?' Marcus asked him.

'Whether we bust them or not,' Whelan replied.

It was a simple reply, and Marcus could imagine these two huge coppers putting the fear of God into hardened criminals.

The three of them sat there for well over an hour, making small talk but saying very little. Marcus had tried to encourage them to open up, but they were not that forthcoming, so he gave up.

They all saw the driver come out of the truck stop and walk across to his lorry. Yorkie gunned the motor into life and waited until the lorry was on the move before pulling away from the parking area.

Their journey was not too long. The lorry drove away from Brandon a short distance and then turned on to the Weeting road. It headed into the country until it came to a sign pointing to the town of Feltwell.

None of them spoke as a sense of tension began feeling its way into the car. Marcus was sure it would not affect the two policemen, but he could definitely feel a slight, skin-tightening sensation creeping over him.

They followed the lorry through the small town of Feltwell. It was beginning to get dark and the street lights were flickering into life. Soon the shops and houses began to thin out as they drove a little deeper into the countryside.

Then the lorry slowed and turned on to a small road. Yorkie pulled the Vectra over and parked.

'Why are we stopping?' Marcus asked.

'Wouldn't do to follow him up there,' Whelan told him. 'We'll have to wait until it gets dark.'

'Aren't you afraid of losing him?'

Whelan shook his head. 'No.' It was all he said.

So they waited until the darkness was complete. Suddenly Whelan leaned forward and reached over the empty passenger seat. Yorkie put his hand out and opened the glove box. He took a Sig Sauer handgun from the compartment, and handed it to Whelan who slipped out the magazine, checked it and rammed it back. Then he put the gun into his inside pocket.

'Wait here,' he said, and climbed out of the car.

Whelan walked carefully along the track, which was in very good condition considering it was probably no more than a farm road. It had a tarmac surface, which surprised him.

He could see the road curving in the moonlight, but the curve was too sharp for him to see much beyond thirty yards or so. On his right the trees seemed to leap up and hang over him like phantoms. He took the Sig Sauer handgun from his pocket, slipped off the safety catch and held the gun firmly, pointing it down.

The road began to straighten and he was able to see a chain-link fence in the distance. He could also see a wide metal gate, which was closed. But, astonishingly, the gateway was flooded in light from arc lamps bearing down from high stanchions above the fence. And just inside the gate was what looked like a sentry post; a security hut. He could see someone sitting at a desk. He was wearing a uniform which Whelan recognized. And then he saw the large, floodlit sign.

'Oh, bollocks,' he said.

The words on the sign read: *United States Air Force. 7th. Logistics Wing. Bonded Warehouse.*

Whelan stopped and slipped the gun back into his pocket. He then retraced his footsteps until he had cleared the curve in the road. Then he quickened his pace and eventually broke into a trot. When he reached the car he was slightly breathless.

Marcus and Yorkie watched him get into the front of the car.

'It's the fucking Yanks,' he gasped. 'A bonded fucking warehouse!'

'What are you talking about, Paddy?' Iverson asked him.

'It's a bloody Yank compound,' he explained, shaking his head. 'Can't go in there asking questions.'

Suddenly there was a tap on the window. The three of them looked over at the window beside Yorkie. There was an American Military Policeman standing there. Yorkie put the window down.

'Yes, Officer?' he asked politely.

The MP's hand came into view. He was holding a standard issue M9 handgun.

'Get out of the car, sir.' He stepped back.

Whelan felt the weight of his own gun in the pocket of his jacket, but before he could make a decision one way or the other, it was made for him: his door was pulled open by a second, armed MP.

'Hands in the air!' was the command, as the three men climbed out of the Vectra.

As Marcus straightened up he saw the Dodge pick-up truck. It was just rolling to a halt about twenty yards from them. He realized that the MPs must have approached their car on foot, although he had absolutely no idea where they came from.

The pick-up truck was a long-wheel-base wagon with a passenger compartment. The MPs frisked the three men, removed the gun from Whelan's coat pocket and marshalled them to the rear door of the Dodge and made them get in.

Once they were seated along the bench seat, the doors were locked and the truck motored up the side road to the compound where they knew the contraband had been delivered. The gates were now wide open. The driver took the Dodge up to the large doors of the warehouse and parked in front of them.

The three of them were made to get out and taken through a pedestrian door which opened into the warehouse. On one side was an office. The lights were on and sitting there was the man they assumed to be the lorry driver. Facing him from behind the desk was Danny Grebo.

The master sergeant looked at the three men through the glass window of the office. His posture was fairly relaxed and the expression on his face one of authority and control.

Then it changed: he recognized Marcus.

Grebo stood up slowly as recognition dawned on him. His eyes darted swiftly to Iverson and Whelan, and then back to Marcus as the two MPs brought them into the office. He said nothing straight away, but Marcus knew he had recognized him. And Marcus was intelligent enough to know that once Grebo discovered that Iverson and Whelan were policemen, he could not afford to let them go.

Not now.

Cavendish was shown into the prime minister's private office. It was almost midnight and the prime minister, not one for spending too much time in bed, had agreed to the meeting with the intelligence chief even though it was quite late.

Cavendish had explained that he wanted a private meeting, no notes, no record and no parliamentary private secretaries to sit in on the conversation.

Cavendish sat down in an armchair to wait. He had no qualms about what he would discuss with him, and knew it would certainly give the man a problem. But that was the price of holding down the top job.

The door opened and the prime minister walked in. He was still dressed in his daily attire of bespoke suit and knitted tie. His hair, as usual, was a shambles and his appearance was that of someone who is always in a hurry. But what Cavendish knew of the prime minister was that the man had a very keen intellect, a razor-sharp mind and did not suffer fools gladly.

'Good evening, Sir Giles,' he said, holding out his hand.

Cavendish stood up and shook the prime minister's hand.

'Would you like a drink?'

'No thank you, Prime Minister,' Cavendish answered. 'I don't intend staying long.'

'Very well,' the PM said, and sat down in an armchair that had been placed at a right angle to the one Cavendish had chosen. 'So, what is it you wish to see me about?'

'It's about the James Purdy assassination, Prime Minister.'

The PM's facial expression changed, bringing his eyebrows closer together.

'Bad business, that,' he said. 'The police commissioner assures me that he will find the perpetrators. I've asked him to keep me informed of course. Do you have anything to add, Sir Giles?'

Cavendish nodded briefly. 'Purdy's assassination has uncovered a whole nest of vipers and unfortunately it implicates the minister in a way that could be very damaging to the government, I'm afraid.'

'Go on.'

'Some very senior and important people in this country are involved in drugs and pornography.' He put up a restraining hand. 'I know; it's something we all know, but often we shake our heads and tut tut our opinion, and tend to mentally sweep it all under the carpet. But with James Purdy it reached a point where national security could have been threatened.'

'Go on,' the PM said again.

'James Purdy was photographed engaging in pornographic sexual activities with three under-age girls from Pakistan. One of the girls subsequently died from the injuries she received.' The prime minister gasped out loud, but Cavendish continued, 'The two girls who survived have disappeared and are now most likely to have been sold into a paedophile or prostitution ring.'

The prime minister's face was now almost white.

'Let me understand this, Sir Giles, you say Purdy was photographed. Does that mean you have seen the photographs?'

Cavendish nodded. 'Yes, it was my department that took them.'

'You knew this was going on?' The prime minister seemed shocked.

Cavendish leaned forward to make a point. 'Prime Minister, it's my job to make sure no foreign government can blackmail, threaten or intimidate any member of your cabinet. We had our suspicions about Purdy, but even then we didn't know just how deep he had got himself. So deep in fact that he was actually working against our interests.'

'Are you saying, Sir Giles,' the prime minister interrupted, 'that James Purdy was working for a foreign government?'

Cavendish shook his head. 'Not exactly a foreign government, Prime Minister, but a group who have a great deal of power and can use that power to influence decisions made by government ministers.'

'So why was Purdy assassinated?'

Cavendish shifted in his chair. 'He was about to tell me who his co-conspirators were; who else was involved in the gang rape of those three young girls and who is responsible for smuggling huge quantities of drugs into this country.' He almost took a deep breath when he added the next line. 'And who is responsible for shipping arms out to Al-Qaeda and the Taliban in Afghanistan.'

He let it sit there, allowing the prime minister to digest the import of his words and the real damage that men like Purdy can do, simply to feather their own nests and indulge their own, misdirected passions.

Eventually the prime minister spoke.

'So you believe that Muslim terrorists assassinated James Purdy because he was about to name names?'

Cavendish shook his head. 'No, Prime Minister, it wasn't the Muslims who murdered James Purdy; it was the Americans.'

The police radio in the Vectra had been left on because there had been no reason for Iverson to turn everything off when ordered out of the car by the two American MPs. A metallic voice filled the empty car.

'Whisky India, come in please.'

Back in the call control centre in Thetford, the officer tried several times to raise Iverson and Whelan without luck. He turned to his supervisor and told him he was having trouble raising the two men.

The supervisor came over to the desk and looked at the controller's console.

'They're not on an incident,' he muttered, as he checked the screen. 'Where is Whisky India, by the way?' he asked.

The controller selected a sat nav screen which showed the exact location of the police car. 'Two miles west of Feltwell.'

'Who's closest?'

The controller scanned the screen. 'Boon and Manning.'

The supervisor straightened up. 'Get them to check it out.'

The controller pressed the call button on his desk console. 'Bravo Mike, control; come in, please.'

In the bonded warehouse, Grebo continued to stare at Marcus. All Marcus could do was hold the American's gaze and wait for something to happen. There were seven men in the room. Two of them, the American MPs, were armed. It was unlikely that Grebo would be carrying a weapon but he could have one in his desk drawer. Marcus felt confident he could take care of one of the armed MPs, but he wondered who would take care of the other one.

Boon and Manning received the call to investigate why Whisky India was not answering the call from control. They were on their way within seconds of being directed to the location. Boon switched on the flashing blue warning lights and put the hammer down. Manning estimated it would take about ten minutes in their BMW to reach Whisky India's Vectra.

It was Whelan who spoke first. 'Whoever you are,' he said to Grebo, 'I think you should know that we are police officers.' He lifted his hand up, keeping it open. 'I'm going to get out my warrant card,' he told him.

Very slowly, Whelan pulled out his warrant card and laid it on the desk in front of the American. 'Detective Sergeant Whelan. And this,' he pointed to Iverson, 'is Detective Constable Iverson.'

Grebo looked away from Whelan to Marcus. 'And who is this?' he asked.

Whelan turned slowly to Marcus. 'He is a trainee police community support officer.'

Marcus wondered how Whelan could have come up with such a preposterous idea in such a short time.

'Is he now?' Grebo responded acidly. 'So what are we going to do with you all?'

'You're going to do nothing,' Whelan told him. 'We are going to walk out of here now.' He reached forward to pick up his warrant card.

One of the MPs put an arm out to stop him. He had a gun in his other hand.

Whelan stared at him with an iron-hard look. 'You be careful, sonny,' he warned him and picked up his warrant card.

Grebo flicked a cautionary look at the MP. Marcus could see his dilemma: Grebo could not afford a shoot out, nor could he afford to let any of them go. There was also something else behind that look – like a rabbit trapped in the headlights.

Boon and Manning came up beside the Vectra. They peered through the windows of the car but could see no one inside. Manning climbed out of the BMW and checked the Vectra. He turned round to Boon and showed him a pair of empty hands.

Boon pointed towards the side road and indicated to Manning that he would drive up there. Manning nodded and waved him forward, preferring to walk up behind him. Boon turned into the side road and cruised slowly towards the curve in the road. Manning kept pace behind him.

Grebo was about to say something when the phone on his desk rang. He looked a little startled as he picked up the phone.

'Grebo.'

He listened briefly then slammed the phone down. 'There's a police unit at the gate,' he said in disbelief. 'What the fuck are they doing here?' For a moment Grebo looked like a man lost. Then suddenly he made up his mind. He pointed at Marcus and the two policemen.

'Keep them here,' he ordered, and opened a desk drawer. He then pulled out an M9 handgun and hurried out of the office.

The two MPs immediately waved their guns at Whelan and Iverson, pointing to the far side of the office. They shuffled across to the far wall.

Marcus was told to join them. It looked like the execution wall in front of a firing squad; Marcus had no intention of moving over there.

He turned his head suddenly towards the MPs and was about to say something, hoping to distract them so he could get at them, when they all heard several shots ring out. The two MPs automatically turned in the direction of the shots. At that moment Marcus knew he had the window he needed and launched himself at the nearest MP.

He kicked the man's gun from his hand as the other MP lifted his gun to shoot him. But Marcus dived beneath the first MP and lifted him bodily into the air, holding him on his shoulders in a fireman's lift. He then spun and dropped the man at his colleague's feet, intending to knock the man off balance.

The man was still trying to get a shot at Marcus but was hesitating because he was afraid of shooting his colleague. The sudden opening gave him the chance, but at that moment, Iverson had thrown himself forward and lifted the desk, bringing it up as a shield and pushed it at the MP who was about to shoot Marcus.

The man saw it coming and turned and fired at Iverson instead. Now Whelan joined in the fray and came forward with the intention of grappling with the man who had been tossed to the ground by Marcus, but the shot aimed at Iverson caught Whelan on the arm. He cried out and fell on top of the MP, clutching his arm.

Iverson stood up and reached over the desk which was now on its side as the American swung the gun round to fire off another shot. He grabbed the collar of the second MP, swung his arm down on to the man's gun hand and dragged him over the desk. On the way the MP dropped his gun. Immediately the lorry driver, who until now had been a spectator, picked up the gun and fired a shot into the ceiling.

Everybody stopped. Except Marcus; he gambled on the man not being a gunman and leapt over the top of Whelan who had collapsed and kicked the driver with a classic, straight leg right into the rib cage.

They all heard the sound of the man's ribs crack, and he dropped into a heap letting the gun fall from his hand.

Iverson picked up the gun and walked round the overturned desk. He picked up the other M9 and handed one to Marcus.

'Cover them, and try not to shoot anyone,' he said. 'I'm going outside to see what's happened.'

Whelan staggered to his feet. His arm was bleeding from where he had been shot. He looked at the damage caused by the sudden explosion of violence and shook his head.

'What a fucking mess,' he muttered to himself. 'God knows how we're going to write this one up.'

He then leant down and searched the two MPs until he found his Sig Sauer handgun that had been taken from him outside the compound. He tucked it into his waistband. Using his good arm, he pulled the desk upright and dragged it away from the two MPs and the lorry driver until it was pushed up against the far wall. He then propped himself up against it and looked at the scene in front of him.

The lorry driver was lying on the floor nursing a cracked rib or two. One of the military policemen was lying on the floor too, but he looked as though he had been winded. The other MP was on his knees, but Marcus was standing well clear with the M9 pistol pointing at them.

Whelan took the Sig Sauer from his waistband and held it loosely in his good hand.

'Marcus, see if you can give Yorkie a hand,' he asked, 'I'll keep an eye on these three.'

Marcus was about to go outside when the door flew open and Iverson burst in. He looked devastated.

'The bastard's shot two coppers; one of ours and one of his own.'

'Where is he now?' Whelan snapped.

'Gone,' Iverson told him. 'He took the local's BMW, shot the MP in the gatehouse. There's another copper out there, he's OK though.'

'Put out an APB,' Whelan told him.

'I'm on it,' Iverson replied, 'Can you manage here?'

Whelan nodded. 'Oh yes, we can manage here.'

Thirty minutes later the area around the compound was like a scene from a Hollywood movie; there were several police units, British and American, ambulances from the American base and the local hospital at Thetford, flashing blue lights from stationary police cars and policemen marking off the area with police tape. There were also several American officers of various ranks with very grim-looking faces.

The two American MPs who had been involved were in the back of a police wagon along with the driver of the lorry. Grebo was now on the run after shooting Boon and the American MP in the gatehouse.

Manning had come across the shooting just as Grebo was hauling Boon out of the police car and using it to make his getaway. Boon was not mortally wounded, but the poor unfortunate American in the gate-house was dead.

Whelan had been seen by a paramedic and was waiting to be taken to hospital in one of the ambulances. Marcus sat beside him on a chair outside the office which had now been cordoned off as a crime scene.

Inside the bonded warehouse was a team of men, British and American, checking the crates, opening each one carefully. It was an unhappy scene, Marcus thought. He knew Grebo had run because he couldn't see any other way out. In a way that had saved the lives of Marcus, Whelan and Iverson, but sadly had cost the life of the poor guy in the gatehouse. He probably didn't even know what was going on.

Now the whole world was about to find out as the first of many television vans appeared at the gate; tomorrow it would be on all the front pages and the major news networks worldwide.

And Marcus knew that this time Cavendish would not be able to send a team in.

THIRTEEN

SIR GILES CAVENDISH went ballistic; or his version of it anyway. Sitting alone in his office with the first editions on his desk he felt extremely angry that decisions he had made, and those made by others, had resulted in such a woeful outcome. He couldn't really fault any one person for causing what the red top tabloids were describing as a shoot out at the OK Corral, but each person in the chain was culpable. And being at the head of that chain, Cavendish felt responsible for having a coach and horses driven through his careful, methodical investigation into the corrupt practices of some people in very high positions of authority.

He felt he had reached a crossroads and didn't know which way to turn. His investigation was now dead in the water and common sense told him that those people involved in the vicious trade he had been looking into would close ranks and probably lie low for a while. The trouble with that was that he needed them to be active so he could penetrate their organization and reach the head. He swore and called down curses on those people who dealt in misery, violence and death.

The phone rang. It was the prime minister.

'Good morning, Sir Giles. Could you come over to Downing Street right away?'

There was no ambiguity in the request; he expected Cavendish over there immediately.

'I'll be there in thirty minutes, Prime Minister,' Cavendish promised, and put the phone down.

He had two guesses: one was a conference, the other was dismissal. Not that being dismissed would be so terribly painful, he mused. After all, he would pick up a gold-plated Civil Service pension. A statement on his retirement would be couched in prosaic terms and he could retire to the country where he could tend his roses or whatever it was retired civil servants did. And meanwhile men in high places would continue to pursue their misguided foreign policy and feather their own nests with millions of dollars drawn from the pain and suffering of the victims of their obsessive lust for wealth.

And men like him would know the truth, but never be allowed to reveal it either through stealth or any other means. To do so would mean no more tending of roses, no more gold-plated pension, no more of anything.

He arrived at Downing Street and was shown into the cabinet office where the prime minister was waiting. With him was Andrew Butler, the Metropolitan Police Commissioner, and James Faulkner, the director of SOCA. SOCA was the Serious Organized Crime Agency – Britain's equivalent to the American FBI.

'Ah, Sir Giles, take a seat.'

It was clear from his body language that the prime minister was keen to get on with the meeting and dispense with any niceties.

'I've no need to apprise you of last night's events,' he began, 'but I would like your take on it.'

Cavendish had just about made himself comfortable and responded immediately. 'My take on it, Prime Minister, is that a huge hole has been blown in my investigation; one from which I cannot see us recovering.' He helped himself to a glass of water. He took a sip and put the glass down on to a small table. 'At the moment all I can think of is damage limitation and trying to keep the Press out of it.'

'Was your investigation the reason we ended up with a shoot out, as the papers put it, at an American depot?' the police commissioner asked him.

Cavendish gave it a moment's thought. 'I wish it wasn't but, yes, that was the reason there was a shoot out.'

Butler frowned. 'I find that a little flippant,' he told Cavendish. 'There must be a convincing reason why you were there. And why on earth were the Americans involved?'

Cavendish bridled at Butler's assertion that he was being flippant, but held his tongue; the last thing he wanted here was a slanging match and point scoring over other security departments.

'The reason my men ended up at the American depot was because they were following a suspicious cargo which we believed contained drugs.'

Faulkner butted in. 'What on earth was your department doing investigating drugs?' he asked testily. 'We have a dedicated drug squad for that very purpose. Why weren't we informed?'

'It wasn't so much the drugs we were interested in,' Cavendish replied, 'but the result of where those drugs were going, and who is behind the operation.'

Faulkner made a guttural sound in his throat. 'Hmmph! Come to my office, Cavendish, and I'll give you a list of known dealers a mile long.'

'Do they deal in arms as well?' Cavendish put to him. 'And do they deal in child pornography, trafficking young children for the delectation of men in high places? Do they put this country's security at risk because they are involved in one of the vilest, vicious, demonic and lucrative operations?'

'What on earth do you mean?' Butler asked, his mouth twisted into a grimace.

Cavendish glanced at him and then back across the table to the prime minister.

'This is not a drug cartel that smuggles drugs into our country for the sake of making money,' he said sharply. 'This is an organization that trades under the protection of very powerful men who hold positions of authority in politics, the armed forces and terrorism.' He was holding their attention now. 'They bring drugs into our country, sell them on and use the money to buy arms which they ship out to Al-Qaeda and the Taliban. They use young girls as sweeteners so that these twisted men can use them for their own purposes.'

'Where are they buying the drugs from?' Faulkner asked. 'We've just about destroyed all the poppy fields in Afghanistan.'

Cavendish gave him a withering look. 'The drug harvest in Afghanistan is extremely healthy. The annual crop is worth about a hundred million pounds. A lot of that funds the weapons traffic.'

'I was under the impression, Sir Giles,' interrupted the prime minister, 'that we had all but secured those provinces where we operate and halted all drug production.'

Cavendish looked askance at him. 'Then your sources are unreliable, Prime Minister. Perhaps your information is deliberately false. This continuous rotation of drugs and guns is a fact and is kept going by men in high positions of authority.'

'Preposterous,' declared Butler. 'We would know about it immediately. Our men out in Afghanistan are without question the most dependable and reliable.'

Cavendish looked at Butler, but before replying he stole a quick glance at the prime minister. Directing his eyes back to the police commissioner, he said, 'Our soldiers in Afghanistan are underpaid, under-equipped and undermanned. They rely heavily on human intelligence in the field which comes from some Taliban commanders, when it suits them,' he added, 'and from local Afghani tribal chiefs. Our soldiers cannot be in several places at once, and they are often led to believe that the poppy field they destroyed a year ago is no longer producing when the fact is the farmer is still growing the poppies and the drug factories are making pure heroin.'

'What you are implying, Cavendish,' Faulkner said, 'is that there are corrupt men at the top of the chain. Do you have any proof of this?'

Cavendish shook his head. 'Unfortunately I cannot always deal in proof; it's something that our department sees very little of. Even with facts, we often have to use them in trade offs; tit for tat exchanges. Promises made by one party to another. Someone wants his name kept out of it so is willing to sell his soul. We can only stop this corrupt practice by getting at the heads of the chain and cutting them off. That is what we were trying to do at the American depot at Feltwell when the whole thing blew up in our faces. And I assure you, gentlemen, it was no one's fault but mine.'

'There's no need to fall on your sword, Sir Giles,' the prime minister told him abruptly.

'Why did this have to involve the Americans?' Butler asked Cavendish.

'Because the Americans are involved,' he replied simply. 'It's really they who are calling the shots.'

'What do you mean the Americans are calling the shots?'

'They have the scope and the size to hide an operation like this within the parameters of their own legitimate operations,' Cavendish told him.

'But you've no proof.' It was a simply stated fact, and the police commissioner seemed confident now that Cavendish's explanations were based largely on supposition and wishful thinking. 'And they could only run a clandestine operation with the knowledge and connivance of some very well-placed men.'

'Precisely.' It was all Cavendish said because the police commissioner had simply reiterated what he had been trying to tell them all along.

The commissioner realized what he had just implied and the expression on his face changed. It was as if he finally understood the solution to a problem that had been dogging him for some time, only in this case it wasn't a problem that he alone could solve.

'Sir Giles,' the prime minister said, breaking the slight impasse, 'I am seeing the American Ambassador later today along with Commodore Deveraux, the Military Attaché. I need something to tell them, but I also need something to ask them. If you cannot furnish me with something positive, it looks like they will be asking the questions and I will have to provide the answers.'

Cavendish shrugged his shoulders. 'In that case, Prime Minister, I can only ask you to tell them what you know.'

'Which is precisely nothing without facts,' the prime minister commented.

Cavendish nodded. 'Exactly, but you could labour the point about Chief Master Sergeant Danvor Grebo going missing after wounding one of our police officers and shooting dead one of his own American comrades.'

'I must say that's hardly a senior rank to be considered as a man in high authority,' Faulkner put in. 'I understood from what you have been saying, Sir Giles, that you were looking for men in high places.'

Cavendish turned to face Faulkner. 'Chief Grebo is a logistics man. He has attained the highest, non-commissioned rank in the American Air Force. It gives him an element of power and control. Four nights ago, Grebo shot and wounded one of my operatives. He is a dangerous man. He is also the cousin of Milan Janov; a man we believe is heavily involved in drugs and people trafficking. The more we look into the connections between individuals here, the worse it becomes.' He then spoke to the prime minister.

'I would ask you, Prime Minister, to be very circumspect during your meeting with the Ambassador and Commodore Deveraux.'

The police commissioner interrupted Cavendish. 'You're not suggesting the links with this Grebo go further up the chain of command, are you?'

'I hope I'm wrong,' Cavendish told him, 'and I have no proof, but I know I'm right: the Americans are in it up to their necks.'

Marcus was lying on his back with his hands behind his head looking up at the ceiling. He had been doing some thinking, and he wasn't convinced that he was cut out for intelligence work. He seemed to have a habit of attracting violence and being forced to dish it out, when all he really wanted was a quiet life. The events twelve hours earlier had taught him a salutary lesson: people like Danny Grebo and his associates were to be avoided at all costs. But then, he reasoned, the world is full of people like that, and they encroach on your life whether you invite them to or not. In his case, Marcus had to accept that he had been largely responsible for his own situation, and it was this that made him decide to split from Cavendish.

Marcus had reached that decision earlier, shortly after waking up in the holding cell in Thetford where they were keeping him. He had asked if he could make a phone call. The station officer had agreed, so Marcus phoned his father and asked for a lawyer to get down to the police station to get him out. He was sure there wouldn't be a problem; not that he understood the law, but he was fairly convinced the police couldn't hold him without charge. He was sure the lawyer would post bail or whatever they do; get a magistrate or judge to sign some release papers. And bugger Cavendish, he thought resolutely, he could play his own silly games.

He had had a wash and cleaned his teeth; toiletries provided by the station sergeant, and had a fairly decent breakfast. Lunch passed by as well, and so far no one had come to see him about the events of the night before. It was strange, but perhaps there was a conflict between departments, he decided, and neither one had won the argument. He was sure Cavendish would have him out of the nick in two seconds, and he was equally sure that a normal police investigation would have him remanded for some time. So all he could do was wait.

With nothing to do, Marcus began to think again of his decision to split from Cavendish. He also thought of Susan and her brother, David. Susan wanted nothing more than to see her brother free. When she had come to Marcus she only wondered if David was still alive. Now she knew because she had received a letter from him. That meant a line had been opened between David and Susan by whoever was keeping David prisoner.

Marcus also began to think about Grebo and the whole American connection. Just how deep, he wondered, were the American military involved? Afghanistan was not really Britain's bag; more the Yanks'. The kind of organization Grebo was running, if he was running it, had to have some powerful backers. How else could Grebo make use of a bonded warehouse right under the noses of the American military?

Marcus was reconsidering his options when he heard footsteps in the passageway. He swung his feet off the bed and sat up as a police sergeant, accompanied by a civilian, appeared at the door of his cell.

'Time to go, Blake,' the sergeant sang out, as he rattled the keys in the lock.

Marcus jumped to his feet and stepped through the open door. He presumed it was the lawyer with the sergeant, although he didn't recognize him.

'Hallo, Marcus, I'm Covington. Your father sent me to get you out of here.'

Marcus shook the lawyer's hand thinking as he did that there was something odd in the way the lawyer had said 'out of here'. It was more like 'outa here'. He put it to the back of his mind and followed the lawyer to the desk where he had his personal effects returned and his release papers were signed.

Marcus followed Covington out to the car-park towards a black Mercedes parked in a visitor's slot. Covington aimed the key fob at it and the hazard lights on the car flashed several times as the door locks were released.

Covington turned to Marcus and smiled, gesturing to the passenger door on the far side. Marcus did as he was bid and climbed into the soft leather upholstery. Covington settled himself into the driver's seat and gunned the motor into life.

Reversing out of the parking slot, Covington swung the wheel effortlessly. Marcus immediately felt a familiar sensation as adrenalin began pumping into his system.

'Where are we going?' Marcus asked him.

Covington turned and looked at him. 'We're going to meet your father,' he told him. He accelerated out of the car-park and into the main high street. As he did, Covington reached forward and pressed a button on the dash. Marcus heard the sound of the door locks closing.

They cleared Thetford within twenty minutes or so and were soon heading up the A134, passing through the amusingly named Two Mile Bottom. Marcus had no idea where they were going, but he knew he would have to come up with something if he wanted to see the rest of the day out.

Suddenly Covington slowed and turned into a side road. About a mile or so later he pulled into a lay-by and stopped.

He then turned to Marcus and was about to say something when Marcus hit him.

Marcus knew there would almost certainly be a little preamble; something like 'This is where you get off', or 'Get out of the car because I'm going to blow your brains out'. But whatever Marcus did, he had to make sure he did not give the man who called himself Covington an opportunity to kill him, because he knew that was the man's intention.

Marcus hit him again and again, pounding his fist into the side of Covington's head until the bogus lawyer sagged unconscious into the seat.

Marcus quickly removed his seat belt, reached forward and pressed the button to release the door locks and then looked out through the windows to see if there was anybody about.

A car drove by fairly quickly, rocking the Mercedes. Once that had gone, Marcus got out and went round to the driver's side. He released Covington's seat belt and pulled him out of the car. Then he checked the road again to make sure it was clear and lifted him on to his shoulder, back heeled the door shut, then carried him into the woods lining the side of the road.

Once clear of the road and out of sight, Marcus dropped Covington on to the ground and immediately searched through his pockets. He took his wallet and a Walther PPK handgun. He left him there and went back to the Merc and settled himself into it, switched on the ignition and started the motor. Then he glanced over at the trees where he had dumped Covington.

'Sorry about this, Mr Covington,' he shouted. 'But I gotta get outa here!'

He powered the Merc away. Ten minutes later Marcus pulled up beside a public phone box in the village of Munford and phoned his father.

Sir Henry Blake answered the phone with little else on his mind other than what he and his wife Emily would be doing later in the day. It was one of the pleasantries of retirement, where one could make plans at one's leisure. But there were times, naturally, where circumstances tended to blunt even the most quiescent moments. And this was to be one.

'Sir Henry Blake,' he said, as he pressed the phone to his ear.

'Hallo, Dad, Marcus here.'

Blake's eyes lit up as they often did when his son called. 'Marcus, my dear boy, you're free.'

'Yes, but there's a problem,' Marcus told his father. 'The man who came to get me out claimed to be Covington, your lawyer.'

Blake nodded. 'Yes, I sent him.'

'It wasn't your man. The guy who came here was an American, and he had no intention of letting me go free.'

'What do you mean he had no intention of letting you go free? That's the reason I sent him up there.'

'Look, Dad, I'm free, I'm OK, but I have to lie low for a while. I'll explain later. But I think you need to check up on something.'

'Marcus, you're not making sense,' Blake told him sternly. 'What are you gabbling about?'

'When did you speak to Covington?' Marcus asked him.

'Shortly after you rang, why?'

'Well, somehow, the Yanks intercepted Covington and sent one of their own men. And they could only have done that because they knew you had called him.'

'What are you suggesting, Marcus?' Blake had a feeling he wasn't going to like what he was about to hear.

'The Yanks must have a tap on your phone line; it's the only way they could have known about Covington. I suggest you get in touch with Cavendish and nobody else. Tell him I've called and what has happened.'

'I think this is preposterous,' Blake replied strongly.

'In that case, Dad, phone your lawyer. I'll be in touch.'

The line went dead and left Blake staring into space. He replaced the handset and flicked open a phone book which lay on the table beside the phone. He found the number of his lawyer and dialled it. It was picked up within seconds.

'Cope's legal services. How may I help you?'

'Judy, this is Sir Henry Blake. Can you put me in touch with John Covington?'

'I'm sorry, Sir Henry, we have been trying to get in touch with Mr Covington on another matter, but he's not answering his mobile. It's most unusual for him not to answer. Perhaps he's lost it, but we won't know until he phones in. Is there something Mr Cope can help you with, Sir Henry?'

Blake didn't answer for a few seconds; his mind was beginning to move into overdrive.

'Ah, no, no, thank you, Judy,' he said hurriedly. 'Just ask Mr Covington to ring me as soon as you can. Thank you.'

He put the phone down and his heart sank. Blake's gut feeling was that Covington would not be getting in touch with his office or anybody else for that matter.

Covington was almost certainly dead.

FOURTEEN

DANNY GREBO HAD dumped the BMW in north London and walked through the streets until he came to an all night taxi rank. Grebo's knowledge of the city was scant so he simply asked the taxi driver to drop him off at Oxford Street. Once there, he made his way round to Grosvenor Square in sight of the American Embassy and located a public phone booth.

The call he had to make could mean a way out of the jam he had got himself into. Any other option simply didn't exist. Grebo knew he would be indicted for murder and almost certainly extradited to America because he had killed a serving American military policeman. It meant the electric chair and that just didn't bear thinking about. He was hoping that the man he was about to ring could get him into the American Embassy in the first instance. This would give him a relatively safe haven, providing the American authorities didn't know he was there, until it could be decided which would be the best way to get him out of the country.

The ringing phone was answered fairly quickly.

'John Deveraux.'

'This is Grebo. Can you talk?'

There was no reply for a couple of seconds. Then, 'I think so; Marjorie is in the shower. What do you want?'

'You know about last night?'

'I didn't get to bed until four o'clock this morning, thanks to you. Of course I know about last night.' Deveraux sounded terse.

'I need a way out, Commodore. You're the only one who can help me.'

'And what makes you think I can help you?'

'The Chapter can,' Grebo answered desperately. 'Get them to me; they can get me out.'

'They may not want to, Danny. After all, you've messed up big style.'

'They're my only chance, Commodore. You've got to help me.'

'You should have thought of that before you murdered one of our own men.'

'I didn't plan it that way, I swear.'

'Planned or not, Grebo, you killed one of our serving airmen. I think The Chapter will probably want to wash its hands of you from now on.'

'Don't let them do that, sir. I need help and I need it bad. I've made a lot of money for those guys, including you. They owe me.'

'Nobody owes you anything, Grebo. You're the one who has come unstuck; nobody else. And why should they owe you?'

Grebo could feel the sweat gathering round his neck. It was like a noose. 'If I get picked up, the whole organization could go to the wall. I know the names, places, everything. How long do you think it would take them to get all of that out of me? I know about rendition, Commodore, and it ain't nice.'

He listened for an answer and could hear the sound of Deveraux's breathing coming down the phone line. Eventually the commodore spoke.

'Very well, Grebo, I'll see what I can do. Call my office at ten o'clock. I will give you an address in London. That's all I can offer at the moment.'

'Thank you, sir, thank you.' Grebo felt his whole body begin to shake in relief. 'Ten o'clock.'

He put the phone down and stepped out of the phone booth. It was still early and he wondered what he could do to fill in the next few hours. Ordinarily he would have drawn some money out of an ATM machine and bought himself a breakfast and maybe a wash and brush up. Trouble was, though, he wasn't sure it was a good idea to use his ATM card in case the police were looking out for any transactions he might make so that they could pinpoint his location. He still had a few pounds in his wallet so he decided instead to wander around the department stores in Oxford Street, grab a coffee and a donut (he had enough money for that), and make the call at ten o'clock.

When Grebo made the call, he was given an address in Ealing

Broadway. He knew he could get there by tube and using the ATM machine for the fare money wasn't too big a risk because the police would never know where he was going if indeed they did pick up the transaction.

Grebo arrived at the address he was given about ninety minutes later. The road was a typical pre-war residential area. Fairly run down now, but probably a very up-market neighbourhood in its heyday. Grebo didn't bother to knock at the front door; he simply turned the knob and pushed the door open.

He stepped inside and closed the door behind him. He waited for a moment and then called out. A voice answered.

'Hi, Danny, come through to the kitchen.'

Grebo walked down the passageway towards the back of the house. He reached the door that he believed would open on to the kitchen. It was partly closed. Gingerly he pushed the door and it swung open. He couldn't believe what he was seeing at first, but the entire kitchen was covered in plastic sheeting. For a brief second he thought someone was in the process of decorating.

Then he felt a hand push him in the back. The barrel of the gun came up on to the back of his head and Grebo was dead before he hit the deck.

James Faulkner and Randolph Hudson were enjoying a beer together at a riverside pub overlooking the River Thames. It wasn't unusual for the two men in their capacity as security chiefs to share some interdepartmental gossip and swap detail on any joint investigation their relative departments might be undertaking. But this time their conversation had little to do with national security, British or American; it was to do with the disappearance of Marcus Blake and the demise of Danny Grebo.

'Grebo was a liability anyway,' Faulkner was saying, 'such a pity really because he was important to The Chapter.'

'We had no choice, James,' Hudson said. 'Once he'd told Deveraux that he would probably crack and spill the beans ...' He shrugged with a hopeless gesture.

'At least he was honest,' Faulkner observed. 'Too honest for his own good.' He lifted his beer and took a mouthful. A river cruise boat went by and Faulkner looked down at the tourists with their cameras and colourful outfits. 'Poor buggers don't know the half of it,' he said, putting his glass down. 'So, how are you going to fill the gap left by Grebo?' he asked the CIA chief.

Hudson reflected on that for a while. 'It will be difficult, but not impossible. We have to be prepared for people dropping out, so I'm sure we'll cope.'

'It shows how quickly a plan can fall to pieces,' Faulkner lamented. 'I haven't been able to figure out where this man Blake fits in, but I think he was largely responsible why things fell apart so rapidly.'

'Who is he anyway?' Hudson asked the SOCA chief. 'We sent a specialist to deal with him, but he gave our man the slip.'

Faulkner arched his eyebrows. 'Hmm, I've spoken to Cavendish; asked him if Blake was working for him, or doing a bit of freelancing.'

Hudson laughed. 'Some freelancer; he seems quite a guy.'

Faulkner conceded. 'Yes, but we've underestimated him. If he shows up again we'll have to make sure we finish the job this time.'

'Well, we know he phoned his father. He was clever enough to realize there was a tap on the old man's line.'

Faulkner nodded. 'It's off now; too bloody risky. His old man has some clout in the City; could cause us some problems.' He put his hand up and smiled. Hudson had looked like he was about to make a suggestion. 'No, I don't want it taken care of,' Faulkner told him. 'Sir Henry Blake is untouchable, OK?'

Hudson laughed a little too and lifted his beer, and to all the world they were just a couple of men enjoying a quiet lunchtime drink, not two of the most dangerous men in Britain.

The Metropolitan Police Commissioner, Andrew Butler, did not normally bother too much with crimes committed within the London area that would normally be dealt with by his very able senior officers. From his lofty position, his daily round was often briefings with politicians, leading journalists, policy groups and often chief constables from other divisions. But at the early morning brief with his own senior officers, one name had been mentioned that had drawn his attention away from more administrative matters and focused it on the recent events that had drawn him into the world of Sir Giles Cavendish. And that name was Blake.

After the meeting, he asked his secretary to contact Cavendish, wherever he may be and ask him to phone. It was late that afternoon when Cavendish rang. The commissioner's secretary put the call through to Butler.

'Good afternoon, Commissioner, Sir Giles Cavendish here.'

'Hallo, Sir Giles, good of you to call. Something has come up that will probably interest you. It's not part of your remit, I would think, but I am sure you will want to be kept informed.'

'Thank you, Andrew.'

'A body has turned up in a public toilet in one of the main underground stations. It has been identified as a lawyer by the name of Covington. He happens to be Sir Henry Blake's lawyer. The time of death has been put at about ten-thirty yesterday morning. Yesterday afternoon a lawyer by the name of Covington presented release papers at Thetford Police Station and had Marcus Blake released, four hours after the real Covington was murdered. I'll keep you informed of any developments in the case, Sir Giles, but my division superintendent will obviously want to keep this in house. If there is any proven link to your investigation, he will almost certainly prefer to hand it on to SOCA. I'm sure Faulkner will want to be kept informed too.'

In his office, Cavendish mouthed an obscenity. Then he composed himself and put a request to the police chief.

'Commissioner, would you try to keep this out of the hands of SOCA? For the time being at least?'

'Would you like to tell me why, Sir Giles?'

'I'm afraid I can't; not yet anyway. And if I did, it would be in private; not over the phone. I hope you'll understand.'

'I will do my best,' Butler promised, 'but if the superintendent feels he wants to pass this on, I will try to hold it up for forty-eight hours.'

'Thank you, Andrew. I'm sure we'll talk again.' He put the phone down.

Cavendish was reluctant to have SOCA involved because of something Faulkner had said during the meeting with the prime minister. On its own it wasn't incriminating, but it managed to ring an alarm bell in Cavendish's mind, and that was all that was needed in his murky world of secret intelligence.

Marcus left the Mercedes at the truck stop where he had met up with the two policemen, Iverson and Whelan. He then drove the Mondeo that Cavendish had provided and motored back to London. He didn't go back to his own flat, but found a three-star hotel and booked in there for the night. The following morning he put together a plan that he

hoped might get him closer to the organization that sent the bogus
Covington to release him from the jail in Thetford.

Marcus had the hit-man's wallet and the car keys to the Mercedes.
With the car's documents and the driving licence, he now knew where
he lived, and decided to go to the man's address.

Marcus knew the score: not to approach the house until he was
convinced it was empty and he wouldn't be noticed. To that end he
needed to spend some time watching the premises without being seen;
the watcher being watched.

The house was in Elgin Avenue at Maida Vale. Marcus found somewhere to park his car and walked to the Elgin public house. The pub was
situated on the corner of the street. There were tables and chairs outside
and from there Marcus was able to sit and watch with a soft drink in his
hand. He knew he couldn't sit there all day, but he had to spend as much
time as possible until he could be certain it was safe to enter the house.
He had bought a daily paper so was able to adopt the classic stance of
pretending to read while keeping an eye on the place.

His patience was rewarded when he saw someone leave from the
front door. It was a woman whom Marcus assumed to be the man's wife
or partner. When she had gone, Marcus got up from the table and
walked down to the front entrance. He walked up the short garden path
and rang the doorbell. There was no reply, so Marcus tried again. When
it was obvious there was nobody in, Marcus walked away and went
back to the pub.

Marcus gambled that there would be nobody watching the house, so
he retraced his footsteps and went back, but this time he walked up to
the front door and opened it with the key that was on the Mercedes key
ring.

He pushed the door open and stepped over the threshold, pulling the
door closed behind him. He then waited for at least two minutes, not
moving, but listening carefully for any sound that might suggest there
was still somebody inside.

There was a staircase in front of him, which he assumed led up to the
bedrooms. He went up as quickly and as quietly as he could and opened
the doors that all faced on to the landing running alongside the upper
stairwell.

There was nobody there so he went back downstairs and into the
front room. It was furnished tastefully and expensively, which didn't

surprise Marcus considering the profession of the man who, he believed lived there. He saw a bureau against a far wall. He went over to it and began looking through it, lifting out letters, documents and the odd receipt and bill.

He then went through to the dining room and began searching through the Welsh dresser that was in there. Once again the drawers were haphazardly filled with impedimenta relating to bills, addresses, TV licence and the like. But there was nothing he could see that could link the man to the organization he knew Cavendish was investigating.

Marcus began to realize it was a reflection of the man's professionalism that he would leave nothing incriminating that could link him to any organization involved in anything illegal. It was disappointing to say the least that he could find nothing that he could take to Cavendish.

He closed the drawers and cast around once more before trying the kitchen and the bedrooms. But his search was fruitless there too; nothing. He came down the stairs and went back into the front room for one more look in the bureau. And that was when he came across something he least expected to; something that shook Marcus to the core.

It was a photograph jumbled up with a few others that Marcus had ignored. It was of two men. They were standing in front of what looked like an Indian temple or something of that nature; Marcus couldn't be sure. But what he could be sure of was that one of the men in the photograph was the bogus Covington who had planned to kill him. The second man in the picture was a Pakistani; of that Marcus had no doubt.

It was Maggot.

Susan had settled herself down in front of the television to watch her favourite soap when the doorbell rang. She moaned to herself and went to the front door. When she opened it she saw Marcus standing there.

'Marcus! What on earth are you doing here?'

Marcus didn't wait for an invitation but brushed past her and waited for her to close the door, which she did.

'I'm sorry about this, Susan,' he told her. 'Are you alone?'

'And what if I'm not?' she snapped at him. 'Haven't you heard of the telephone?'

He thought about the phone tap on his father's line but said nothing about that. He thought that might scare her more than she could bear.

'Please forgive me, Susan, but I have to talk to you.'

Susan pushed past him and went through to the part of the house that she rented as a flat. She stood by the door.

'Well, are you coming or not?'

Marcus went inside and sat down on one of her armchairs. Susan came in, set the DVD to record and switched the television off.

'I'm sorry if I'm interrupting something,' he said.

Susan shrugged and tossed the remote control on to the sofa. 'It's nothing,' she told him. 'Now, what is it you want?'

'Why are you angry with me, Susan?'

The question was unexpected. Susan didn't know what to say for a moment so she settled herself down in an armchair facing Marcus and composed herself.

'I'm not angry with you, Marcus,' she began, 'but things happen when you turn up. My life hasn't been the same since we met. Just when I think I might make some sense out of everything, you somehow manage to … oh, I don't know, break the moment.'

He agreed and was sure Cavendish would agree as well. 'Fair enough, Susan, but hear me out this time and I'll walk out of your life altogether. Promise.'

She sighed. 'What do you want?'

'Do you remember the first letter, or writing that you received from your brother?' he asked her.

'The one that Cavendish brought to me?'

He nodded. 'Yes. Do you have it?' When she said she did, Marcus asked her if she would fetch it so he could read it.

She brought the pages to him and he read through them. When he had finished he lowered them on to his lap and closed his eyes.

'Maggot,' he whispered softly. 'I can't believe it.'

Susan peered at him. 'What's the matter?'

He looked at her and passed the pages back.

'Maggot would go back to Pakistan from time to time,' he said softly. 'Always on family business, so he said. He would never explain; just say, "something like that".'

'Marcus, what are you saying?' she pressed.

He had been looking at Susan but not seeing her. It was as though he was staring straight through her. He shook his head and drew himself back to the present moment.

'A man tried to kill me yesterday; a professional.' Marcus was talking in a matter-of-fact way, as though it was an everyday occurrence. 'He didn't though, obviously. I found out where he lived and went to his house.' He saw Susan's mouth open as she began to say something. He put his hand up. 'There was no one there. I looked around, found nothing incriminating. Then I came across a photograph. It was the hitman, the guy who tried to kill me, and a Pakistani guy. The picture was taken somewhere in India or Pakistan. They were standing together, smiling. Lovely picture really. Maggot would have been proud of it.'

'Maggot?'

Marcus nodded. 'Yes, he was the other man in the photograph. Did you know, Susan, that Maggot has the little finger of his left hand missing?'

'Yes,' she answered, looking surprised. 'I noticed it the other day.'

'I remembered reading that your brother was shot by a man with his little finger missing. It's not conclusive, Susan, but when you see a photograph of him with a man who has just tried to kill you, and when you read what happened to your brother, and when you think of how often Maggot goes away …' He leaned back in the chair. 'Maggot's a hitman; that's what he does.'

'He's also a terrorist,' Susan said, her voice cracking a little.

Marcus's eyes widened. 'What?'

'He's a terrorist, Marcus; and the police know.'

She then told him about her trip to the local police station and what Detective Chief Inspector Rendell had told her.

'It was Maggot who delivered my brother's second letter. The police took pictures of him doing it.'

Marcus sagged visibly in the chair. His deductions about Maggot had saddened him immensely, and now he wasn't sure what he could do about it.

Susan could see that the news of Maggot had affected him. She knew they were both very good friends. Maggot had spoken very warmly of Marcus, too.

'Would you like a drink?' she asked suddenly.

Marcus smiled weakly. 'I don't fancy a drink, Susan, but I will have a coffee, thank you.'

Susan spent ten minutes making coffee and putting some quick snacks on a plate. She brought them through to him and watched as he worked his way through the lot. When he had finished, Susan took his plate from him and set it down on the coffee table beside her.

'What are you going to do?' she asked.

He shrugged. 'To be honest, I'm out of my depth. This is a job for the professionals. I was better off where I was before: running my own agency in the way I know best.'

'Marcus, your agency doesn't exist anymore.'

'What do you mean?'

She told him how she had turned up at his office and found it empty.

Marcus was stunned. Then he realized why Cavendish had to have the place cleaned out. He told Susan what had happened.

A look of concern clouded her face.

'You really ought to get out of the country for a while, Marcus. Lie low, as they say.'

He laughed. 'They'll have my picture at every departure point in Britain. I wouldn't even get a foot on a boat or an aeroplane.' He stood up. 'But I can do as I promised and get out of your life, Susan.' He put his empty cup down.

She stood up and put her hand on his arm. 'I don't want you to get out of my life. Even if it's only as a friend, I want you in it.' She reached up and kissed him on the forehead. 'But I want you in it in one piece. So, please, try and sort things out. If you stay in this, you never know, we might learn the truth about David.'

'Did you go to the Press about him?'

She nodded. 'They're not interested; hostages aren't newsworthy anymore: too many of them.'

Marcus was about to say something when the doorbell rang. He looked round and Susan told him to wait there. She went through to her front door and opened it. Marcus heard her greet someone disconsolately and then he heard footsteps. The door opened and Cavendish walked in.

'Good evening, Marcus,' he said cheerfully. 'My boy, you have given us a difficult time.'

Marcus looked over Cavendish's shoulder as Susan walked into the room.

'Did you phone him when you were outside making coffee?' he asked sharply.

Susan shook her head. 'No, Marcus, I didn't. He's been watching this house for some time now. You just walked into his trap, that's all.'

FIFTEEN

DAVID ELLIS LOOKED out through the windows of the Toyota as Abdul drove through a flat plain of rock and sand. They were in a natural basin that nestled in the foothills of Kondoz in northern Afghanistan. Outside, the temperature was in the high forties, while inside the Toyota they rode in air-conditioned comfort.

They had been driving for about five hours, with Abdul and his minders taking turns at the wheel. Abdul had said very little to David, but with each day David was becoming more and more familiar with the Persian language that Abdul and his men used. It was basically the *lingua franca* of Afghanistan, although in some of the more remote regions of the country, the farmers used local dialects. So with David's increasing knowledge of the tongue, he was able to understand a great deal of what was being said. But whenever he spoke to Abdul, he made sure he always spoke in English.

Abdul had been following a river for several miles that flowed through the basin from the upper reaches of the hills, and it was soon evident to David where they were going when he saw the drying pans laid out in rows in the sun. These were pans of raw opium. Each pan held about twenty-five to thirty kilos. David knew they wouldn't be far from a poppy farm now and the preliminary processing plant.

A few houses came into view as the ground gave way to a scattering of trees that screened the poppy fields. Abdul pulled up beside one of the houses and killed the engine. He sounded the horn and got out of the car followed by David and the two minders. Abdul said nothing to either of them but waited until someone came out of the house. It was the poppy farmer.

Immediately the two men began the ritual of greeting each other before venturing into the house where David knew they would be obliged to eat according to the traditional hospitality of the Afghani people.

After the meal, Abdul got up from the table and beckoned David to follow.

'We are going out to the sheds,' he told him. 'It will be good for you to see the work these men do to make your people rich.'

David got up and followed him out with the farmer. The two minders stayed behind.

They walked some considerable distance from the house before coming to the first of several sheds. David could smell something in the air. It reminded him of the smells of his schooldays in chemistry lessons.

Inside the first shed David saw several containers marked 'ammonium chloride' and 'sodium carbonate'. He knew from titbits of information he had picked up that these were essential chemicals used in the initial process of converting opium sap into pure heroin.

There were several pots of boiling liquid adding to the overpowering acidic aroma in the shed. On top of the boiling liquid he could see all manner of debris and scum collecting there.

Elsewhere men were straining the cooled liquid from other pots through cheesecloth filters, leaving a sticky residue behind. Abdul told David that the residue would be heated and condensed down to leave a paste, and it was this that David saw drying in pans out in the sun. Abdul explained much of the process to David as they walked through the sheds.

'The paste will be shipped out across the border from Kondoz into Turkmenistan for processing into pure heroin. We have other processing sites spread all along the border.'

'Why Turkmenistan?' David asked him.

Abdul almost snarled when he answered. 'That is Janov's part of the operation. It is less trouble shipping it over the border into Turkmenistan than trying to get it through into Pakistan. There are too many British soldiers in Helmand Province.'

'What about the Americans?'

Abdul allowed himself a wry smile. 'We have no problems in Nuristan where the Americans are.' He slapped his thigh a couple of times. 'They are in our pockets as you say in England.'

'What about NATO troops?'

Abdul laughed out loud. 'They are babies; they will not fight, so we have no problem with them.'

They walked out of the shed and into the hot sun. In between talking to David, Abdul had been having a business-like discussion with the farmer. David knew it wasn't going too well, but he couldn't figure out why. The farmer stopped on the track and faced them. He bowed his head slightly and said farewell. They shook hands and the farmer went back into the sheds.

'Abdul,' David said, putting his hand on Abdul's arm; something that would have encouraged a severe beating some months ago. 'Why are you dragging me round like this?'

He considered his reply for a while. Then he put his hands together in an attitude of prayer and began to walk along the track. David fell into step beside him.

'I want you to learn to trust me, that is why I am keeping you with me,' he began. 'I am having many problems now with my suppliers, my farmers. They are holding out on fixing a price.'

'What has that got to do with me?'

'You will see. You remember the attack on the compound?' He waited for David to say he did. 'It was Janov's doing. One of my farmers who is loyal to me has told me that Janov wants to cut me out.'

'But you are doing business with Janov,' David reminded him. 'You met him a few days ago.'

Abdul looked hard at David. 'Janov is an ambitious man, an evil man.' Abdul seemed to conveniently forget the kind of business he himself was in, the same as Janov. 'But he is working for his cousin, Danvor. And his cousin works for the American CIA; one day they will run this country. Soon, if I am not careful, the Americans will come and I will be taken out. That is why I keep moving and why I keep you with me, because I want to exchange you for something.'

David stopped. 'Exchange me for what?'

'Your freedom and my freedom.'

There was a moment's silence.

'I don't understand,' David admitted.

Abdul put his hand on David's shoulder. 'Your freedom means you can go home and live your life without hindrance, am I right?' David nodded. Abdul continued, 'But for me I want something else. I want your country to give me political asylum so I can live my life free from the threat I face from the Americans.'

David was stunned to hear him say that he wanted to get out of the lucrative and criminal business he was in, and that he expected the British to help him achieve that. He feared Abdul was in for a big disappointment.

'Well, you won't get that in exchange for me, I can assure you.'

Abdul smiled. 'No, but I will if I offer to give them the names of those who are involved here in Afghanistan and in Britain.'

They found Grebo's body. It had been dumped in a fairly quiet area beside the river. A man walking his dog came across it. The police could not identify the corpse easily because the face wasn't there. The bullet into the back of the head had taken Grebo's face clean off. All the police could do was to cordon off the area and wait for the forensic boys to get to work.

There were no identifying documents on him so they had to rely on dental records, but there was no way of locating a dentist with those records. It was a chicken and egg situation: they had the teeth, but no records, and whoever had the records would not know about the teeth. But eventually it was suggested that they check on all Americans living in the area because the dead man was wearing clothing that had probably been purchased in America. Then someone thought of the American Forces stationed in Britain, which widened the search.

This link brought them to the United States Air Force base at Lakenheath and it was there they found the dental records they were looking for, and subsequently identified one Danvor Grebo, Chief Master Sergeant in the USAF, as the dead man.

It was fairly obvious to the investigating officer that Grebo's murder had the hallmarks of a gang-style killing, and there were only two possibilities that rang alarm bells: one was drugs, the other was terrorism; the possible slaying of a member of the American Forces as a terrorist-style revenge attack.

The connections were then passed to various departments within the Metropolitan Police divisions which included the narcotics and terrorist departments of SOCA, Special Branch and eventually the desk of James Faulkner.

It also crossed the desk of Andrew Butler, the Metropolitan Police

Commissioner who phoned Sir Giles Cavendish as a courtesy. And so the loop was completed, and all the interested parties made their own choices on how they were going to deal with this particular crime.

James Faulkner made his choice; he phoned Randy Hudson, the CIA Station chief and asked for an urgent meeting. The meeting took place at the same riverside pub as before, but this time they were being observed and filmed by a member of Sir Giles Cavendish's department. Cavendish was taking no chances with Faulkner since their meeting with the prime minister. It was because of something the SOCA chief had said after Cavendish had told them about the drug smugglers bringing in drugs and young girls, then smuggling arms out. Faulkner had declared that he believed all the poppy fields in Afghanistan had been destroyed.

It was a simple enough assumption to make, that the drugs were coming in from Afghanistan, but Cavendish hadn't mentioned that country; the drugs could have been coming in from the Far East. It was a small error, but one that immediately raised the bar, and Cavendish decided to keep a discreet surveillance on the SOCA chief; hence the camera filming his meeting with Hudson from across the river.

'I've got very little time,' Hudson warned Faulkner. He looked at his watch and sat down opposite him. 'I don't know if I can give you anything new; the boys at Lakenheath are in a flat spin over this. Your English newspaper guys are already calling it "Gunfight at the OK Corral".'

Faulkner raised his eyebrows a notch. 'Our headline writers have vivid imaginations.'

'But they do at least stir things up and get the public interested. This has taken them away from their soap operas.'

'Well, hopefully, your country folk will give our Press something to feed on. But I want to know if you have any contingency plan?'

'Milan Janov is flying in tomorrow,' Hudson told Faulkner. 'I contacted him through the usual channels to tell him of his cousin's disappearance. He doesn't know yet what's happened.'

'I'm more concerned about how we are going to replace Grebo,' Faulkner said levelly. 'At the moment we don't have anybody in place.'

Hudson shook his head. 'Don't worry; I'll fill that gap. And I'll talk to Janov.'

'What can he do?'

Hudson shrugged. 'Nothing really; I think he wants to ride in and flex his muscles.'

'I won't be able to do anything if Immigration stops him at Heathrow,' Faulkner told him. 'Probably better if they do stop him and send him home.'

Hudson laughed lightly. 'Well, we'll let him have his moment if he does get in. But I suspect there's another reason for his visit.' He looked at his watch. 'Look, James, I really have to go. I'll catch up with you later.'

Faulkner drained his glass and stood up. 'OK, Randy let me know if anything develops.'

Hudson stood up and shook Faulkner's hand. 'Deveraux has already had to close the operation down,' he said, 'For now anyway. It might mean I'll have to make a trip back to the States for a while, but I'll let you know.'

'Thanks, Randy, keep in touch.'

And with that the two men went their separate ways.

Cavendish had kept Marcus under virtual house arrest for a couple of days. He had taken him from Susan's house and made sure there was no way he could disappear again. During that time he did his best to debrief Marcus and find out as much as he could about the events that had happened while Marcus had been operating unofficially.

Marcus had told Cavendish as much as he could, even to the extent that he believed the police would find the gun that killed Covington in the Mercedes he had dumped at the truck stop.

He also told Cavendish about the killer's house and, most painfully of all, the fact that he now believed Maggot was a hitman for the organization that was smuggling drugs into Britain.

Cavendish told Marcus that there was a growing conviction that the CIA was running the organization and smuggling arms out to Afghanistan to keep the insurgent warlords happy and to maintain a constant supply of heroin into the West. He told Marcus that the heroin trade world-wide was worth in the region of $120 billion a year, and that a great deal of money was going into the pockets of people in very senior positions of authority.

'And remember this, Marcus,' Cavendish added, at the end of one of his short lectures. 'They have killed a cabinet minister, a high-flying lawyer and one of their own key men in order to maintain a very lucrative business. And they would have killed me if you hadn't intervened.'

'And they have tried to kill me,' Marcus mentioned.

Cavendish almost smiled. 'Yes, you annoy them, and they spoil your day anyway, so both of you had better watch out.'

For the moment, Marcus failed to see the rejoinder. He was thinking instead of why he was this far in.

'Is there going to be any end to this, Sir Giles?' he asked.

Cavendish nodded firmly. 'Mark my words, Marcus; it will end. One way or the other,' he added ominously.

Milan Janov flew into London and waltzed through Immigration at Heathrow with his false passport. He was met by an inconsequential-looking youth and immediately taken by car to an address in north London. He was dropped off at the house with his overnight bag and left standing at the front door as the car disappeared into the late evening.

Janov waited no more than a few seconds before the door was opened and he was taken into a room at the rear of the house. Waiting there for him was Randy Hudson, CIA Station Chief in Britain.

Janov was not used to travelling without minders, but his instructions had been explicit, and only by travelling under an assumed name and with a false passport could he be sure of getting into Britain without the security people showing an interest in him and sending him packing.

A meal had been prepared for him, which he ate while discussing events with Hudson.

'Have you found the people who murdered my cousin?' Janov asked through a mouthful of food.

'We've no idea who killed your cousin,' Hudson lied, shaking his head. 'But we will eventually, I'm sure.'

'What happened to the arms shipment?' Janov asked, shovelling in another mouthful. 'My man has told me that it did not arrive at King's Lynn docks as expected. If I do not get the goods, I cannot do business.'

Hudson explained the predicament that faced the organization. 'It was not of our choosing. And I have to say that your cousin acted like a damn fool.'

Janov stopped eating immediately and looked across the table with venom in his eyes. Then he shrugged and carried on eating.

'He was a damn fool to get himself killed,' he spluttered, through a mouthful of food. 'But it could happen to any one of us; it is a dangerous business. Now, what about the arms shipment?'

'There will be no shipment,' Hudson told him. 'The United States Air Force has placed the warehouse off limits until their investigation is complete.'

'Are the goods still there?' Janov asked him.

'Yes, but they had been sealed by the Customs and Excise at the docks, and for that reason the Air Force investigators have no reason to want to see into them. Yet,' he added.

'That is good.' Janov shoved his plate aside. 'So, what is the reason given for the shooting at the warehouse?'

'No reason is being given,' Hudson told him. 'But the real reason is that a security agent had been following your cousin, and this caused him a problem.'

'Danny?'

Hudson nodded. 'Yes.'

Janov gave this some thought for a while. Then he got up from the table and walked over to a worktop and picked up a bottle of *slivovic*, a plum brandy that Hudson knew Janov was partial to. He poured a generous measure into a glass and drank it down. Then he poured another and came back to the table.

'I want another team put in to take care of Abdul,' he told Hudson.

The CIA man was surprised by Janov's sudden request. 'Why couldn't you take care of him yourself?' he asked reasonably.

Janov swirled a mouthful of *slivovic* around his gums before swallowing the brandy. 'It has to look like an American or British action,' he told Hudson. 'It is the only way I can persuade the farmers that I am not a threat to them. If I kill Khaliq, they will know and this will scare them off; it will drive them into the arms of the Taliban.' He finished his brandy. 'And I'm sure the organization would not want that.'

'I will need to talk to someone,' Hudson warned him. 'It isn't something I can do at the drop of a hat. And it costs.'

Janov dipped his head sharply. 'I will pay.'

Hudson looked impressed; it meant that Janov saw the financing of a hit team to take out Abdul Khaliq was a good investment.

'The Chapter will still have to authorize it,' Hudson told him.

'They are good businessmen,' Janov replied. 'They understand profit and loss, and who is making too much profit. They will authorize it.'

'In that case,' Hudson said, getting to his feet, 'I will make a few phone calls and see you back here tomorrow. If you want anything, one of my men will be here until you leave. But remember; the operation has been closed down until further notice. Goodnight, Janov.'

After Hudson had left the house, Janov had a shower and changed his clothes. He then asked Hudson's man to order a taxi. When it arrived he asked the driver to take him to a club in West London.

The club was a popular meeting place for Slovaks and other Eastern Europeans. There were other clubs scattered in the area and the air was heavy with the tortured vowel sounds of a mixture of mid-European languages. It was one of Janov's favourite places whenever he visited London. As it was here at this particular club where some of the girls that the organization provided could be found. Janov's particular passion was for the young Pakistani girls provided unwittingly by the mission in Jalalabad.

But before entering the club, Janov found a phone box and made a call. Then he walked back to the club entrance and introduced himself to one of the security guards who took him inside and handed him over to another member of the staff.

The call Janov had made was to a member of the organization who he knew would call the club and ask them to let Janov in.

Janov stepped inside and looked around at the décor that seemed to swamp the interior. It was a mix of red velvet, draped curtains, cord-edged sofas and chairs, heavy dark tables each with a small lampshade in the centre. The dance floor was carpet free and covered in parquet wood. Screens hid the toilet doors and one other door that led to the rooms upstairs.

He was taken to a small unoccupied corner table, which he guessed had been cleared for him and asked what he would like to drink. He ordered a Pilsner Urquell; the most widely exported Czech beer and sat back to enjoy the music, the dancing and to think of what he might do later with one of the girls in the upper rooms.

There was an unmistakable hint of cannabis smoke in the air, which helped to relax Janov. He finished his pilsner and ordered another, checked his watch and wondered how long he would have to wait until the man he had phoned showed up. Although the CIA chief told Janov he would need to get authorization from The Chapter to send a small team into Afghanistan to take out Abdul, Janov knew that this man would almost certainly lead it.

The double doors on the opposite side of the club opened and the man Janov had phoned came in. He spoke to a security guard who pointed across the floor to Janov. The man nodded his head and walked over to his table. Janov stood up and shook his hand.

'Hallo, Janov.'

Janov smiled warmly. 'Greetings, Rafiq, my friend, it is so good to see you.'

It was Maggot.

Cavendish sat in the darkened room watching the screen in front of him. He was looking at a film recording of the CIA chief, Hudson meeting with the SOCA chief, Faulkner. They were sitting in the beer garden of the riverside pub where they had met the day before. The camera used to film them had been positioned on the other side of the river, using a high-powered telescopic lens.

Despite the quality of the camera and the reasonable conditions in which the two men had been filmed, the pictures were slightly grainy, and for the man sitting with Cavendish, a little tricky to follow. He was a lip-reader, and Cavendish had called him in to interpret what the two men had been talking about.

They had watched the footage once already and were now about to go through it again. One of the problems the lip-reader had besides the grainy images was the fact that Faulkner would keep lifting his hand across his mouth and so giving the lip-reader nothing to read.

'Give you anything new,' the lip-reader began. His words were being recorded as he read what he could understand. 'Gunfight at the OK ... your country ... press ... any contingency plan ... Milan Janov ... tomorrow.' There was a brief silence. 'We are going to replace Grebo ... fill that gap.' Silence again. 'I won't be ... Immigration stops ... send him home.' Another pause. 'Have to go ... Deveraux to close ... trip back to the States.' He stopped and sat up.

'I'm afraid that's it, Sir Giles,' the lip-reader told Cavendish. 'Very difficult to follow the patterns: too grainy and too much hand movement.'

Cavendish got up and switched on the lights. 'That's fine. I'll send a copy of what you've managed so far and then you can look at the tape a few more times; see if you can fill in any gaps.'

The lip-reader stopped the DVD player. 'I'll be off then, Sir Giles. Hope there's enough for you to go on.'

Cavendish nodded. 'Couple of things,' he answered non-committally. 'And thanks again.'

Cavendish sat alone in his office after the lip-reader had left wondering what his next move was going to be. He had little scope to fill the investigation with countless agents working to ferret out information that was more or less well known to him but of which he had no proof, because of limited funding; a burden all government departments had to live with, and the fact that all avenues out of his office seemed to come up against people in authority who were in the pay of the organization known as The Chapter.

Cavendish had penetrated The Chapter with an agent working undercover, right in the heart of the organization's clearing centre in Jalalabad, in the mission, but the agent's identity had been discovered by the organization.

His second agent, David Ellis, who had gathered valuable intelligence, was now in captivity, a hostage, and it was this fact that was beginning to puzzle Cavendish. Ellis had been shot and almost killed, but had been snatched from the hospital only to resurface almost a year later. Contact had been made with Ellis's sister from an unknown source. At first, Cavendish could not set too much store in that first packet of grubby pages that had turned up. But the second, the letter which was now in Susan Ellis's possession was the more puzzling; why had it been sent, and by whom?

With today's internet technology, he knew it wouldn't be beyond the wit of the kidnappers to put a video on the web and read out their demands with David Ellis sitting forlornly in the foreground. But that wasn't the case, which led Cavendish to believe that whoever was holding Ellis hostage either wouldn't or couldn't resort to that tactic. Why?

Could it be, he wondered, that the kidnapper was afraid of revealing his or her identity? The kidnapper had nothing to fear from the British authorities; rather the opposite: the British would gladly take Ellis off the kidnapper's hands for nothing. So the kidnapper must have something to fear from his own side.

A picture was beginning to emerge in Cavendish's mind. The Chapter had proved how ruthless they were when it came to dispatching men who posed a threat to them. People like James Purdy, the cabinet minister, or Danvor Grebo, one of their own.

It meant that if the kidnapper was a member of The Chapter, part of the drug and arms-smuggling cartel Cavendish was trying to penetrate and smash, he would have every reason to fear for his life.

He wanted to talk! That was it; it had to be the reason Susan had received the second letter. But how on earth was Cavendish supposed to unearth the person who wanted to make contact without advertising the fact, and putting that man or woman's life in danger, and that of David Ellis?

It was something he had to think about, but an idea began to germinate in his mind and he wondered if he might be able to pull it off.

Three days later, Cavendish rang James Faulkner and asked for a meeting. Faulkner sounded reluctant, but because of their overlapping responsibilities he knew he was obliged to. Cavendish gave him no idea of why he wanted the meeting, but pressed him on its urgency.

Faulkner duly arrived at MI6 headquarters and was shown up to Cavendish's office. He was surprised to see Andrew Butler there, the Metropolitan Police Commissioner.

Cavendish greeted him, a touch formally Faulkner thought, and invited him to sit down. He then produced a manila envelope from which he withdrew two sheets of paper. He passed one to Faulkner and the other to the Commissioner.

'I would like you to read that for me if you would,' Cavendish asked the SOCA chief. 'I'll be interested in your reaction.'

Faulkner frowned and pulled the sheet of paper towards him. He took a pair of half-moon glasses from his jacket pocket, perched them on the bridge of his nose while holding them with one hand, and scanned the document. He could feel the colour and heat flooding into his neck as he looked through the typescript.

What Cavendish had given the two men was an almost complete script of the conversation that had taken place between Faulkner and Hudson at the riverside pub a few days ago. Cavendish's man, the lip-reader had pored over the film many times and used his own skills and inclination to fill in the majority of empty spaces that had prevailed after his first attempt. The result was an almost complete copy of what had been said between the two men.

Faulkner kept his face fixed firmly on the paper, his mind working furiously. Eventually he put his glasses back in his pocket and looked across the table at Cavendish.

'What is this, Sir Giles?'

Butler peered over the top of his glasses. 'Yes, what is it?'

Looking at Butler, Cavendish said, 'Our SOCA chief had a meeting with Randolph Hudson, the CIA Station Chief a few days ago at a pub alongside the river. We filmed that meeting and used lip-reading techniques to produce that transcript of what was said between the two men.'

Butler dropped his eyes down to the script. 'It's nothing but a piece of paper with a jumbled narrative.'

'I agree,' Cavendish told him. 'But with the film it makes an awful lot of difference.' He turned his attention back to Faulkner. 'Have you anything to say?'

Faulkner dropped the paper on to the table top. 'Well, what is it? All I can see is what appears to be a script of some kind.' He shrugged his shoulders. 'So, what are you saying?'

Cavendish did not want to go along with what he knew was play-acting from Faulkner. He decided to nail this and force the man into a climb down and possibly a confession; although he considered the latter unlikely.

'You and the CIA chief are part of an organization known as The Chapter of Mercy.' Faulkner said nothing. 'Along with other men of authority, holding very senior positions, you are actively engaged in smuggling heroin and people into this country. You are also engaged in supplying arms to our opponents in Afghanistan; namely the Taliban and Al-Qaeda.'

Faulkner jumped up. 'Rubbish! Absolute rubbish! I'm not sitting here listening to this scandalous trash,' he said sternly, and turned away to walk to the door.

'You won't get out,' Cavendish told him, 'the door is locked.'

Faulkner spun round, his face a picture of anger. 'What on earth do you mean by holding me against my will, Cavendish?' he shouted furiously. 'I insist you open this door immediately.' Cavendish shook his head and maintained a fixed stare at Faulkner.

The SOCA chief glared at Butler. 'Andrew, are you going to sit there and be a party to this … this kidnap?'

The commissioner held the sheet of paper in his hand. 'I think, James, under the circumstances, you should at least listen to what Sir Giles has to say.' He looked at Cavendish. 'I for one would certainly like to know what's going on.'

Faulkner came back to the table and sat down. 'This is complete tosh,' he told Cavendish. 'And an absolute insult to my integrity.' He picked up the sheet of paper and waved it at him. 'For your information, Hudson and I were discussing a case that we are investigating; nothing more than that.'

'At this moment,' Cavendish said, without waiting for Faulkner to add anything else to his tirade, 'Randolph Hudson is being spoken to by my opposite number in MI5. He is being advised to seek retirement on medical grounds seeing as it's unlikely we could hold him here in UK. After all, he would probably claim diplomatic immunity.'

Faulkner looked nonplussed. 'Why are you telling me this?'

Cavendish ploughed on. 'Commodore Deveraux has been apprised of the situation by the American Ambassador. The fact that he is being told that his accomplices are under suspicion should be enough for him to seek early retirement as well, don't you think?'

Nothing was said for a while because Faulkner was considering his options and the vague signals being sent out by the MI6 chief.

'Why do I think there is more to it than this?' he asked Cavendish. 'Or am I supposed to know that too?'

Cavendish allowed himself a smile. 'We shall see,' he told Faulkner. 'But at the moment we have succeeded in stopping the organization in its tracks. We know the CIA have been sanctioning the operation for their own sordid reasons. We also know the part played in it by some members of the American Air Force. What we need now, Faulkner, are names. We want names that will help us in breaking the so-called Chapter of Mercy into a thousand pieces and protecting so many innocent people here in Britain and elsewhere.'

Butler spoke then. 'James, I think you should co-operate. I think there is some *quid pro quo* here. Am I right, Sir Giles?' he asked, turning to Cavendish, who nodded. He then looked back at Faulkner. 'If this crosses my desk officially, then I will be compelled to act. It will cause an enormous stink all the way back to the White House; you know that, don't you?'

Faulkner could see he was trapped, even though it appeared that he was being offered a way out. He would have to resign on health grounds, of course, or family reasons, but would his co-operation ensure his freedom? It was possible he would always live in fear that some rogue elements of The Chapter would come looking for him.

Finally he looked over at Cavendish. 'Give me a few hours. I'll go back to my office, sort some things out. *Quid pro quo*, right?'

Cavendish nodded. '*Quid pro quo*.'

Faulkner was allowed to leave and Butler spent about twenty minutes with Cavendish. They discussed the case briefly and Butler managed to extract a promise from Cavendish that he would keep the Met informed of anything that be useful to the police once Faulkner had been debriefed.

When the police commissioner left, Cavendish began planning the next stage of his campaign to kill the organization stone dead. He now had some work to do with Susan and Marcus as part of the scheme he was considering. He managed a quick lunch at his favourite eatery and returned to his office a little after two o'clock in the afternoon.

At ten minutes past two his phone rang. He picked it up. It was the commissioner.

'Sir Giles? Andrew Butler here. I'm afraid I have some bad news for you.'

'Oh, and what is that?' Cavendish asked.

'It's about James Faulkner. He has committed suicide; he shot himself.'

SIXTEEN

SUSAN SHIVERED AS the wind blew suddenly with swirling gusts that made walking difficult. The hammering rain forced her to keep her head turned away and from time to time the strength of the wind almost blew her off her feet.

Susan had caught the tube to Charing Cross and was now battling her way along the Strand to the Starbucks coffee bar where she had first met Cavendish. The rain and the wind were totally unexpected, as was the call from Cavendish. He said he had a proposition to put to her, and that he hoped she would not mind if he didn't call on her at her home.

It had been something like three weeks since Susan had seen him. It had been the evening that Marcus had turned up unexpectedly at her house. She hadn't seen Marcus since that day either, and had wondered if her association with those two was at an end. What Susan did not know at the time was that Cavendish was keeping Marcus off the streets for his own safety.

Summer was turning into autumn and giving in too easily as it did in England. Susan had no umbrella and could feel the cold wind pushing the rain at her as she dodged one pedestrian after another and wondered what on earth it was that Cavendish wanted to see her about.

She turned towards the large, double doors of the coffee house and pushed them open, welcoming the sudden shelter from the weather. She let the doors swing shut and stepped aside as someone made a move to go past her, his face a picture of gloom as he caught sight of the sudden squall that had sprung up outside.

Before Susan had finished running her fingers through her hair to flush out the wetness, Cavendish was by her side.

'Let me take your coat, Susan,' he offered.

Susan thanked him and allowed him to pull her coat from her shoulders.

'We're over there,' he told her, pointing to the same corner in which they had sat on their first meeting.

'We?' Susan said, looking at Cavendish in surprise. Then she glanced across the room and saw Marcus sitting there. He smiled and waved at her.

Cavendish was grinning. 'What would you like? Coffee?'

Susan said she would and then tried not to make it look as though she was in a hurry to get across the room to Marcus, but she felt so good at seeing him there that she just wanted to rush over and say hello.

But she walked.

'Marcus, what a surprise,' she admitted to him, as he stood up like the perfect gentleman he was. There was plenty of noise in the coffee house and she had no qualms about saying it loudly.

'I'm like a bad penny, Susan; I keep turning up.'

Susan laughed and sat opposite him. 'It's lovely to see you, Marcus. Where have you been?'

Marcus glanced across at Cavendish. 'He's been keeping me under lock and key.' He lowered his voice conspiratorially. 'It's for my own good, so I'm told.'

'Or is it for Cavendish's good?' she asked him, her nose wrinkling in that same sense of impish fun that Marcus was displaying.

'You know, Susan, it really is good to see you. How are you?'

She gave a kind of so-so shrug. 'I'm OK, Marcus. I just wish I could have done more to find David.'

He put his hand over hers. 'Don't ever give up,' he said softly.

Susan liked the feel of Marcus's hand on hers. 'I won't, but it's difficult. Anyway,' she said brightly, 'why are we here?'

He grinned. 'I could tell you, but then I would have to kill you; it's a state secret.'

Susan laughed. 'Now come on, Marcus, what are we doing here?'

He winked at her. 'All in good time,' he told her. 'All in good time.'

Cavendish came up to the table and put Susan's coffee down in front of her. He then sat down beside Marcus. The two men were now facing her. There was still a great deal of movement and general noise around them but Susan focused her mind on the two men.

'My dear,' Cavendish began, 'we've been doing an incredible amount of work behind the scenes since we saw you last, and you haven't been forgotten.'

Susan sipped her coffee as Cavendish spoke, her curiosity level rising.

'But, first, a little background before I come to the reason for asking you here.' He glanced away for a moment and Susan wondered if he was play-acting; putting on a show for her benefit.

'When your brother was shot, he was working for me.'

As a statement it carried little weight, but it staggered Susan. She almost burnt her mouth as she dipped her head and gasped. Cavendish put up a hand.

'It happens, Susan; men work undercover for the state, but they are not always allowed to reveal that. Your brother was a very good field agent; it was why he was on assignment at the mission in Jalalabad.'

'I thought he was a journalist,' Susan said weakly.

'So did The Chapter.' Cavendish arched his eyebrows. 'Well, for a time they did. We believe it was that organization which tried to kill him.'

'So this meeting is about David, isn't it?' Susan asked him, feeling a little surge of optimism rising inside her.

'To a point, yes,' he told her. 'But more importantly, it's about stopping the organization and their insidious business.'

Susan looked at Marcus. He just seemed to be sitting there gazing at her with a poorly concealed smile on his face. She felt her colour come up and looked back at Cavendish.

'So,' the intelligence chief went on, 'I've asked you here to put a proposition to you.'

'What's that?' Susan asked warily.

Cavendish shifted in his seat. He leaned closer. 'I believe the reason you received that second letter from your brother is because someone is trying to contact me.'

'You?' Susan interrupted. 'Why didn't they send you the letter then?'

'Too obvious,' he told her. 'I believe from intelligence I have received from Afghanistan that there is a problem within the organization. I'm not too clear on exactly what it is, but I believe that there is an element of unrest somewhere in their loop, so to speak.'

Susan was nodding her head as he spoke. She stopped and lifted the coffee to her lips. Marcus watched her closely. She looked over the top of her cup at him, her eyes almost sparkling. Once again she felt conscious of her own behaviour and glanced away.

'So I want to try to develop that weakness, so to speak. It might just be someone giving us an opportunity to get your brother out.' He paused for a moment. 'But I have a gut feeling that there is more to it than that.'

'So why have you asked me to come here?' Susan asked him.

Cavendish studied the tips of his fingers for a while. Then he looked up at her.

'When your brother was working under cover at the mission, there was another agent there also, but your brother did not know. That agent has never been replaced because the risk of exposure was too great; the organization would have known immediately. But now I think we have someone who could be ready to work for us in Jalalabad; a case of seeing an opportunity present itself and grabbing that opportunity.'

Susan was curious and, for some reason, alarm bells began ringing in her head. She stared at Cavendish with a frown gathering over her lovely dark eyes.

Cavendish dropped his gaze away and looked into his cup. When he saw that it was empty he wrinkled his nose in disappointment.

'Do you want another coffee, Sir Giles?' Marcus asked him.

'Thank you, Marcus, yes.'

Marcus got up and went across to the counter. Cavendish turned his attention back to Susan.

'As I was saying, I believe we now have somebody ready to go to Jalalabad.'

Susan expected him to carry on with his explanation, but when she realized Cavendish had stopped for a moment and was looking directly at her, almost peering deep into her soul, she said, 'Is it Marcus?'

He shook his head. 'No, my dear, it's you.'

Marcus had returned with Cavendish's coffee before Susan finally spoke. He was unaware that the bombshell had been dropped, although he had been warned by Sir Giles that it was going to happen.

Susan felt a weakness in her legs. It was as though they were emptying and losing their strength. In fact, she thought she was going to faint, but because she was sitting down she was able to rely on the chair for support. Then her hands started trembling and she could see her fingers shaking. She tried to say something, but her voice faltered in her throat and simply came out in a husky croak.

She lifted her cup and took a mouthful of coffee, swallowing it down with a certain amount of difficulty. Cavendish could see she was in trouble, but he had seen the same reaction many times before. He knew that if she had an immediate rejection in her mind, it would have resulted in an almost certain display of histrionics and no doubt she would have walked out of the coffee house.

But she was still there.

'It would give you an opportunity to look for your brother,' he told her.

Susan cleared her throat. 'What on earth makes you think I could work for you in Jalalabad? I have no training, no qualifications, nothing.'

He smiled almost patronizingly. 'You have all the qualifications you need; your brother's welfare.'

'But I have a job,' she protested. 'I can't just walk out.'

He shook his head. 'Of course you can't. But it has already been taken care of.'

Her mouth fell open. 'You've spoken to my manager?' She could hardly believe it, but, then, Cavendish seemed to do whatever he wanted.

'Not quite. Let us say that his superiors have been apprised of a situation that has developed in your life, the need for discretion on his part, and the need for a certain amount of shall we say, *laissez faire*, so that you may travel to India in search of your brother. I can assure you that your job is safe and will be there for you when you return.'

'You told them I was going to India?'

That certain kind of smile slid across his face. 'I couldn't tell them the truth now, could I?'

'What makes you think I want to go anyway,' she asked him, haughtily.

'Because you haven't said no.'

Susan looked away from Cavendish and could feel tears welling up at the back of her eyes. Suddenly she was being given a chance to do something to help her brother, but at the same time she was almost certainly being asked to risk her own life. She thought of Cavendish's remark that the previous agent had been killed by the organization. It made her fearful that her own inadequacies might result in her death too.

But as rational as her thinking might be, and as obvious to her as it was that she was not properly trained for such a task, she knew she could not turn down the opportunity to at least get close to her brother.

'What about Marcus?' she asked, glancing across at him.

'Later,' was all Cavendish said.

'Your previous agent was murdered?' she asked warily.

Cavendish nodded but said nothing.

'Was the agent a woman?'

He nodded again.

'Who was it?' she asked, knowing already what he would say.

'It was Shakira.'

Shakira had arrived in Jalalabad shortly after enjoying a holiday with her parents in Mumbai, India. She had told them that she had managed to get a job with The Chapter of Mercy; a charitable organization that took in orphans and unwanted children at their orphanage in Jalalabad. And because of the traditional bigotry against infant females, there were many young girls growing up there.

Shakira had no problem getting used to the customs and way of life in Afghanistan. Because she had Indian parents, Shakira might have been expected to wear the traditional *burqa* or *chadri* to give it the correct name, but she chose to dress as a westerner because she had been raised in England before returning to India. Her only sop to tradition and culture was to wear a headscarf at all times.

Shakira's first day at the mission was spent being introduced to the children, of whom there were many, and to the staff of course, who were mainly nuns of a local order. The office where Shakira was to take up her duties had not been used for a few weeks, and it was clear to her that tidying it up was her responsibility.

It took Shakira about a week to settle in to her job which was programme development co-ordinator. At first she wasn't really sure exactly what was expected of her, but it soon became apparent that the nuns had little time for administration because they were either battling away with the children by tending to them, playing with them, nursing them, feeding them and bathing them. After their devotions there was little time left for anything else.

The mission was situated on the north-east approaches to the city about ten miles beyond the well-defined city boundaries. A dirt road wound its way up through the foothills, following a river course for a short while before rounding a sharp bend and leaving the river behind. It overlooked a valley lush with vegetation and vineyards, and each morning the sun would lift its head above the ridge between two adjacent hills and shine down like God's eternal bounty.

In the winter the sun could be a blessing, but, in the middle of summer, it was more of a curse which plagued the lives of the young and old who lived and worked there.

Shakira knew she had to juggle two jobs at once: one she had been employed to do by The Chapter of Mercy, and the other to feed information back to Sir Giles Cavendish at MI6 whenever she had something to send and whenever she had the opportunity.

Her brief had been short and without too much information, but she had been told by Cavendish that the organization known as The Chapter of Mercy, usually shortened to The Chapter, was actively taking young children from the mission, the majority of whom were in their very early teens, and passing them on to another group which smuggled children into the Western countries for use in prostitution and paedophile rings.

The child smuggling was merely an addition to the core business of The Chapter – the smuggling of drugs out of Afghanistan and the import of arms into that country. Shakira had to put faces to names and then attach blame and guilt. It was a tall order, but she was a trained agent. She was also very clever and with a great intellect. Shakira had an honours degree in Ancient Greek, which established in the minds of people like Sir Giles Cavendish that she was capable of compartmentalizing problems in such a way that she could get right down to the meat on the bone, and leave out the trash.

Shakira had been there for one week when a visitor turned up and demanded to see the nuns. When Shakira pointed out that she was the programme development co-ordinator, her visitor laughed and brushed past her, calling out for one of the sisters.

Shakira was annoyed to say the least, but in a way, not surprised. Her visitor looked quite brutal, and she was not about to invite an argument, particularly as she was only supposed to observe and report. She kept her temper and asked who he was.

He told Shakira that his name was Abdul Khaliq. He said he was a regular visitor to the mission, but he only ever spoke to the nuns. His name meant nothing to Shakira, but she filed it away in her memory to add to a list she was putting together.

Once she had taken him into the office, and he had come to understand that she was indeed running the orphanage, he agreed to sit down and state his business.

Khaliq told her that he had found several childless couples who wished to adopt a child from the orphanage, but who were unable to do it legally in their own countries. So, because of the way in which the orphanage operated, he asked Shakira to prepare several girls whom he would pick to be made ready for their new lives.

Shakira had great difficulty in not telling her visitor to get lost. She had to remember that he was one of the reasons why she was there and it wasn't for her to moralize on the child smuggling; her job was to nail people like him and undo the damage his organization was doing to countless young children.

What appalled Shakira was the absolute gall of the man that he could walk into the orphanage and 'order' several children. But what she did know was that each child was prepared with the correct paperwork by the nuns to be presented to the Afghanistan authorities so that they could be released into Khaliq's custody. Or whoever it was that came calling, which she was to discover in time.

She also learned, to her horror, that girls as young as twelve or thirteen were being brought to the orphanage as orphans and transferred out again within a matter of weeks. The nuns were given money provided by The Chapter every time children were brought in, but Shakira discovered that a great deal of what they received was passed on to their order, which left very little to support the children.

It was about three weeks after Abdul Khaliq's visit that five children were made ready for collection by the obnoxious man. Shakira had been warned by the nuns that her presence during the handover might not be desirable. They didn't explain, but Shakira had a good idea why, and reasoned that the nuns were really turning a blind eye to what was going on. Either that or they were being deliberately naïve.

So, on the evening of the appointed delivery, Shakira parked her car in a convenient spot down the mountain road where she hoped she could remain unobserved until Khaliq went by with his new charge of vulnerable children.

The transport had arrived at the mission just after sunset and, within an hour, the Toyota Mini-bus came down the mountain road. Shakira immediately pulled on to the road as the Toyota passed by. She noticed Khaliq was not in the vehicle. This gave her some hope that the man who was driving would not think he was being followed.

The bus motored into the town of Jalalabad, not in a hurry judging by the care with which the man was driving. Shakira followed resolutely until the bus came to a halt outside the house that served as a consulate to the Turkmenistan nation. The children were immediately taken from the bus and bundled in through a side entrance.

Shakira waited, keeping the motor running until the driver came out. He climbed into the bus and pulled out into the sparse flow of traffic. She followed until the bus came to a halt in the car-park of a small restaurant.

Although Shakira did not smoke, she needed a reason for going into the restaurant, so she purchased a packet of cigarettes from the cigarette machine. She saw the driver order a meal, so she decided to call it a day and left.

For the next three months Shakira followed people, whether they were innocent parties or suspect. To her it was a matter of complete indifference; she needed to build up a picture of the people who had reason to come and go at the orphanage.

Then one day Shakira was introduced to a journalist who had been commissioned to do an assignment on the work of the orphanage. His name was David Ellis, and Shakira took to him immediately. It wasn't long before he was telling her silly jokes which made her laugh. He had a way of making her feel energized whenever he came into her presence. He was also very interested in the work of the orphanage and spent a great deal of time with her, particularly in the evenings, when they would spend some time up on the hillside watching the sunset and talking small talk.

Every two or three days, after spending some time with David, Shakira would shut herself in her office and write a short report for Sir Giles Cavendish. She would encode the report and then send it on her mobile phone via the recently launched Mercury 6 British military satellite. The satellite pass time was in the region of ninety minutes, which gave Shakira plenty of time to prepare her report and send it.

What Shakira did not know, and would never know, was that the

CIA, in and around the Middle East, used that satellite as part of its overall communications cover, under the auspices of Her Majesty's Britannic Government. And although she used a one-time pad for obvious security reasons, no one in MI6 considered the CIA posed any threat, or represented any risk as compliant sharers of that satellite link.

But it was that very naïve thinking on the part of British intelligence that led to the murder of Shakira and almost fatal wounding of David Ellis. Since the attacks on the twin towers in New York, remembered all over the world as 9/11, the National Security Agency, the NSA, in America had eavesdropped on all communications traffic originating in the Middle East as part of its terrorist surveillance programme. And the British intelligence authorities assumed that all their traffic would be sacrosanct, and left untouched by the NSA.

It was this blunder that led to the CIA being made aware of short bursts of traffic emanating from the heartland of Al-Qaeda and other Muslim terror groups in Afghanistan itself.

The signals were intercepted and decoded, then passed on to the CIA in London, because this was the tracked destination of the coded messages. Ordinarily the message would have been identified as British military traffic and deleted, but for reasons best known to the Americans, they were filed into a dead box.

Because the United Kingdom came within the overall responsibility of the station CIA chief in London, the knowledge of these signals was passed to Randolph Hudson, a covert member of The Chapter.

Hudson took this information to Commodore Deveraux and between them they made the decision to launch an attack on the mission and make sure an insurgent group were blamed for the atrocity.

And it was just a few days before the attack that a man Shakira had never seen before, walked into the mission and introduced himself as Rafiq. She noticed the little finger on his left hand was missing. He was posing as a potential customer, wanting to adopt one of the children, but was keen to get to know a little more about the orphanage before making up his mind.

Shakira thought he was a very pleasant man, but despite the fact that he was a complete stranger and his business seemed perfectly normal, she included his name in the report she was to send that evening.

Three days later Shakira died and Rafiq's name, meaningless to the

British at that time, was filed away in the dead box of the CIA in London and, perversely, it was filed away in the file marked 'Mission' in Sir Giles Cavendish's office.

SEVENTEEN

SUSAN ARRIVED IN Kabul with her nerves in shreds, despite the fact that Marcus had been with her since leaving England. It had been Cavendish's idea that they travel together. He thought Marcus would provide some kind of inner strength and support for Susan, but privately, and uncharacteristically, he was hoping that Marcus's penchant for invention when things got out of hand might just help win the day for them.

The flight from Heathrow by Air India had stopped at Dubai and Delhi before arriving in Kabul almost twenty-four hours after leaving London. All Susan could think of during her flight was the way in which she had been persuaded by Cavendish that this was well within her capabilities and that she had nothing to be afraid of. And with Marcus with her, she should feel relaxed.

The security chief had explained how she could walk freely around Kabul and make it known to the local press and radio stations that she was in Afghanistan to look for her brother. He convinced her that the men who were holding her brother would come looking for her and would probably be prepared to do a deal.

When Susan pointed out that she was not a trained negotiator, neither did she carry any clout in the same way a British politician might, Cavendish said that intellect often gets in the way of a good cause, and that she was perfect for the role of appeaser, negotiator and rescuer. He said she had it in her heart to find her brother for no other reason than he was of her blood and she loved him as any sister would. A politician would never be able to speak from the heart because the only goal on the horizon that a politician could see was personal *kudos* and elevation amongst his or her peers.

As for a negotiator, he or she would be conducting a business deal, and would do that in a particularly mercenary fashion, putting his country's politics and aims first before the welfare of the hostage. Cavendish insisted that Susan was perfect for the task, and at no risk to herself.

During the flight Susan kept thinking of Terry Waite, the Christian minister who had been taken hostage in the Lebanon and kept captive for five years. His only crime was to go openly to Beirut and try to win the freedom of the hostage John McCarthy who was held for five years in the Lebanon. Ironically it was the selfless effort of McCarthy's friend, Jill Morrell, who campaigned tirelessly for his release that finally got McCarthy free. Could Cavendish see another Jill Morrell in Susan Ellis, she wondered?

That thought teased at her for some considerable time, but did little in effect to calm her nerves and stop her from seeing all kinds of demons waiting for her in Afghanistan. From time to time she would take hold of Marcus's hand, squeeze it and just sit there, taking some kind of comfort from the contact.

Marcus said very little during the trip because he could see that Susan was walking a mental tightrope. He understood that there was nothing he could do or say that would make things easier for her.

Susan would keep thinking of David and telling herself that it was for him that she was doing this, not for herself, or for Cavendish, whatever the security man's ulterior motives were. And she thought how badly David must be suffering, shackled as he almost certainly would be in some insufferable dark hole somewhere in the distant hills in that sad country.

She pledged to keep control of herself and fight to regain David's freedom as the plane touched down on to a steaming hot evening in the city of Kabul.

David threw his head back and roared with laughter, the wine in his glass spilling on to the table as his hand jerked with the sudden movement. Abdul Khaliq was beaming at David through his beard which was stained red from the copious amounts of wine he had drunk. His bodyguards were in the room, enjoying the ribald jokes that Abdul was telling them all, but for them not the luxury of wine because of their dedication to serving their boss.

David had been fluent in Farsi for some time, but now he was fluent in the garbled dialect of Abdul's countrymen because of the amount of time he had spent in his company. He was now treated almost like one of the family, hence the ribald humour being bandied about in that room. But if David felt like he was accepted now, he knew the reality was totally different.

They were in a farmhouse many miles from the nearest town, and probably a hundred miles or so from Kabul. He might just as well have been on the moon. He was allowed the freedom to move about as he wished and hadn't been shackled for some weeks now. And, from time to time, Abdul would hint that his freedom was not too far away. But all this meant to David was that he was still a hostage, but being kept in an open prison that ranged from one border to another.

There were also times, in amongst the humour and good-natured behaviour shown by Abdul and his men that the warlord would confess to David that all was not well. It had taken Abdul many months to figure it out, but now he could state with some certainty that he was being edged aside by the influence of the Americans and the British in Afghanistan. By that he meant there were factions within the occupying forces, his words, who were trying to gain control of Abdul's side of the operation.

At first David told Abdul he was imagining things; that he was probably getting paranoid. But, as a result of the previous few weeks, David was beginning to see a pattern emerging; one of almost open hostility to Abdul from the same farmers who used to show almost reverential respect.

There had also been some seemingly opportunistic attacks from wandering bands of Taliban. Abdul had always kept a small group of men with him, and they had shown they were particularly competent in dealing with the attacks. But, as time went by, the band of men began to dwindle in numbers.

That evening, before Abdul let the wine get to him, and he was drinking a lot more, David noticed, David asked him if he had any idea who was responsible for the attacks, and why.

Abdul muttered something about the Americans, which didn't make sense to David, but he also mentioned Milan Janov.

David recalled that the last meeting between the two men had been very tense, but both men had brought a small army with them at that time, and it was this that had almost certainly prevented any bloodshed. But now, Abdul was travelling fairly light, and this worried David. He wasn't concerned for Abdul's safety but his own.

When David had asked why he was not travelling with his usual band of warriors, Abdul had not been able to answer immediately, and it was obvious to David that some things were beginning to come to light. Abdul's armed group was crumbling slowly. Men were leaving him, citing all manner of reasons for doing so. And in the customary manner that seemed to linger within even the most savage breast, the men would return to their families.

Abdul's strength had always been in the number of his static followers, namely the farmers, and in the knowledge he possessed of others involved in the drugs and arms traffic. But that strength seemed to be diminishing and, with the news of the disaster that had struck in England, Abdul knew his power was ebbing away fast. And that was why he kept hinting that David might one day be free. What David couldn't see was exactly how Abdul could give David his freedom without exposing the two of them to further danger.

The conversation, the subjective arguments and collective reasoning of the four men in that room began to wane as the late evening wore on. Eventually David declared that he was going to bed and left Abdul with his lieutenants still talking.

The wine had taken its toll on David and he fell on to his bed, fully clothed. Within minutes he was fast asleep, the noise from the three men no longer audible in David's sub-conscious.

About two hours after falling asleep, David was woken by a full bladder. He clambered out of bed and wandered out into the yard where he relieved himself. When he had finished he went back into the house and into the kitchen to get a drink of water from the jug that was always filled.

It was there that he noticed a mobile phone lying on the kitchen table. The moonlight funnelling through the small open window glinted off the bright metal that decorated the phone.

He stood looking at it for several seconds before picking it up. He flipped it open and stared at the keypad. How long, he wondered, was it since he had used that number; eight or nine months, a year perhaps? He wasn't sure, but he hoped the injury to his head would not stop him from recalling it.

He walked out into the courtyard to find more light from the moon. He then entered in a short text message followed by the number he hoped was correct and pressed the 'send' key. Then he went back into the kitchen, put the phone back on the table and finished his drink. Ten minutes after waking David was back in his bed with a contented smile playing on the corners of his lips.

Marcus gave the taxi driver the name of the hotel and sat back in the battered Toyota with Susan and tried to relax for a while. They had travelled with minimum luggage because Cavendish had supplied them with travellers' cheques and cash in Afghanis, and they planned to spend her first day doing some shopping. Marcus hoped this would go some way to breaking the tension Susan was feeling.

Cavendish had also given Susan a mobile phone for Afghanistan. He told her it was expensive and would allow her to phone UK all expenses paid. It was a useful gift, one which Susan was determined to use as often as she liked.

Cavendish had given them a copy of Nancy Hatch Dupree's pocket guidebook, first published in 1965 together with a list of does and don'ts, plus a reminder that Kabul was the most mined city in the world. To wander off the beaten track could mean being blown up. Neither of them had any reason to suspect they might want to walk in unseen places. All Susan wanted to do was talk to people in positions of power and influence and begin her search for David.

Her immediate priority, once she had enjoyed a good night's sleep, was to make her way over to the British Embassy and arrange an appointment with the ambassador. She believed that the mention of her brother's name would be enough to interest him and agree to see her. Marcus had agreed to let Susan do the talking and searching, while he kept a low profile.

Susan was disappointed that she was only granted an interview with a diplomatic aide. She explained that she had come over to Kabul to begin searching for her brother. The idea was met with a great deal of condescension, which infuriated her but also let her know the kind of obdurate obstacles she was likely to encounter.

Once she had left the embassy, Susan met Marcus in an internet café they had picked out earlier in the day. Together they looked up the addresses of the local Kabul newspapers. There were many listed, and plenty who published in the English language. Susan made a note of those she believed would be willing to listen to her and perhaps give her some column inches to tell her story.

They agreed on the *Cheragh Daily* first, and phoned the editor who turned out to be a woman. Susan believed a female would listen with sympathy and understanding and probably include something in the paper.

Following that, Susan contacted the editor of the *Daily Outlook Afghanistan* and enjoyed the same warm reception and the promise of an interview.

Her third choice was the *Kabul Weekly*, a magazine that, like the other newspapers also published in English.

All the appointments were lined up for the following day, so the two of them took the opportunity to explore Kabul with a guide recommended by her hotel, and it was during a lunch stop that they learned the bare truth about Kabul and the chances of ever finding her brother alive.

Their guide was called Ali Seema. He spoke excellent English and proved to be a valuable guide. It was Ali's accommodating way that relaxed Susan and encouraged her to ask many questions about the chances of ever seeing her brother alive. His reply was disappointing.

'You will not have noticed how many extra police there are in Kabul because you have just arrived,' he told her. 'But in the last month they have moved seven thousand policemen into the city because of the infiltration of Taliban spies and suicide bombers. Although our president denies it, we know that the Taliban are taking up positions just a few miles outside the city; just like they did twenty years ago after the Russians left.' He looked around with an expression on his face that seemed to be looking ahead to the terror to come and the past they would have to say goodbye to.

'The Taliban cannot be beaten. They will have a complete stranglehold on the city within six months. No one will be able to leave the city without their permission. The only people allowed in will be those who fly in on the commercials airlines or with the military. For all your posturing, you Westerners can do nothing; the Taliban will win.' He made an empty gesture with his hands and shrugged his shoulders. 'It is unlikely that you will be allowed to find your brother. If you get a mention in the newspapers, you will be lucky.'

Susan protested. 'But I have already spoken on the telephone with the editors. I have told them why I am here and they have all agreed to see me. Surely they would have said no if they didn't intend printing anything?'

'It is not like that here. They are being polite.' He dipped his head slightly. 'Yes, they may print something, but it will be very little and probably tucked away in the middle of their papers. Don't forget, there are suicide bombings almost daily here and in Pakistan, which is just a few miles away. There are Afghani policemen and soldiers from the United Nations being killed by roadside bombs and suicide bombers, not counting innocent civilians. What value is your brother's situation against that of those brave men who are laying down their lives to protect Afghanistan? No, the newspapers have much to choose from, and I think your brother will be of little interest to their readers.'

'I'm not going to give up,' Susan told him a little indignantly. 'My brother is important to me. I do understand the awfulness of the situation, but I won't let that get in my way just because of a few Taliban.'

Ali pulled a face and pursed his lips. 'Please, please do not underestimate them; they are ruthless.' He leaned forward as if to add meaning to his next remark. 'And they do not like Western women, believe me.' He straightened. 'My advice to you is complete your enquiries, your search, quickly and leave. Your brother has been missing a very long time; it is unlikely you will ever find him.'

Susan looked at Ali with a sad expression on her face. 'What can I do?'

He shrugged. 'There is nothing either of you can do because it will be very dangerous for you both. Already the American Embassy is providing secure accommodation for its employees inside the embassy because it is so unsafe for them in the city. Believe me; if the two of you do not leave Afghanistan soon, you will never leave.'

Milan Janov had been left kicking his heels by the events that had unfolded in London. His request to the CIA chief to send a hit team in to take out Abdul and his group had yielded nothing, and in frustration he had contacted Maggot to find out why. Maggot was unhelpful, not because he wanted to be but because he knew nothing; he had not been contacted by Hudson, the CIA man. At that stage, neither of them knew that the organization had been seriously compromised and effectively shut down, probably for good.

Janov asked Maggot to make some phone calls. He was afraid his own, heavily accented English might give him away, so Maggot had agreed to take on that task. He contacted the American Embassy and asked for Randolph Hudson but was told that Mr Hudson had returned to the United States. He then asked to be put through to the military attaché's office to be told that Commodore Deveraux had also returned to America.

The alarm bells began to ring and Maggot had that uneasy feeling that the game was up; the security forces were closing in on members of the group. He contacted Janov and they met again in the nightclub in West London.

'From what you have told me,' Maggot said to Janov, 'The Chapter has stopped operating. Well, here at least, and I think it is getting dangerous for anyone who had dealings with them.'

Janov was sat hunched over his Urquell lager. He held the glass firmly and shook it gently so that the amber liquid spun inside the glass.

'If I take care of my end of the operation,' he said eventually, 'could you take it on here in Britain?'

Maggot shook his head firmly. 'The operation is too big. And even if I wanted to, there will be other members of The Chapter who would prevent it. Someone will pick it up again, but not me.'

They sat in silence as the music drifted over them and dancers moved gracelessly about the pocket handkerchief dance floor. Janov cast around; his bottom lip protruding as he pondered the impact of what Maggot has said. His thoughts were no longer on what pleasures awaited him in the rooms upstairs, but how he could repair the break in their import/export business.

'Rafiq,' he said after a while. 'I have control from Turkmenistan up to all the European ports. Abdul Khaliq has control in Afghanistan, but it is weakening and I believe he is preparing to break away from us. I think it is because of him that we have reached this situation.'

'If this is true, how can you prevent it?' Maggot asked him.

Janov shook his head. 'I cannot, but I can make him pay.' He lifted his glass and drained it. Maggot turned round towards the bar and attracted the attention of one of the barmaids. He pointed to Janov's empty glass. The girl nodded.

'How can you make him pay?'

Janov belched and put his hand to his mouth. The sound was swamped by the noise pounding out from the speakers.

'When I go back I will go to Kabul. Abdul goes there often.' He pointed at Maggot. 'That is where it will finish; I will see to it.'

'How will you do that?' asked Maggot, doubting whether Janov had the support in Kabul that he would need. 'It isn't your territory. You don't have the people in place there.'

Janov smiled slowly. A shadow fell across him as the barmaid put a full glass in front of him. Janov put his hand up her skirt and squeezed her thigh. She pulled away sharply and looked daggers at him. Maggot laughed.

'It isn't always necessary to have people there, as you say, Rafiq.' His face brightened. 'But so long as I have someone with me who I can rely on and trust, I can get the job done.'

'Who's that someone?' Maggot asked, sensing the direction the conversation was going.

'You, Rafiq.'

Maggot laughed. 'Why me?'

Janov opened his hands in an empty gesture. 'Because you are no longer safe here in England. You have to be there.'

'I don't have to be anywhere,' he told Janov, shaking his head.

Janov nodded vigorously. 'But you do, Rafiq. You are no longer safe in England.' He leaned closer, repeating his point. 'How much longer will it be before they connect you with The Chapter?' He leaned back in his chair but kept his gaze fixed firmly on Maggot. 'Don't you see? You will be safer with me in Afghanistan than you are here in your own country.'

Maggot could see a modicum of sense in what Janov was saying. He thought back to the day he had met Susan Ellis in Marcus's empty office and began to see one or two pointers into the way things were changing. He had told Susan that if Marcus was involved in the big boys' games, he could be in trouble. He linked that thought to Susan's reason for contacting Marcus, namely her brother David, and he could see where those pointers were going: all the way to Afghanistan.

He put all this into the melting pot of supposition and conjecture, including Janov's assertion that he might not be safe in England, and realised that it might be time for another trip to Pakistan, or even Afghanistan, simply to keep away from the security forces in England.

'How easy would it be to hit Abdul?' he asked carefully.

A huge smile blossomed on Janov's craggy features and thumped the table top with his huge fist.

'That's it, Rafiq; the old Rafiq that I know.' He came closer. 'First of all we must get you to Kabul, and then we can plan everything else once you are there.'

'How will you know where he is?' Maggot asked.

Janov tapped the side of his head with the tip of his finger. 'I have somebody close to him. He tells me what I wish to know. So when we get to Kabul I will find out where Abdul is and you and I will finish it.'

EIGHTEEN

DAVID WAS ASLEEP on a small bed when the sound of his bedroom door opening woke him. He had been given a very tiny room to sleep in, much like a prison cell but without bars. Despite being allowed certain freedoms, David still found himself being contained rather than confined, and knew that his existence depended purely upon Khaliq's state of mind. He had made precious little mention of the so-called freedom he had told David to expect, and wondered if it was some delusion that he carried around in his head all day.

David opened his eyes and rubbed the sleep from them, allowing himself a moment to get accustomed to the orange sunlight filtering through the small opening in the wall that served as a window. He blinked away the sleep and opened his eyes fully as the door burst open and Abdul Khaliq walked into the room.

'Get dressed!' Abdul shouted, flicking his arm in the air. 'We leave in ten minutes.' He stormed out of the room.

David sat there staring at the back of the door which was closing slowly. He had no idea why he had done that, and he knew it would do no good asking. He stood up and pulled on a pair of trousers and then went out into the courtyard of the farmhouse in which they were staying. There was a small, square bathing area which was little more than a low walled box into which water was hand pumped from a subterranean well.

David operated the handle of the pump and doused himself in cold water. It brought up goose bumps on his skin in the chill morning air. Water ran from his beard and he shook his head vigorously sending droplets flying like a dog shaking itself after a dousing.

He straightened up and looked around the small courtyard. It was strangely quiet, as though an air of expectancy had suppressed any life. He guessed it had something to do with the dramatic order to be ready to leave.

As he walked across the yard he could hear the sound of a Toyota Landcruiser starting up. He guessed it must be Abdul's wagon. David quickened his step and hurried back to his room where he finished dressing.

Seven minutes after Abdul had left his room, David walked out of the house eating an apple which he had picked up from the table in the kitchen. He had grabbed a drink of water from a jug that was always kept full, and hoped it wouldn't be too long before Abdul explained what the drama was all about, and then perhaps he could get a satisfying meal inside his belly.

Abdul had seemed nervous lately, not that it was too obvious, but David had been in custody long enough now to know that something was worrying him.

As usual, the two lieutenants signalled David to join them in the Toyota. He clambered in and took up his accustomed position in the rear passenger seat, sandwiched between the two men.

Abdul came hurrying out of the farmhouse and looked quickly at another Toyota that had lined up behind his car. He gave a satisfyied nod of the head and clambered into the Landcruiser. The driver slipped it into gear and hit the accelerator, spinning the wheels on the sandy ground and throwing up clouds of dust.

The second Toyota followed and the two vehicles motored away from the farmhouse in which the men had stayed overnight. David peered through the window and watched the dwelling grow smaller until it was lost from sight behind the rising ground they were leaving.

But if David had looked up into a sky that was coming to life in a mixture of reds and dark blues, he might, just might, have seen an American MQ-9 pilotless drone watching their progress, 8000 feet above them.

Cavendish was standing behind a United States Air Force colonel who was sitting at the control desk of the MQ-9 Reaper unmanned drone. The aircraft was flying above the Landcruiser, looking down from the sky at an easy target. They were inside the MQ-9 control station that had been fitted into a windowless, air-conditioned trailer at the American Air Force base at Khost.

Immediately in front of the USAF officer was essentially the cockpit of the MQ-9, with hand controls to fly the unmanned drone. In front of him were two, large coloured screens that gave him a camera shot looking down towards the ground, and a moving map on which he could track the drone's progress. With the camera view he was able to maintain contact with the target which, in this case was the Toyota Landcruiser.

Beside him was the sensor operator who operated the sensors that were essential to fly the aircraft. Between them the two men were like the flight crew of a two man jet. Fortunately for Abdul Khaliq, this was not a hostile surveillance.

Cavendish was at Khost base at his own request; he had flown out the moment he had received the most unexpected text message on his phone just a couple of days previously, and had been met at the base by the Base Security Officer, Lieutenant Brad McCain.

Cavendish now knew that David Ellis was alive and well. Although Cavendish had put a trace on the call, the number was unlisted, but he was now convinced that the search for his man would end in Afghanistan.

Cavendish believed he knew the reason Susan had received those letters; it was because someone was definitely trying to contact him without making it known in Afghanistan. And David had named Abdul Khaliq in the text message. Putting two and two together was fairly simple logic, but Cavendish knew he was not quite touching home base; there was still plenty to do.

He stayed in the MQ-9 trailer until he had seen enough, and told the young officer at the cockpit controls that he was leaving. He said he would check with the operations officer on the time of the next MQ-9 over flight of the suspected target.

On his way back to his quarters, Cavendish passed by a great number of service and civilian personnel all walking from one place to the other, intent on their business, getting on with their own lives in that hostile environment.

As he walked past the base headquarters, Cavendish saw two men come out of the building and get into a waiting car. One of the men was wearing the uniform of a pilot. The other was a civilian and Cavendish thought he recognized him. He watched the car pull away but was unable to get a closer look at the man because of the darkened windows of the car. He shrugged and thought no more of it, and continued his progress towards his own accommodation block, hoping it would come to him later.

Janov had no trouble crossing the border between Turkmenistan and Afghanistan. It was something he had done countless times before and would probably do countless times in the future. It crossed his mind at the time that he might even move the centre of his operation into Afghanistan once he had disposed of the troublesome Abdul Khaliq.

Sitting beside him in the Nissan 4×4 was Maggot. He had travelled with Janov to Turkmenistan, leaving behind the good life in England for a while. He hoped it would only be temporary, but deep inside his instincts told him it was for good.

With Janov were two men; his permanent minders. The four of them were on their way to Maymaneh, a small town about fifty miles inland from the border. It was one of Janov's safest towns, simply because of its closeness to the Turkmenistan border and the fact that the opium fields like the war did little to interfere with the lives of the local Afghani people.

They reached Maymaneh in time for lunch, and Janov's driver pulled up at a small hotel. He killed the engine and the four men climbed out and went into the hotel for a meal. Janov wasn't keen to stay too long, so within the hour they were on their way again, driving down the single carriageway that divided the town.

On the way to the airfield they passed a white armoured scout car with a Finnish emblem emblazoned on the side. It was part of the United Nations security force. The Finns were there alongside their Norwegian counterparts. Janov almost felt sorry for the poor sods who had to serve in such a godforsaken wilderness.

They reached the airfield and left the car in a parking lot. Then they walked through to the airport waiting room and took a seat while one of Janov's men went in search of their flight crew. Because they were flying internally, there were no formalities to complete other than logging a flight plan and a passenger list.

While they were waiting for the formalities to be concluded, Janov received a text on his mobile phone. He read the message and grunted in satisfaction. He now knew where Abdul was heading.

Within thirty minutes of arriving at Maymaneh airfield, Janov, his two minders and Maggot were on their way to Kabul and a final show-down.

Susan was sitting in an armchair in her hotel room reading a book. The television was tuned into Sky News, but the sound was off. It was early evening and Susan was more or less at the end of her personal quest to find her brother. She had spoken to the editors of the three newspapers she had chosen at random from the internet, and received much the same condescending attention she had experienced at the British Embassy. Sure, there would be press coverage, but with so much happening, so many people being killed and injured by suicide bombers and roadside bombs ... Blah, blah.

She had no real idea what to do next. Perhaps she would go up to the mission at Jalalabad, but wondered if there was anything to be gained by doing that. It might bring her closer to her brother, but it was almost a year now since the attack. She gave up the thought and stared sight-lessly at the page of her book. Then she got up, threw the book on her bed and wondered if she should ring Marcus and suggest they share a drink downstairs in the hotel bar.

Just then there was a knock at the door. For a moment she wondered if it was Marcus. Perhaps he had come up with the same idea. She felt a little excited and hurried across to the door and opened it.

Ali Seema, the interpreter, was standing there with Marcus. Seema bowed his head a little.

'Miss Ellis, please forgive this intrusion, but I would like you both to come with me please.'

'What on earth for?' she asked.

He glanced left and right along the corridor. 'It will be in your interest to come with me. Please,' he added solemnly.

Susan felt nervous and didn't know quite what she should do.

'Is this about David?'

He dipped his head again. 'Please.' He even held out his hand to her.

She hesitated for a moment, then thought about the reason she was there.

'Give me five minutes,' she told him. 'I will meet you downstairs.'

'Thank you.' He glanced at Marcus. 'We will wait outside the front of the hotel.'

He turned and walked away as Susan closed the door.

She went across to the small chest of drawers that graced one wall and opened the top drawer. She took out her handbag and from that she pulled out the mobile phone Cavendish had given her. His instructions were quite explicit; any change in circumstances, any change in plan, or anything she might be concerned about, she was to phone or text.

Susan dialled the number she had been given and waited for the connection. When it came she left the simple message explaining that she was going out of the hotel with Marcus and their interpreter, Ali Seema. She switched off the phone, put it back in her handbag and spent the next five minutes getting ready to go out.

She walked past reception and tossed her key on to the counter, then walked out through the front doors of the hotel. Ali Seema was there with Marcus. He was leaning up against the wall smoking a cigarette. As soon as he saw her, he pushed himself upright and threw his cigarette on to the ground. Then he waved his hand at somebody and stood there as Susan walked up to him. She stopped and waited for him to speak, but just then a car pulled up alongside them. Seema hurried forward and opened the door.

'Please,' he said, with urgency in his voice. 'Get in, quickly.'

Marcus and Susan exchanged glances and climbed into an old, Indian Tata saloon car that had seen better days.

Seema slammed the door shut and climbed in beside the driver. Suddenly the engine roared into life and the battered old car sped away from the hotel and disappeared into the teeming streets of Kabul.

NINETEEN

'WHERE ARE WE going?' Marcus asked, after a brief silence.

'I am taking you to see someone who can help you find your brother,' Seema told him.

'David?' Susan's voice sounded harsh and breathless, gushing out of her mouth.

Seema nodded. 'Yes, but please, we must be cautious.' He turned round and faced them. 'There could be many problems ahead.'

Susan shook her head gently. 'Why are we acting like fugitives?' she asked.

He smiled. It was almost condescending. The car lurched in the darkness and threw her sideways into Marcus's arms. He pushed her gently upright as the driver apologized after letting out a stream of Afghani abuse.

'There are always eyes and ears around us here in Kabul,' he explained. 'It isn't always sensible let your adversaries know what you are doing.' He held his hand out, palm upwards. 'Someone is always listening. Once they knew you were in Kabul to look for your brother, you became valuable to certain members of our society.'

'I can't believe we are that valuable,' Marcus put in. 'We are just two civilians who have no allegiance to anyone except David Ellis.'

'It's a point of view,' Seema told him, 'but a peculiarly British one. Just trust me and try to relax.'

Susan tried to relax a little but was still not sure whether to trust him.

'Who are these people who may know about David?' she asked, trying to keep the tone of demanding inquisition out of her voice.

'I cannot say,' he replied. 'But you will meet them soon.'

Susan glanced out of the window, peering into the darkness. 'Where are we going then?'

'We are going where you will find your answers,' he replied, cryptically.

As they journeyed on, conversation became limited until it eventually stopped. Marcus and Susan were left with their own thoughts, each one feeling a little apprehensive. Seema would say something from time to time, but to the driver and always in Farsi. The two men would chuckle and this display of ease between them actually unsettled Susan. Marcus didn't seem the least bit affected by it, although Susan did notice that he was not his usual lively self.

She felt the car slow until it eventually stopped. Seema turned round and looked at them over his shoulder. He told them they would have to wait a few minutes. Then he got out of the car and disappeared in the darkness.

Five minutes later he was back. He looked satisfied and Susan wondered if he had used the time for a comfort stop. She asked him.

'Telephone,' he told her. 'I used the public phone in that hotel,' he said pointing out of the window. 'Safer.'

'Who were you phoning?' Marcus asked him.

'The mission,' he answered, and tapped the driver on the shoulder, barking out something unpronounceable. 'We are going there now.'

Suddenly Susan felt incredibly nervous. The mention of the mission, where David had almost died was like a shock to her system. She had never in her wildest dreams, or her nightmares, thought she would ever walk over the ground where David had almost been murdered. She thought of the poor woman, Shakira, and David's admitted love for her. It made her feel so sad. Her nervousness trickled through her like a growing storm and she hoped she would be brave enough to face whatever was to come.

About half an hour later the driver pulled up outside the mission and switched off the engine. Susan and Marcus waited to be told that they could get out before opening the door. Seema beckoned to them as he slid from the front seat and stepped out into the moonlight. Susan got out her side and looked around her. Across the other side of the car she could see Marcus doing the same.

All Susan could clearly see was the mission building in front of her. It was a single storey, bungalow style. Behind it, dark and brooding, was the mountain that dwarfed the building. The outline of the hills continued; picked out faintly by the moonlight. There was little definition to anything because of the darkness.

The silence was broken only by the clicking sound of the hot engine of the battered Tata and the sound of Ali Seema's sandals on the gravel as he walked up to the main entrance. Susan turned around slowly, full circle, trying to get some sense of the solitude that wrapped itself around the place. Marcus walked over and slipped his arm around her shoulder.

'Soon,' he whispered. 'Soon we'll know the truth.'

Cavendish had enjoyed an evening meal and splendid company in the officers' mess, one that was bereft of the glamour and grandeur of some of the more eloquent messes he had been in during his years in security. He had enjoyed a few glasses of Jim Beam Bourbon Whiskey over ice and felt the consequences of indulging his passion; the result being a little awkwardness when he stood.

Cavendish had been dining with the Lieutenant McCain, and had been joined later by a couple of officers from one of the operational squadrons. Talk had been informative but strictly legit; no secrets being divulged, and much of it humorous anecdotes of past misdemeanours and also thoughts on how the war in Afghanistan was progressing.

It was close to midnight when Cavendish took his leave of the company and decided to take some fresh air before turning in for the night. He made sure he kept to the domestic area, keeping away from the technical site, which included the airfield and perimeters. He had been warned that it wasn't unusual for the insurgents to send in some hopeful shots, both of gunfire and RPGs, rocket propelled grenades. It was all more of a nuisance factor than serious threat, but Cavendish heeded the warnings and kept his walk in the safe area.

He had his flak jacket with him; something he had been advised to wear at all times. So his evening stroll was only made supposedly safer by the addition of the jacket; something he felt was totally unnecessary. But he had it on, loosely fitted and with the collar up.

He had reached a particularly quiet area when he heard footsteps behind him. He stopped and turned round, expecting to see someone like himself, either out walking or perhaps returning from a social gathering at one of the on-base bars.

It was then he saw someone walking quickly towards him. In the darkness it looked like he was wearing combat fatigues. He then saw the upraised arm. It came swinging down and something smacked him on the side of the head.

Cavendish yelled out in pain and collapsed, striking his head on the ground. As he began to fade into unconsciousness he was vaguely aware of someone kicking him and then the sound of footsteps running away.

Ali Seema came out of the front door of the mission and walked across the gravel to where Susan and Marcus were waiting. When he reached them he pointed back towards the building and told them that they could go in.

'Aren't you coming with us?' Marcus asked him.

Seema shook his head. 'No, my work is done here. It would not be right for me to be here when contact is made.'

'Why ever not?' Marcus asked him.

The interpreter looked at Marcus rather sheepishly. 'My job was to bring you here; nothing else.' He took a step towards the car. 'I must go now.'

Marcus grabbed his arm. 'No, Seema, you're not walking away just like that.'

Seema began to struggle but Marcus wouldn't let him go. 'You're not going anywhere, Seema. There's no way we are walking into that building without you. Do you understand?'

Seema's attitude was one of belligerence, but against the powerful grip that Marcus had on him, his belligerence was wasted.

'Very well,' he said at last, 'I will go back in there with you.'

Marcus relaxed his grip and let the man go. He said nothing but nodded his head towards the building. Seema took the hint and led them in.

Susan fell into step beside Marcus. She was extremely nervous now and that little show of belligerence from Ali Seema did little to help her nerves. She knew that Marcus would probably sense it. Her breathing sounded laboured, but in fact she was beginning to hyperventilate. Seema's attitude had scared her and she wondered what they might find once they stepped inside.

They walked in through the double doors, which creaked as Seema pushed them open. Immediately in front of them was a corridor which ran right and left the entire length of the building. Seema turned right and took them a few steps along the corridor before stopping and opening a door which they found led into an office.

It was simply furnished. A large old desk dominated the room. Behind it was a chair. On the walls were posters of various descriptions, all in Farsi. There was a calendar which would have made no sense to a European, plus a planning schedule, the kind of which would be found in most modern offices.

A single light bulb hung from the ceiling with no benefit of a lamp-shade. And up against one wall were a couple of chairs that had seen better days. The floor was plain wood, and lodged against the open window was an old air-conditioning unit. Marcus wondered if it ever worked.

Standing beside the unit, her arms folded, was a nun. She tipped her head in greeting and asked them, in English, to sit down. Then she looked beyond Marcus and Susan to Ali Seema and nodded. The inter-preter bowed his head, said a few *salaams* and backed out of the office.

Marcus and Susan did as they had been asked and sat down. Meanwhile the nun took her place in the chair behind the desk. They heard the car engine start up and listened as the Tata drove away, the sound of its engine fading into the night.

Then they heard something else; the sound of footsteps on the gravel outside, then the creaking of the main door as it swung open. The foot-steps sounded again in the corridor outside the office. Suddenly the door opened and an Arab walked in. Marcus and Susan both gasped in surprise; it was the driver of the Tata.

'Good evening,' he said to them in passable English. 'I'm sorry for the ...' – he stumbled on the word for a moment – 'how do you say, tricks? But I have to be careful.' He bowed his head. 'Please allow me to intro-duce myself; I am Abdul Khaliq.'

Cavendish woke up, his head throbbing like mad. He opened his eyes and looked around him. He could see white walls and smell disinfec-tant and soap. The ache in his head reminded him that he had been drinking Jim Beam, but there was something else he couldn't quite put his finger on.

He lifted his head off the pillow and looked around the room. It was like a private room in a hospital, but without the personal touches he would have associated with such a place. There was a bell cord beside his bed which he pulled. A nurse appeared. She was wearing a white coat over army fatigues. She lifted Cavendish's arm and checked his pulse, then put his arm down and put her fingers to her lips.

'Back in a while,' she told him, and left.

The nurse came back with a doctor. He also was wearing camouflage fatigues beneath a white coat. He had the traditional stethoscope hanging round his neck.

'Good morning, sir,' he said cheerfully. 'How are you feeling?'

Cavendish couldn't tell him the truth, which was that he didn't want to give the doctor a reason to keep him there.

'I'm fine,' he lied. 'Too much to drink, I guess.'

The doctor smiled and pulled a pen torch from his top pocket. He shone it in Cavendish's eyes.

'You fell over and banged your head, they tell me.' He peered closely at Cavendish's eyes. 'But these tell me something different,' he muttered.

'What, my eyes?'

The doctor laughed. 'No, these,' he said, and touched Cavendish on the side of the neck. The doctor's touch made him yelp, pulling his head away.

'It looks like something hit you on the side of the neck.' The doctor was moving his head around as he spoke, carefully examining the bruising. 'I think the collar of your flak jacket saved you. Wonderful things, flak jackets.'

He straightened and put his torch away. Then he finished examining Cavendish and told him he could go whenever he felt able.

Cavendish was mightily pleased; eager to get out of the base hospital and speak to Lieutenant McCain. He was also curious to find out who the man was he saw coming out of the headquarters building. The bang on the side of the head hadn't exactly cleared it, but neither had it diminished his sense of urgency nor his sense of intrigue. Something was nagging away at him and he needed to find out what it was.

And quickly.

Khaliq sat facing them across the desk. The nun had left the room after asking them all if they wanted something to eat or drink. They settled for water which the nun brought in. She had put the jug and three glasses on the desk before leaving.

'Why the subterfuge then?' Marcus asked him. 'Why couldn't you have come up to the hotel room, avoid all this drama?'

Abdul studied him with the air of someone who feels sympathy for one who understands so little. 'We are at risk even now,' he explained. 'If I had approached you openly in Kabul, I would never have left the hotel. And nor would you.'

Susan twitched at that last statement. She tried to keep thinking of David and not let her nerves get the better of her.

'What can you tell me about my brother?' she asked Abdul. 'Is he OK?'

Abdul smiled at her, his teeth flashing brilliantly white beneath his beard. 'I can promise you he is alive and he is well.'

'Why didn't you bring him here?' Marcus asked him.

Abdul glanced across at Marcus knowing that he still did not understand. 'He is too important to be brought here and handed over to you two.' He held both his arms forward across the desk, his hands open. 'Surely you can understand that?'

Marcus could see the logic; anybody seriously opposed to Khaliq would have no problems wiping them all out. The sense of danger, of risk, was beginning to stir something in Marcus; he was beginning to feel that strange sense of displeasure that often surged through him whenever anyone spoiled his day. He wanted David Ellis free, back home with Susan, unhindered by the warlords and the drug barons, and he was beginning to get a little tired of all this posturing he was witnessing from Khaliq.

'So when are you going to take us to see him? I presume you are, Abdul,' he said. 'Or is this just a bloody game to you?'

Susan turned sharply. 'Marcus!'

Marcus stared at her with hard eyes. There was steel in them which Susan recognized and she began to wonder if Marcus might blow it for them all because of his latent temper.

'I'm sure he will take us to David in good time,' she insisted, trying to bring a calming influence to bear. She looked across at Abdul. 'Well, will you take us to see my brother?' she asked.

Abdul sat forward, his manner changing a little; it was more business like. 'The reason you are here is to get your brother released, is that right?' Susan nodded. 'And you are here because you have been sent by your government, is that correct also?'

Susan hadn't been given any real mandate from Cavendish other than to keep him informed of developments over the phone.

'Yes, but I'm not sure I have any real authority,' she replied weakly.

'Then let me explain something to you.' He paused and cleared his throat. 'The war here in Afghanistan cannot be won by the Americans or the British. The Americans do not like our president; they see him as weak and ineffective. And when our so-called democratic elections come in the summer, they expect him to be re-elected; in which case they plan to install someone in the government who will have the real power. He will be pro-American. He will be the top man.'

'What's your point?' Marcus asked him.

Abdul frowned. 'He will be a CIA man. He will run the country, and he will want complete control of the poppy fields.'

'So men like you will be an obstacle to the Americans, is that it?'

He nodded. 'To the CIA. And even if I withdrew, they would find me and kill me. In fact, they are trying now.'

'And that is why you want our help?' Susan asked incredulously.

'Yes!' He slapped his hand on the table making Susan jump. 'So you can tell your government that I will exchange your brother for my freedom. I want political asylum.'

TWENTY

S USAN CAREFULLY COMPOSED the text message using cryptic language that she hoped Cavendish would understand. When she was satisfied that she had written the text out correctly on a scrap of paper, she punched the letters into her mobile phone and held her finger over the 'send' button.

'You promise we will see David?' she asked Abdul again.

He nodded, but said nothing. Marcus thought the man looked quite nervous.

'It's done,' Susan said, breathing out sharply and lifting her finger off the key. She looked guardedly at Marcus. 'All we can do now is wait.'

Abdul leaned on the desk and pushed himself upright, shoving the chair back with his legs. It scraped noisily on the bare floor.

'When we receive the reply I want, I will take you to see your brother.' He walked round from behind the desk. 'Now we must see about getting some sleep.'

He left Marcus and Susan sitting together in the room. They said nothing for a while. Marcus yawned which made Susan do the same thing. They were both very tired. It was past midnight and the talking had gone on for such a long time, neither of them had been aware of their tiredness creeping up on them.

When Abdul came back he motioned them to follow him. He took them both along the corridor to an open door. He stood there and pointed into the room.

'You will sleep here,' he told them. 'Keep your door shut. If you need anything urgently, there is a nun sleeping in that room there.' He pointed along the corridor to a closed door.

'Where will you be sleeping?' Marcus asked.

He smiled. 'I won't be far away.' He put his hands together in an attitude of prayer and bowed his head. 'May the one, true God be with us all tonight. *Salaam.*'

When he had gone, Susan and Marcus looked around the room. It was sparsely furnished. There was a single bed and a very small table on which a jug and bowl were standing. It looked like the room was almost certainly intended for a nun because of the crucifix tacked to the wall above the bed and the complete lack of character in the room.

They exchanged glances. Susan could see the unasked question in Marcus's face and put her hand on his arm.

'Marcus,' she said softly, a tremor in her voice. 'Please don't misunderstand me, but I don't want to be left alone tonight.'

He shook his head. 'You won't be; I'll be sleeping on the floor beside you,' he told her.

Susan gripped his hand tightly. 'No, Marcus, you don't understand. I'm scared and I need you to be close.'

She then pulled Marcus towards the bed and lay on it. She looked up at him then turned to face the wall. He lay full length behind her, then put his arm around her and slipped his hand beneath her blouse. He felt her stiffen and put her hand over his. Then she relaxed and he moved his hand over her breast and squeezed it gently.

Susan sighed and breathed in deeply. For a brief moment, both of them thought of nothing else but each other. But the truth was, neither of them felt safe.

Cavendish watched the military policeman leave his room with Lieutenant McCain. They had questioned him about the unprovoked attack the previous evening, but offered no clues as to why it had taken place. The MP suggested lamely that because of the number of people on the base, it was possible that one or two criminal elements might have been attempting to mug him and been scared off.

Cavendish was quite happy to go along with that, but didn't believe it for one minute. He said nothing of his fears to either of them, and they were happy to record the incident as an unprovoked attack by person or persons unknown.

It was as they were leaving the room that he found himself staring at the back of the MP. The uniform the man was wearing was common enough, but it took Cavendish's mind back to the attack on Marcus and the two policemen at the bonded warehouse at Feltwell. It wasn't the police uniform so much as the events and the personnel surrounding it. Everybody seemed to get in on the act afterwards, including the CIA.

And that was when it struck him: like the sudden realization that he had interpreted a vital clue in a complicated crossword puzzle. Except that this was no crossword; it was a deadly game of murder.

The civilian he had seen coming out of the main entrance of the base headquarters with an American officer was Randy Hudson, the expelled CIA station chief in England.

Cavendish's heart sank as it dawned on him that The Chapter must have very powerful allies within the military to be able to send Hudson out to Afghanistan, without any sanctions, where he would be at the heart of the sinister work the organization carried out.

Hudson should have been languishing in a police cell in America right now, awaiting charges of conspiracy, drugs and arms smuggling, and most other crimes that would send him to the electric chair, or at least many years on death row hoping he would beat the death penalty.

Hudson must have seen him; it was the only explanation Cavendish could think of. He was attacked last night to stop him; nothing else. He knew then that his own life was in jeopardy if Hudson learned that he had not succumbed to the attack, but was in fact recovering in the base hospital.

He threw the covers from his bed and swung his legs round, sitting up at the same time. He was wearing a standard issue hospital gown, which barely covered his backside as he stood up and went in search of his clothes.

As he reached into the slim tall locker beside his bed, he heard his mobile phone ringing and vibrating. He put his hands into the pocket of his trousers which were hanging up and pulled it out. A text message had come through from MI6 in London. The message had been sent in 'clear', so Cavendish read the actual letters that Susan had entered; there was no code.

Five minutes later Cavendish walked out of the base hospital knowing that the next phase of the game had shifted; it had now become critical.

*

Shortly after Cavendish had read the text message from Susan, the CIA liaison officer at Khost base punched in a selection of numbers on his desk phone. He only waited a few seconds when he heard the voice of Randolph Hudson on the line.

'Sir, I have something I think you will want to see.' He put the phone down without waiting for a reply. Five minutes later Randy Hudson walked into the liaison officer's room.

'We picked up a transmission,' the young official told him. 'It's from somewhere in Afghanistan to MI6 in London. We listen in on their Mercury 6 satellite, sir,' he reminded Hudson. 'The message wasn't coded but transmitted in clear. Headquarters at Langley interpreted the message and sent an encrypted version here.' He picked up a sheet of notepaper. 'I've written the message down, sir.' He passed it to Hudson.

The CIA man read the message nodded briefly and thanked the young CIA official. 'Time to kick ass,' he said, and left the room.

Milan Janov was watching an Arab channel on the hotel room TV when the phone rang. It was Hudson. He told Janov that his informer, an interpreter who was paid by the CIA, had told him where Abdul was heading and he passed the details on.

Janov's face broke out into a broad grin as he put the phone down. He switched off the TV and picked up his leather jacket from the foot of the bed. Then he went to the room next door to his and knocked gently on the door.

'Rafiq, it's me, Milan!'

Maggot opened the door and let him in. Janov closed the door behind him.

'I know where Abdul is going; north from here, about twenty miles.'

Maggot looked surprised. 'That was quick.'

It should have come as no surprise to Maggot that Janov had picked up the information quickly; there were that many spies in Afghanistan and people in other people's pockets that it was amazing that they didn't publish daily bulletins in the local press concerning the whereabouts of people.

'I'll go and pick up a hire car now.' He looked at his watch. 'I'll meet you down in the lobby in one hour.'

'What about manpower?'

Janov shook his head. 'No extra men this time; just you and me. It's better that way.' He put his hand on Maggot's shoulder. 'We will make our way to Charika and then, after dark, we go to where he is hiding and, when they are sleeping, we will finish Abdul Khaliq and his friends.'

Cavendish hurried over to base headquarters and called in at the base security office. He asked to see McCain. Cavendish hadn't known the head of security very long, less than forty-eight hours in fact, but he was about to put a lot of trust and faith in his own instincts and tell Lieutenant McCain the reason why he had paid an unexpected visit to Afghanistan.

Brad McCain was a ruddy-looking character, reaching his mid-forties and wearing well in the manner of many Americans in the armed forces. He hailed from Kentucky and had told Cavendish many yarns the previous evening about the state, the horses and the whiskey during their encounter. Cavendish had taken to him quite quickly.

'Come in, Sir Giles. Have a seat.' McCain had risen from his chair and was pointing to the single chair facing his desk.

Cavendish sat down. 'Please call me Giles,' he said. 'It is so less formal.'

McCain smiled and threw a wink at him. 'Anything you say, Giles.' He sat down. 'Now, what can I do for you?'

'Have you ever heard of The Chapter of Mercy?' Cavendish began.

McCain's expression changed instantly. Gone was the ruddy, smiling, hail-fellow-well-met countenance, replaced by one of caution. He said nothing, just nodded his head.

Cavendish tried to read something in the man's face, but still had to go with his instincts. 'They run a mission here in Afghanistan for deprived children. They also operate in Pakistan and India. They do terrific work for the underprivileged and deprived kids in those countries.'

McCain picked up a paper knife and began tapping out a gentle tattoo on his desk top. He looked thoughtful for a while. Then he nodded and told Cavendish that he knew of The Chapter of Mercy.

'And did you know that they smuggle drugs out of the country and into Europe?

'I have heard the rumour,' McCain admitted.

'And did you know that they smuggle arms back into Afghanistan to keep the armed *jihad* going?'

McCain's eyes narrowed and a frown dived from his forehead into deep creases like furrows across his eyebrows.

'Can you substantiate this?' he asked.

Cavendish shrugged and gestured with his hands. 'Of course not, but how often have you, as a security man, known facts that you couldn't prove either because of lack of evidence, or because you were under strict orders from your superiors to keep your mouth shut?'

McCain nodded his head and a smile of recognition wandered across his face. He hunched forward, lifting his head slightly.

'Why don't you just come right out with it, Giles? Make it so much easier.'

'Do you know Randy Hudson, the CIA chief who was in England until a week ago?'

McCain tilted his head slightly and looked up as though he was trying to recall something lodged somewhere in his brain. He snapped his fingers and pointed at Cavendish with the paper knife.

'Randy Hudson; flew in a couple of days ago. Yeah, that's the guy. Why, what's he done?'

So Cavendish told him; as much as he dared. When he had finished, McCain whistled softly through his teeth. He got up from his desk, put the paper knife down and went over to a water cooler. He filled a plastic cup from it, holding it towards Cavendish as an offering. Cavendish shook his head.

What's your next question?' he asked, lifting his jaw.

'I think he had something to do with the attack on me last night,' Cavendish told him. 'I saw him coming out of this building with an officer in uniform. I want to know if they were with you and who the officer was.'

McCain pushed himself away from the water cooler and went back to his desk. He tossed the empty cup into his waste basket and sat down.

'I could tell you to go to hell,' McCain told him.

Cavendish agreed, and deep down he knew this would be the point at which his *raison d'être* would either fail or succeed.

'But you won't, will you?' he put to McCain carefully.

McCain shook his head and gave a short, snuffling laugh. 'I hate those cocky bastards,' he said with venom. 'They act like they're top guys; look down on us. Probably call us all grunts, I shouldn't wonder.' He wrung his hands together, working the knuckles into each palm.

'What's your call on this then, Sir Giles?' he asked suddenly, forgetting Cavendish's suggestion that he dropped the formality. 'You wanna get even with him because you got socked over the head?'

Cavendish shook his head. 'No. What I want to do is bring some signal traffic through your resources, and I don't want any CIA officer looking in on it. I also want to know the names of any officers that Hudson might be friendly with.'

'The signal traffic's not a problem; I can give you clearance on that effective immediately. But collecting names?' He shook his head vigorously. 'The CO would have my balls if he thought I was going round collecting names.'

Cavendish put his hand up. 'OK, Lieutenant, sorry I asked.'

McCain opened a drawer in his desk and pulled out a folder. He extracted a small form from it and passed it across the desk to Cavendish.

'Just jot your particulars on there. It will be needed for your clearance once I've signed it.'

Cavendish took the form and filled in the blank spaces. Then he signed it and handed it back to McCain who countersigned it.

'Give me one hour and I'll take you over to the ops room; you can send your signal then.'

Cavendish got up and shook McCain's hand.

'Thank you, Lieutenant. One hour.'

'By the way,' McCain said to him, as he was making his way to the door, 'the guy who was with Hudson? His name is Berry. Lieutenant Chuck Berry; posted in recently. He was on transports, the Hercs, but he had a problem and had to be medically downgraded for a while, so he's been assigned to the MQ-9 Reaper Flight. I'll see you in one hour.'

TWENTY-ONE

I T WAS LATE afternoon as Abdul pulled off the main highway north of Charika and brought the Landcruiser rumbling down on to a dirt road. They were immediately surrounded in a cloud of dust as the wheels bit into the dry sandy rock that had seen the passage of weather and traffic over many years and had crumbled beneath the onslaught. The hills rose up on either side of the road, but soon those on the east side began to lose their height against the mountains that were rising up in the west.

The green valley they were driving into began to lose its colour as the light faded. Although they passed several dwellings, most of them looked unoccupied. Marcus wondered idly how much of that was to do with the war, and how much was to do with the locals going off in search of work in the towns and cities.

Their journey up to Charika had been uneventful. It had taken them about five hours. There hadn't been much talking; mainly small talk when they did open their mouths. From time to time they passed small convoys of army trucks and armed vehicles. Most of them were American. Occasionally they would see a British convoy, but because they were not travelling through the British Zone, they didn't expect to come across many.

Susan had been thinking of her brother more and more as the journey progressed. Abdul had assured her that her brother was alive and well, and would be released to her as soon as he had received instructions from the British when and where they could complete the handover – providing the guarantees had been put in place.

Marcus had asked him why he could even contemplate leaving

Afghanistan and seeking political asylum in England when he had such a powerbase in this country. Abdul had explained that he was under threat from what he called 'discontents' in his province, and that he believed his life was forfeit because of the increasing pressure from the American and British presence in Afghanistan.

He didn't elaborate, but he did believe the Americans had been actively trying to kill him. And he also believed that Janov was jostling for position and had the Americans on his side. For Abdul that was too powerful an opposition; asylum in Britain was the only way out.

Suddenly he spun the wheel of the Landcruiser and it tilted over as he drove on to a rutted track. Susan clung to Marcus as the Landcruiser bucked and rolled over the uneven ground. After what seemed like an eternity, Abdul pulled into a yard and up alongside a plain wall, about two metres high. The rudimentary brickwork could be plainly seen even in the half light.

The dust swept past them in a cloud as Abdul stepped on the brakes and brought the Landcruiser to a halt. He killed the engine and got out of the car. Then he turned to Susan and Marcus and beckoned them to follow him.

Susan now felt extremely nervous and excited. She knew she was about to see her brother, the man she believed long ago to be dead. And, as she followed Abdul through the open gateway, she prayed that this would not be a false dawn for her or for David.

There was a light burning inside the single-storey dwelling. No sound could be heard save for the occasional sound of an animal somewhere behind the house. Abdul walked up to the front door and rattled his fist on it noisily, calling out something in Farsi.

The door was opened almost immediately by one of his lieutenants. They greeted each other warmly. The man stepped back and let the three of them pass through the door. They then followed him in to a room which was sparsely furnished. Abdul asked them to sit down. Marcus sat on an old wooden chair, leaving the one remaining chair that had a cushion for Susan. She sat on it, rigid and bolt upright. Abdul left the room saying nothing. Two minutes later he returned with a stranger.

The man was dressed in traditional dress: a *pakol* hat and *chapan* jacket over baggy pantaloons. He had a full beard that showed some grey. His eyebrows were dark and shaggy and seemed to merge with the deep furrows across his brow. Beneath those eyebrows were eyes of piercing blue, and just to the side of one eye was a scar that climbed up beneath the hat.

Susan rose slowly to her feet.

'David?' she said softly, the question in her voice showed her disbelief. 'Is it really you?'

He stepped forward and held his arms out wide. 'Susan.' He couldn't get another word out, because the tears burst from his eyes and his voice choked on his sobs.

Susan ran across the room and threw herself at him, sobbing wildly. 'David! David!'

Marcus stood up. What he was witnessing, no one would ever have believed possible. But he saw it with his own eyes – Susan and David reunited. What was it, he wondered had brought Susan this far, her own dogged perseverance? Chance encounters?

He thought back to his office in Oliver's Yard in London and the grubby letter she had with her. Now the writer of that horrifying passage was standing in front of them, alive and well. But not yet free.

Susan stepped back from her brother's embrace. She put her hand to his face and wiped his tears with her thumb, brushing them aside like a doting mother.

'Oh David, what have they done to you?'

He took hold of her hand and held on to it. 'I never thought I would live to see this day.' He looked over at Abdul. 'He has looked after me well because I was worth something to him.' He looked back at her. 'Believe me, I'm fine. All I need is to get home to England and pick up my life again.'

Abdul stepped forward and separated the two of them. 'Time for talking later; now we must eat. Tomorrow I want to know what your government intends to do.'

Susan felt a ripple of fear in her stomach. She had absolutely no authority whatsoever to negotiate David's release on her government's behalf, and she had no idea how Abdul would react to that. She looked at David and thought how dreadful it would be if she was unable to persuade him to release her brother.

Susan spent the next hour sick to the stomach. She tried to eat the food put before her, but her appetite had disappeared. David was in very high spirits, naturally, and kept her and Marcus entertained, if that was the right word, with details of his captivity. He never mentioned Shakira once.

But one thing Susan did notice, despite her fretful condition, was that Marcus was unusually quiet. Whenever he responded to something David had said, it was monosyllabic. And, when David told them something funny, she thought that Marcus's laugh was affected. She knew how she herself felt, but had a suspicion that Marcus's thoughts were not in the room but elsewhere. It was as if he was planning something.

After the evening meal, Abdul allowed Susan and David to spend a little more time together before taking him away and shackling him in one of the rooms in the house. Then he returned and showed Marcus and Susan where they would be sleeping.

Marcus couldn't sleep; he daren't sleep because of what he was planning. He knew that Susan would not be able to negotiate her brother's release simply because she had sent a text message to Cavendish; but, no, it was much more involved than that.

His best guess was that someone in the government would ask to meet Abdul on neutral ground, which was hardly likely in Afghanistan. Abdul would sense duplicity in that because that was the way governments played the rules. This would antagonize him and he would more than likely take Susan and himself as hostages and use the three of them, David included, as bargaining chips.

He thought about Cavendish and realized the man had sent them into the lion's den deliberately and was probably relying on some inspiration from Marcus. Perhaps he thought that David would help, but then Cavendish had no idea how fit and strong his former agent was.

The more he thought about it, the more Marcus realized that their lives were almost certainly forfeit unless he could think of something. And it was these thoughts that had been running through his mind the moment he had seen David. And the more he thought about what would probably happen, the angrier he became.

He looked at his watch and could see from the luminous dial that it was almost four o'clock in the morning. Soon the dawn light would begin to fill the house. He hoped everybody in the house would be asleep, although he guessed that Abdul would have posted a guard. It surprised him that he didn't have a small army with him, but then if Abdul was expecting to be welcomed into the arms of the British

Government, he probably would not have wanted his loyal band of thugs watching.

Marcus got out of bed and tiptoed to the door. He opened it carefully, surprised that it was not locked, and peered out along the corridor that ran the length of the house. He saw a shadowy figure walking towards the short passage that led to the front doors of the house. Marcus had no idea who it was.

He slipped quietly out of the room and closed the door behind him, then went carefully down to the corner of the short passage. Peering round the corner he saw the figure closing the front door. From his body language, he was closing it like a thief would when entering somebody's house and didn't want to be heard.

As the figure disappeared from view, Marcus walked quickly up to the door and edged it open. He looked through the narrow gap and could see the front yard bathed in the half light between night and dawn. He could see one of Abdul's men, Habib, apparently asleep on a log, judging from his crumpled shape.

What followed next, Marcus could hardly believe. The figure he had watched leaving the house was Kareem. He suddenly thrust something into Habib's neck. Then he wrapped his arm around the man's head and stabbed him again. He let him slump to the ground.

Marcus knew then that they were all in terrible danger and his earlier misgivings about Abdul had taken on a new twist; although he doubted that Abdul had anything to do with what he had just witnessed.

Marcus kept the door open just a little and saw Kareem drag Habib's body into the sparse undergrowth that struggled for survival alongside the track. As soon as he had disappeared, Marcus stepped out of the house and sprinted across the yard into the undergrowth and threw himself at Kareem.

It was over within seconds; Marcus had achieved the element of total surprise and knocked Kareem senseless with a chopping blow to the jawline beneath the ear. Kareem slumped on to the bloody body of Habib in a gruesome parody of endearing friendship.

Marcus stripped Kareem of his clothes and tied him to the body of his comrade in arms, shoving the tails of the man's shirt in his mouth and gagging him securely. All the while Marcus was doing this, he kept asking himself the same question; why had he killed Habib?

Marcus could only make guesses and ponder on the imponderable, but that would not get him any further. His next problem was how to tackle Abdul and secure David's and their own freedom. He had no idea where Abdul was sleeping. Nor did he have any idea where David was, but he intended finding him.

He went back into the house, holding the AK47 that he had picked up from the dead man across his chest, finger across the trigger guard and went back to his room. Once he was in there he knelt beside Susan's bed, kept the AK47 out of sight, and shook her awake. As she sat up he put his fingers to his own lips and one hand on hers.

'Get dressed,' he whispered. 'We're leaving and we're taking David with us.'

Susan caught on very quickly. She, too, had realized that they had been taken into a situation which was beyond them, and she guessed that Marcus was taking matters into his own hands. She nodded at him and scrambled out from under the single blanket that covered her.

Marcus took a little time to admire Susan's delightful curves before leaning over towards her and planting a big kiss on her lips. Then he went over to the door before she could say anything in protest.

Marcus reasoned that Abdul would have put David in the room furthest away from the front door. And he also believed that Abdul would probably sleep in the adjacent room. So he walked to the far end of the passageway and tried the door at the end.

It was locked.

He tried the door opposite. That, too, was locked.

It left him with no alternative. He crashed his foot against the first door, bringing it hard against the lock. The door was old and weak; it gave instantly, opening with a resounding crash as it swung back and hit the wall.

Marcus ran into the room. It was empty.

He turned and lashed out at the other door which gave in, too. As he rushed into that room he saw Abdul reaching across to the chair beside his bed. Marcus could see his AK47 hanging across the back.

He kicked the chair away and shoved the barrel of his own weapon into Abdul's face.

'Don't move!'

Abdul froze. 'You're going to die,' he muttered, through gritted teeth.

Marcus slugged him. He slumped back on the bed, not quite

unconscious but certainly dazed. Marcus then knelt on top of him with one knee and held him like that until he had regained some of his senses.

'Now listen. I am going to stand up. You are going to tell me where the key is to David's chains. Then David, Susan and I are going to leave.'

Abdul shook his head. 'No, you are going to die.'

Marcus hit him again. 'Don't keep saying that. Where's the key?'

David was sitting up by this time. 'It's on the table over there,' he told Marcus, pointing to the table at the far side of the room.

Marcus picked up the weapon from the back of the fallen chair and passed it to David. 'I hope you know how to use this,' he said. He then went across to the table and retrieved the key. Within two minutes, David was standing beside Marcus. Both men were looking at Abdul.

'Well,' David said, a little breathlessly, 'you seem to have control of the situation. What do we do now?'

Marcus glanced quickly at David. 'What we do now is tie him up, and then we leave with Susan.'

'What about his men. Where are they?'

'One is dead and the other is tied up.'

'You?' David said, without finishing.

Marcus shook his head. 'No, one of Abdul's faithful minders killed the other one. I watched him do it.'

Abdul's expression clouded over when he heard what Marcus had said. He began to sit up but Marcus shoved him down again. 'Stay there!'

'Why are you lying about my men?' he asked.

Marcus shook his head. 'I'm not, believe me. One of your men is a traitor to you. He killed his friend. Watch him while I tie him up.'

Marcus spent a couple of minutes making sure Abdul could not move. Then he took the gun back from David. He was about to say something to him when suddenly there was a crash and a scream. Marcus spun round and made a quick sprint for the door.

He got out into the passageway and stopped. At the far end, now reasonably light because of the dawn beginning to seep into the sky, he could see Susan. She was struggling fiercely trying to free herself from the man who was holding her.

In the man's other hand was a gun. He lifted it and pointed it at Susan's head. Then he called down the corridor to Marcus.

'Put your gun down, or I will shoot her.'

Marcus felt his whole body slump in despair and disbelief. He knew the voice of the man who had just spoken to him.

It was Maggot.

TWENTY-TWO

CAVENDISH WAS STANDING in McCain's office. It was just after 4.30 in the morning and McCain had woken him by phone to tell him there was a signal waiting for him. Cavendish had asked that he be told the moment his signal came in, no matter what time of day or night it was. He apologized to McCain for inconveniencing him. McCain simply shrugged.

Cavendish read the coded transmission from MI6 in London. He thanked the security officer for his help and took his leave, hurrying back to his sparse accommodation where he could decode the message safely.

What Cavendish had asked his office in London for was a list of all the suspects, dead or alive that he had on the file marked 'Mission'. The list was not extensive but it included Grebo, Faulkner and James Purdy, the British cabinet minister. It also included the names of Rafiq Shah and Lieutenant Dale Berry.

Cavendish knew the last name as Chuck Berry, now on the Reaper flight, and the other as Maggot, long-time friend of Marcus.

He thought seriously about the association between Marcus and Shah, wondering if Marcus had indeed been pulling the wool over his eyes and was in fact working for The Chapter.

If that was the case, Cavendish believed his master plan was in tatters. All he had wanted was David Ellis's release because Ellis carried in his head an enormous amount of human intelligence, so vital to the security forces in Afghanistan and their battle against Al-Qaeda and the Taliban, that to lose it would seriously jeopardize the outcome of the war.

Ellis had worked undercover in Afghanistan for two years before coming to the mission where he believed his remit would end. What the young man could not have known then was that he had been compromised, and almost certainly by the CIA, which meant Hudson. And it was this that had led to his attempted murder, and the murder of Shakira, Cavendish's other agent.

All this confirmed to Cavendish something he had suspected for a long time: that the CIA were eavesdropping on British Intelligence Security Traffic for their own, duplicitous reasons. It meant that Hudson would almost certainly have known the names of his deeply embedded operators, and it was this that led to the attack on Shakira and David, but not for American security reasons but simply to protect the massive smuggling operation run by The Chapter.

He then thought about Abdul Khaliq's fortuitous kidnapping of Ellis from the hospital. Was it good fortune, luck, or did he know the real value of someone like Ellis? If that was the case then Cavendish owed Abdul something and could afford to cut him some slack; to listen carefully to his demands and find a way of accommodating some, if not all of them.

But rather than think of him as a very clever conspirator, he preferred to think of Marcus as a loose cannon, rather than a skilful agent working for Hudson's CIA. He had to because his reputation and possibly other people's lives depended on it.

He didn't need the list now; there were only two people he needed to watch very carefully, and he would need to take McCain into his confidence. So, before tearing the list up and flushing it down the toilet, Cavendish knew he would have to show it to the lieutenant.

He picked up the phone and dialled Lieutenant McCain's private quarters.

Randy Hudson, the CIA chief, received a call at the same time. Once again the CIA liaison officer had something for him. Hudson dressed and hurried across the domestic compound to the CIA office on the technical site. He had no vehicle so had to put up with a fairly lengthy walk. It was very early in the morning and, thankfully for Hudson, the air was just cool rather than freezing as it often was during the winter months.

He reached the CIA office and showed his pass to the MP at the door. There was a turnstile entrance which the security man opened electronically from within his pigeon-hole office.

Hudson hurried through and found the liaison officer waiting for him.

'I have these co-ordinates for you,' he told Hudson.

The CIA man took them from him, read them and nodded his head in obvious satisfaction.

'Are they there now?' he asked.

The liaison officer said they were. 'We picked them up on the Reaper. My guess is they'll be there a few hours yet.'

Hudson thanked him and folded the note on which had been written the co-ordinates to the farmhouse where Abdul had taken Marcus and Susan. He checked his watch; it was a little after five o'clock. He smiled ruefully; once the figures had been passed on to Chuck Berry the farmhouse would be utterly destroyed on the next Reaper pass. He only wanted to take out Abdul Khaliq, but the collateral damage, meaning whoever was with him, would be perfectly acceptable to a man like Hudson.

He stepped out of the building, a light spring in his step. The dawn light was bright enough now to pick out the silhouettes of the F15E Strike aircraft and the Apache gunships lined up on the pan. Ground crews were out early preparing the aircraft for the coming day's operations. Tractors towed generating sets out to each airplane, and ammunition trolleys were on their way to fill the jets and the gunships with their deadly loads.

None of this attracted Hudson's attention as he hurried over to Reaper flight, intent on a strike of his own. Within one hour he reasoned to himself, Khaliq would be dead.

Cavendish apologized to Lieutenant McCain for the second time that early morning and asked to see him again. McCain agreed, telling Cavendish that he hadn't bothered going back to bed. Cavendish grinned as he put the phone back in its cradle.

He came out of the accommodation block in which he was housed and once again hurried across to the base headquarters. McCain was there before him, which pleased Cavendish. He wasted no time in showing McCain the list with the two names on it that he had highlighted. One of them was Lieutenant Dale Berry.

'Is there any way in which you can put Lieutenant Berry out of action?' Cavendish asked the security officer.

McCain shook his head. 'We need every last damn sonofabitch here, fully fit and working, Sir Giles. Unless you can give me a cast-iron reason for excluding Lieutenant Berry from his work, I'll have to say no. Besides which the base commander would expect me to give a damn good reason.'

Cavendish acknowledged that; he didn't expect anything less, but it had been worth a try. He realized that McCain had no authority other than his police authority to prevent people from working, so it was a lame effort on Cavendish's part.

'You think Lieutenant Berry may be up to something over here?' McCain asked him.

Cavendish had no reason to think so. 'No,' he admitted, 'but I have an uneasy feeling now, knowing that Hudson has turned up here unexpectedly. Seeing the two of them on my list, and knowing that they are here gives me a gut feeling that it's no accident; no chance thing.'

McCain sighed deeply. He had the sense of Cavendish's worries, having often experienced them himself; that same, gut feeling; a policeman's 'nose' for something untoward. He could only see one way to settle the Englishman's nerves.

'What would you say if I arrange for you to speak to Berry, would that help?'

'Yes,' Cavendish replied demonstrably. 'I think that would be a great help.'

'You realize that the lieutenant has every right to refuse?' Cavendish nodded. 'And I can only ask, not demand?' Cavendish nodded again.

McCain picked up the phone. 'Reaper Flight, please.'

He waited. Cavendish looked on. Eventually McCain's body language altered.

'Lieutenant McCain here, Military Police. Could you let me know when Lieutenant Berry will be on duty next?'

Cavendish felt confident about McCain's way of dealing with things, and believed that he had found an excellent contact that he could use in the future. He wasn't about to tell McCain that though.

McCain was nodding his head, his eyebrows lifting in a show of surprise. He thanked whoever he was speaking to and put the phone down.

'Berry has been asked to cover for a sick officer. He's going on duty in five minutes.'

Cavendish felt a sliver of tension run through his body and he suddenly felt helpless. He had a feeling something was wrong, but he couldn't put his finger on it, and he couldn't expect McCain to understand.

But he was mistaken.

'You want to speak to Berry.' It wasn't a question; it was a statement. McCain had sensed the dilemma affecting Cavendish. 'But you don't know how you're gonna do it because this is our patch and not yours, correct?'

'I could not have put it better myself,' Cavendish admitted.

McCain stood up. 'In that case we'll go over to the Reaper Flight and have a chat with the man. We can say that you want to make an appointment to see him; something like that. OK?'

Cavendish knew now that he and McCain were on the same wavelength and McCain was going along with Cavendish's fears. The last thing McCain wanted was trouble on his patch.

He came round from behind the desk, businesslike.

'Come on,' he said. 'Let's go and talk with Lieutenant Berry.'

TWENTY-THREE

MARCUS STOOD STILL in the passageway. He put the AK47 on the floor and held his arms out to show his empty hands. He could feel his heart beating solidly in his chest, but it was not through fear; it was the adrenalin beginning to course through his veins.

Maggot took the pistol away from Susan's head and pointed it at Marcus. He was about to pull the trigger when he had to do a double take.

'Marcus?' He lowered the gun and peered along the length of the corridor. He let Susan go.

As soon as she was released, she ran towards Marcus who grabbed her and pulled her in close. Then he made a kissing motion on the side of Susan's face, but he didn't kiss her, instead he whispered, 'I don't think he knows that David is here. Don't say anything.'

'Marcus?' Maggot called out to him. 'What are you doing here?'

'Abdul is going to take us to see Susan's brother.' He hoped that might persuade Maggot to think that they were on their way somewhere else. 'What are you doing here, Maggot?'

'You don't want to know, Marcus. But I'm going to search all these rooms, including those down there, so you had better move away.'

Marcus said nothing and didn't move.

'Move out of the way, Marcus!' Maggot ordered.

'I'm going nowhere, Maggot,' Marcus insisted. 'Nowhere.'

Maggot smiled, his teeth showing white beneath his parted lips. 'Marcus, you don't want to do this.' He pushed his gun into his belt. 'You never could beat me, Marcus. And you are not going to this time.'

Marcus tensed and pushed Susan to one side. It was true what

Maggot had said: every time the two of them had fought in the gym, Marcus had never got the better of him. Never.

Maggot came towards him, walking slowly on the balls of his feet, a smile teasing the corners of his mouth. Marcus wriggled his fingers in a crab-like motion, trying to get the tension out of his hands.

Maggot came closer.

Marcus pushed Susan away, towards the empty room.

Maggot stopped a few feet from him.

'Make up your mind, Marcus. Concede now, or you'll never leave this building alive.'

Susan gasped. 'You're supposed to be friends.'

'He's a hitman, Susan; he kills. It's what he's paid to do.'

Marcus waited and watched carefully because he knew it would come. It was just a case of being ready for it. Maggot was so quick, Marcus had never seen anybody with faster reactions and reflexes.

When Maggot's arm shot out it was like the long tongue of an iguana lizard; fast and instantaneous. Marcus moved his head to one side as the ends of Maggot's curved knuckles slammed into the edge of his cheekbone.

As Marcus ducked and felt Maggot's arms sliding painfully past his ear, he turned in towards Maggot's outstretched arm, dropping quickly and pushing up with one outstretched hand.

It caught Maggot beneath the armpit and forced his arm up. This gave Marcus the space he needed to duck beneath Maggot's arm and move behind him.

Maggot spun immediately, but, as he did, it gave Marcus a micro second of time to aim a kick at Maggot's kidneys. His foot connected, but Maggot's body was turning and this had the affect of allowing the kick to glance off his body and not do much damage at all.

They were now facing each other, but their positions were reversed. They stood square to each other and waited briefly. Then all hell was let loose.

From the room where Susan had been pushed into by Marcus, she could hear the awful sounds of bone on bone, gristle on gristle, shouts and groans as the two men fought in the confines of the narrow passageway.

She edged herself closer to the open door, compelled to see what was happening but not wanting to see Marcus being hurt. She peered round the corner and saw Maggot being lifted up bodily by Marcus, and then being slammed on to the hard floor like a wrestler slams his opponent down.

Maggot hit the floor, but immediately kicked his leg out straight, catching Marcus in the crotch. Marcus cried out in agony and doubled up as Maggot leapt to his feet and grabbed Marcus round the neck. He then began to throttle the life out of him.

Susan screamed out and ran out into the corridor. She began to pummel Maggot as hard as she could, but it was ineffective. Maggot appeared to ignore her, oblivious to the punches.

But Marcus knew that Maggot would not put up with it for long; soon he would lash out at Susan and it would be over. Just one, swift blow to her throat would crush her windpipe and she would be dead. He had to stop her, but how?

Marcus screamed out at her, his voice almost choked. 'Get out of the way, Susan! He'll kill you!'

But Susan kept raining blows on Maggot's back, ignoring Marcus's pleas.

Marcus tried shouting at her again, but no sound came from his throat. His eyes were blurring and he was vaguely aware of Susan's legs with his fast, diminishing vision. He knew that this would be the only way he could stop her and save her life.

He forced Maggot to swing round a little by pushing his feet against the wall. As Maggot responded to the increased pressure, Marcus swung a foot at Susan's leg, striking her just below her knee. She screamed out and fell to the floor.

Marcus now had nothing to support himself against Maggot's fierce hold now that his foot was off the floor, and his whole body weight slumped in the arm lock that Maggot had around his neck.

This caused Maggot to droop slightly and his grip slackened for a moment, which allowed Marcus to twist his body just a little, enough to move his arm and grab Maggot by the balls.

Marcus squeezed hard. Maggot screamed out and tightened the lock he had on Marcus neck. Marcus squeezed harder until he felt the balls crushing in his hand. Maggot tried ignoring the pain and increased his grip on Marcus neck. Marcus could no longer breathe; he was choking to death, his head was bursting, but he wouldn't let go. He twisted his hand, feeling the scrotum turning. A few seconds more and he would be tearing Maggot's balls away from his crotch.

Maggot yelled at the top of his voice and relaxed his grip on Marcus, who immediately broke away. He straightened, drawing in huge gasps of air. Maggot began to drop towards the floor. Marcus seized the advantage and took Maggot's head in his hands. He held it firmly and looked for a moment as though a terrible sadness had filled his heart. Then he twisted Maggot's head fiercely and yelled out at the top of his voice.

Susan screamed out in terror as she heard Maggot's neck snap and he dropped to the floor. He was dead.

Marcus sagged to his knees and bent over Maggot's body. He was breathing heavily with the tortured sound of someone who has almost been choked to death. He had slumped so far down that his forehead almost rested on his friend's body, weakened by the terrific fight he had put up against him. There was the look of deep sadness and shock in his eyes when he finally lifted his head and looked down at the man who had been his friend. He dropped back on to his heels, tears falling freely down his face.

Susan knelt beside him. Then she put her arms around him very tenderly. She didn't know what to say; she could only try to understand what it must have been like for Marcus.

He turned his face towards her and looked into her eyes. She could see the pain deep inside him. She then reached forward and kissed him gently on the side of his cheek.

'Very touching,' a voice boomed out.

They both looked up immediately, startled. Standing near to the short passage from the front door was Milan Janov. He had a machine pistol in his hand and he was aiming it at the two of them.

'Now you are both going to die. Then I will kill Abdul.'

He raised the gun and a shattering blast of gunfire filled the corridor.

Susan screamed and clutched her ears as Marcus instinctively pulled her to him and sought the dubious cover of the floor.

Janov seemed to burst open as bullet after bullet shredded his body, lifting it high and slamming him against the wall. He was dead before he slithered down the wall to sit, lifeless in a pool of his own blood.

David stepped into the hallway, the AK47 smoking in his hand. He looked at Janov, then down the passage to Marcus and Susan. He said nothing, then walked up to them and looked down at Maggot's dead body. He reached down and lifted Maggot's hand, looking at the joint where Maggot's finger should have been. He nodded and let it drop.

'Where did you come from?' Marcus asked him.

David simply lifted his head in the direction of the room where he had been sleeping.

'I climbed out of the window.' He looked down at Maggot again. 'You know, I remembered his voice. He said something before he shot me in the head. I knew then I had to get out because he would have killed us all.' He turned and looked over at Janov. 'I nearly ran into him.'

'Lucky you didn't,' Marcus commented, 'otherwise we would have all been dead now.'

'What about Abdul?' David asked. 'What are we going to do with him?'

Marcus got to his feet. 'Take him with us,' he said. 'Cavendish can do what he wants then.' He put his arm round David and Susan. 'Time we went home,' he said. 'I think we deserve it.'

TWENTY-FOUR

CAVENDISH FOLLOWED McCAIN out of base headquarters and clambered into the military officer's Chevrolet. The dawn sky was now well lit by the rising sun, painting its glorious colours across the entire horizon. McCain gunned the Chevrolet into life and drove the relatively short distance to the MQ Reaper Flight.

The pilotless drone was remotely controlled from a very nondescript-looking trailer. It stood on its jacks, its wheels clear of the ground. It had no windows so presented a very unprepossessing sight. Its silhouette against the backdrop of the dawn sky simply showed it up as nothing more than a rectangular box on wheels. It was an absurd notion that such an inanimate object could wreak devastation on its unsuspecting victims.

There was also an air-conditioning rig, its huge tubes connected to the control trailer. At the end of the trailer was a short flight of steps. There was another trailer close by, coupled to a generator which hummed quietly beside it.

McCain brought the Chevrolet to a halt in a small parking lot, alongside other military vehicles and jumped out. Cavendish followed him as he bounded up the steps and pulled open the door. McCain waited until Cavendish was inside before pulling the door closed behind him.

The lighting inside the control room was subdued. A narrow strip of floor ran down towards the far end forming a narrow passage and on each side of that was rack upon rack of electronic control equipment.

The far end opened up into a T-shape, the bar of which was the Reaper drone control desk. At a little below head height were two screens, each one showing a different topography of the ground over which the Reaper was flying.

Two men were sitting at the controls. Cavendish knew that the officer on the left was flying the Reaper. The officer on the right was the sensor control officer, responsible for target detection and target lock.

There was another man at the end, sitting on a kind of jump seat. It wasn't until Cavendish got closer that he recognized the CIA man, Randy Hudson.

Marcus asked the others if they were OK; they both said they were, but Susan insisted that she took care of Marcus's injuries. He wasn't aware that he had any, but Susan led him away to the room that served as a kitchen and told him to wait there. She then picked up a bowl and went outside in search of water.

David was shaking like a leaf, but he had a terrific smile on his face. The trembling was simply a reaction to the death of Janov, and the fact that he had been responsible for it. The shaking didn't bother him, but he wasn't keen on the idea that he had killed somebody although he did realize it had been a case of kill or be killed.

He went along to the room where Abdul had been tied up. He sat on the end of the bed opposite, the one he had slept in, and laid the gun down beside him.

'This is where it ends,' he told him, speaking in Farsi. 'I expect we will be taking you with us, but what happens then, I have no idea.'

Abdul couldn't reply because he was still gagged. David realized this and leaned across the space between the two beds and pulled the gag from Abdul's mouth.

'What happened out there?' Abdul asked, lifting his chin towards the door.

David told him.

'So you killed Janov?' Abdul leaned back against the wall. 'It is for the better,' he mumbled. Then he pushed himself up away from the wall. 'When will we be leaving?'

David made a gesture, lifting his shoulders. 'I don't know. But I think we'll probably leave within the next twenty minutes or so.' He pointed towards the other end of the house. 'Susan is fixing Marcus's wounds. When they've finished, we'll go.'

Hudson turned when he heard the sound of footsteps. As soon as he saw Cavendish, he stiffened. Cavendish walked up to him and stopped.

'Good morning, Hudson. Why am I not surprised to see you here?'

Hudson regarded Cavendish in the half light with a contemptuous stare. 'I'm here on business, Cavendish. What are you doing here?'

Cavendish sniffed. 'I hope I'm here to stop you and your dirty little games,' he told him.

Hudson bridled at the remark. 'You're not on your own ground, Cavendish, so have a care what you say.'

'Why?' Cavendish replied. 'Will I get the same as last night?'

Hudson shook his head. 'I've no idea what you're talking about.'

'Of course you haven't, but why are you not surprised to see me here, I wonder?'

Just then the sensor operator called out two co-ordinates. Chuck Berry, who was sitting in the pilot's seat responded by repeating the co-ordinates and operated the controls to bring the Reaper on to a different heading.

Cavendish glanced over Berry's head and saw the map displayed on the screen. Berry looked up at him.

'What can we do for you gents?' he asked.

McCain told him why they were there. 'So perhaps you could arrange to speak with Sir Giles Cavendish later today?'

'You're off track, sir,' the co-ordinator told Berry.

The lieutenant turned his attention back to the screen. 'Back on track. Select missile.'

The co-ordinator responded. 'AGM-114L, number one rail selected, port side.'

McCain turned to Cavendish and whispered out of the side of his mouth, holding his hand there to observe a kind of respectful silence.

'Hellfire Missile,' he whispered. 'Fire and forget. Great to watch.'

'Time over target?' the sensor operator called out.

Berry checked the figures on his screen and then glanced down at a knee pad he had resting on the top of the control panel.

'Time over target is ten minutes.'

Susan finished washing the blood off Marcus's upper body and around his head and ears. She wanted him to let her examine him elsewhere, but he wouldn't hear of it.

'I'm OK,' he told her. 'I can stand; I can walk and, if I have to, I can run.' He got up from the wooden chair as he said it and put both hands on Susan's shoulders, holding her gently. 'When we get back to London, you can examine me wherever and whenever you like.' He leaned forward and kissed her.

Susan pulled away and slapped him playfully. 'There's nothing wrong with you, Marcus,' she laughed. 'Now, how about sorting ourselves out and getting out of here?'

Cavendish knew, for no obvious reason other than a gut feeling, which target the Reaper would be firing a missile at. He also knew that if he tried to prevent it, he would be restrained, not only by McCain, but by Hudson as well. He could think of no way of preventing Berry launching a Hellfire Missile at the farmhouse where Susan and Marcus had gone to meet with Abdul Khaliq and Susan's brother. If they were there when the missile struck, they would all die.

He had less than ten minutes to come up with an answer.

David stuffed the gag back in Abdul's mouth and walked out of the room and down to the kitchen.

'I'm starving,' he complained, as he walked in on Susan and Marcus. 'How about some breakfast before we go?'

Marcus disagreed. 'I don't think it's wise; if any of the locals round here heard the shooting, they could send the local Taliban out here.'

David nodded thoughtfully. 'You're probably right. What about Abdul?'

Marcus and Susan exchanged glances. 'He comes with us,' Marcus answered for the two of them.

Susan was feeling so much happier now. That feeling of anticipation, nervousness, expectancy, call it whatever you will, had left her. She felt so much more secure, and that was probably because she had seen Marcus demonstrate an uncanny ability to look at a situation and unpick it so expertly. And with David showing consummate profession-alism in the way he handled the situation, she saw no reason to worry about anything. Soon they would all be out of the farmhouse and on their way back to Kabul and freedom.

Cavendish kept his hands in his pockets because they were sweating. Despite the cool air-conditioned interior, he was beginning to find the whole atmosphere uncomfortable. They had about five minutes before the Reaper would be over the farmhouse and Berry would fire the missile. He already knew the official reason for launching the rocket – to kill suspected terrorists – but he knew that Hudson was dealing in retribution and plain murder.

He closed his sweaty hand around his mobile phone and an idea came to him. He excused himself to the others and stepped outside the Reaper control room. He then took the phone from his pocket and wrote a simple text on the screen, dialled a twelve digit number and pressed the call button. He closed the phone and slipped it back in his pocket. Then he went back inside.

Susan cupped her hands in the bowl and scooped the water up to her face and over her hair, letting it cascade down over her bare shoulders. It wasn't exactly a shower, but in the circumstances, it was the next best thing. She did it again and again until she felt she could get no more out of it.

There was no towel handy, so she dried herself on her blouse and slipped it back over her shoulders. She emptied the bowl and buttoned her shirt, then went back into the kitchen.

Marcus and David were waiting there when Susan walked in. She was about to say something to them when she heard her mobile phone ringing. It was in the room she had slept in with Marcus. She looked at the two men and frowned, then went through to her bedroom. When she returned, her face was as white as a sheet.

Marcus looked up as she walked in. His smile quickly disappeared when he saw the look on her face. She had the phone in her hand and was holding it out like a gift.

'Look!' she said.

Marcus took the phone from her hand which was shaking. The text message was very clear and unambiguous.

'*Missile. Two minutes. Run!*'

'Fuck! Let's get out of here,' he screamed. 'Out, out!'

The three of them ran out into the yard, but once they were out there, neither of them seemed to know what to do. Then Marcus pointed towards the far side of the track in front of the house. There was a small orchard about twenty yards from the house.

'In there!' he shouted. 'Get as far away as we can. Quick!'

'What about Abdul?' Susan screamed out.

Marcus stopped. It took him a few seconds to make the decision. 'I'll get him. Now run!'

Before either Susan or David could protest, Marcus had gone, running into the house as fast as he could. They had used up one minute.

'Missile armed and locked, and ready to launch.'

Berry brought the Reaper down to its attack height, locked on to the image of the farmhouse and held his thumb over the launch button.

'Fifteen seconds. Within range.'

He brought his thumb down on to the red button.

'Goodbye, farmhouse. And all you boys in there can kiss your asses goodbye.'

He pressed the button.

Marcus sprinted down the passageway and into Abdul's room. The defunct warlord opened his eyes wide in surprise at Marcus's sudden appearance. Marcus tore the bed clothes from him, hauled him out of the bed and threw him over his shoulder in a fireman's lift.

The clamps holding the Hellfire Missile opened on the port rail under the wing of the Reaper. The missile's single-stage, rocket propellant motor fired, bringing the thrust to over 600 pounds at which level the missile left the rail, dropping away until it was 500 feet from the aircraft. It then armed itself automatically and went in search of its target; the farmhouse which was now being hastily evacuated by Susan and David. But Marcus was still in there.

Susan and David sprinted like hell into the trees and kept running until they heard the *whoosh*! as the missile streaked in and blew the farmhouse apart. The blast wave knocked them off their feet even though they were now well in amongst the trees.

Tons of brick debris and dust enveloped everything, raining down on them like a storm. Susan clamped her hands over her ears and just kept screaming. David was close to her but couldn't hear Susan because his ears were ringing from his own screams and epithets too.

They lay together for a long minute before daring to move. Then suddenly Susan sat up.

'Marcus?' she called. 'Marcus, where are you?' She stood up.

'Marcus!' Her voice became stronger, and began to fill with fear. 'Marcus, where are you?'

She started to walk towards the remains of the farmhouse, stumbling over the shattered masonry that lay all over the ground, then her footsteps quickened until she was running towards the house and calling out Marcus's name.

David and Susan reached the ruin together. It could no longer be called a house; it was nothing more than a pile of rubble. The blast fragmentation warhead of the missile had simply decimated the entire building.

Susan began stepping over the rubble, instinctively making her way towards that part of the house where she knew Abdul had been tied up. It was in one corner. There was nothing there.

David took hold of Susan's elbow and tried pulling her away. He could see that no one could have survived the terrible blast. If Marcus had been in that room when the missile struck, there would be nothing left of him. Nor Abdul for that matter.

Susan wouldn't budge; she remained where she was, staring at what was left. David could see the tears beginning to fill her eyes. Ironically the wetness made her eyes glint and sparkle in the dust that covered her face.

Then he heard a sound. It was coming from well beyond the rubble. Susan looked over towards the sound too. Then they both saw him; Marcus! He was covered in dust and what looked like mud. He was on his knees and waving at them.

Susan screamed and ran as fast as she could. David ran as well, but he was laughing as he ran.

When they got to Marcus they could see where he had fallen into a ditch. There was a little water in there which accounted for the mud that covered him. Lying in the ditch, seemingly unconscious, was Abdul.

Marcus pointed at him. 'He didn't want to come at first.' He laughed. 'Bet he's glad he did now.' He looked at what was left of the farmhouse. 'Wow, what a fucking mess!'

Susan fell on him, covering him with kisses and mumbling something about how much she cared.

Marcus just took her in his arms and held her. He had a broad smile planted across his face.

'How did you manage it?' David asked him.

'You left the window open,' Marcus told him. 'When you climbed out after I'd faced up to Maggot. Good thing too. I picked up Abdul and, well, we just bowled out of the window.' He let go of Susan. 'I got about ten yards from this ditch when the bloody missile struck. Goodness knows how I managed to cover that last ten yards so quickly.'

David nodded towards the ditch. 'How's Abdul?' he asked.

Marcus turned round. 'He took most of the blast, but he should be OK.' He got to his feet with Susan reluctant to let go. 'Time we were not here,' he told them. 'There will be people swarming all over this place soon.'

The three of them helped Abdul struggle out of the ditch. He was still tied but his legs were free. He didn't look too good, but that meant he offered no serious threat to any of them.

'So what do you propose we do?' David asked.

Marcus held out his hand. He still had Susan's mobile phone in it. 'I never even let the bloody thing go,' he said, and handed it to Susan. 'Better call your boss,' he suggested. 'Tell him we need help and a taxi for four.'

They all laughed together and Susan flipped the phone open and dialled Cavendish's number.

EPILOGUE

CAVENDISH LOOKED AROUND the table at his guests. They were in the ambassador's residence in Kabul enjoying British hospitality and knowing they were reasonably safe from rogue CIA agents, Taliban warlords and Hellfire Missiles. Susan, David and Marcus were the reason Cavendish was celebrating a remarkable success in his covert war against The Chapter, otherwise known to him as the CIA.

Lieutenant McCain was there as well because of the part he played in helping Cavendish to maintain a secret link to London. Without that they knew that Hudson and his crooked CIA agents there would have eavesdropped on all Cavendish's traffic.

'I think we've just about sewn everything up,' declared Cavendish. 'And now I think it's time I retired. To bed I mean,' he added hastily. 'I just want to thank you all for what you've done. David,' he said, turning to Susan's brother, 'it really is so good to see you. We'll have a great deal to discuss when you're back in London.'

David reached over the table and shook his hand. 'Thank you, Sir Giles. And it's been good to see you too.' David knew that he would have to spend a lot of time with Cavendish being debriefed. He said nothing to Marcus or Susan of the intelligence he had gathered during his time in Afghanistan.

McCain stood up and told them he would be leaving. He wished them all *bon voyage* and wondered if he might ever see them again in the future. There was an understandable chorus of denial from them.

Susan said she would be returning to the bank. Cavendish had assured her that her job was still waiting there for her. She had also been sworn to secrecy by him.

Marcus asked him why they had been targeted by the CIA. 'How on earth were we worth being blown up by a missile? They could have picked us off any time.'

'It wasn't you they were after,' he told Marcus, 'it was David.'

The expression on Marcus's face told Cavendish that his statement wasn't enough, so he went on, 'You see, we knew the CIA was involved up to its neck out here, but we had no names and nothing cast iron to pin on them. I'm afraid the senior politicians in America and in UK were in no mood to listen to my intelligence.' He arched his eyebrows. 'Now we know why; so many of them were lining their pockets. David had picked up a great deal of information which he had been feeding back to me, but, unfortunately, we were using a military satellite which had been compromised by the CIA. They knew what David was up to and set out to stop him.'

'The attack on the mission?'

Cavendish nodded. 'Quite. And when Abdul Khaliq lifted him from the hospital, for his own ends mark you, not the CIA, it left them in a quandary, particularly when I made it known that David was alive.'

Susan sat up suddenly, shocked at that last statement. 'You made it known?'

Cavendish turned towards her. 'That letter from David was an absolute gift. I was able to use it to let the CIA know he was alive. I knew they would go after him. It was the only way I could draw them out into the open, don't you see?'

Susan looked aghast at the MI6 man, and then at Marcus. 'You used us?' she said angrily. 'Why didn't you just tell them David was alive?'

Cavendish shook his hand at her. 'They would not have believed me.' He made an apologetic gesture. 'I know how it must look, Susan, but I needed a spark; something that would open up the investigation further. You and Marcus were like manna from heaven.'

'It very nearly got us killed,' Marcus said drily.

Cavendish agreed. 'But it got David out and back with us. And now I can wrap the whole thing up; kill the operation stone dead.'

'What about Abdul Khaliq, what part did he play?'

'Oh, he wanted David as a bargaining chip. The Americans were getting greedy and wanted him out of the way and their man in place. He needed some kind of assurance, and he believed David was the answer. He believed he could do a deal with us and get out before the CIA got to him.'

Cavendish then told Marcus that it was when he spoke of hearing that the 'station chief' was responsible for the shipment out of the country that confirmed it was the CIA boss who was orchestrating the whole affair. Randy Hudson was the CIA Station Chief in England and perfectly placed to oversee the operation on behalf of his paymasters back in the States. It was another piece of the jigsaw that fell into place.

They spent some time talking about the devious and secretive work that intelligence services perform, and how it impacts on the public perception of what is happening in the hotspots around the world. But eventually Cavendish made his excuses and bid them all goodnight.

When the MI6 man had gone, Marcus told Susan and David that he was going back to his business; Guard Right Security. He said that Cavendish had assured him that his entire office would be refurbished at the expense of MI6. Or the taxpayer! Cavendish had also offered Marcus a job.

'You're not going to take it, surely?' Susan asked in surprise.

Marcus shook his head. 'No,' he assured her. 'I only have so much adrenalin, and I don't want to waste it on Cavendish and his deceitful plans. And I won't miss it either.'

They all laughed at that.

'But there is one thing I will miss,' Marcus said wistfully.

'What's that?' Susan asked him.

'My sessions in the gym with Maggot.'

Susan sat upright. 'Really?' Marcus nodded at her. She leaned back in her chair and studied him for a moment. 'How come you beat Maggot, Marcus? You told me that he always got the better of you, no matter how hard you tried.'

Marcus smiled. 'That's true. But this time there was one difference: we were fighting dirty, and that meant no rules.'

He let it sink in. Then he shook his head gently, tears forming in his eyes.

'You know, I shouldn't say this, but I'm going to: Maggot would have been proud of me.'